FREE THE WOLF

ALEX STEWARD: BOOK 3

STEFANIE GILMOUR

Library of Congress Control Number: 2024908996

Printed in the United States of America
First edition 2024

Hardcover ISBN 979-8-9904623-1-1
Paperback ISBN 979-8-9904623-2-8
E-book ISBN 979-8-9904623-3-5

For the she-wolves.

1

EACH SOLID COLLISION of my boxing gloves caused my body to sing. Standing in front of me, my friend Nate moved the mitts to prompt the different punches I threw. A light sheen of sweat coated my skin and kept me cool despite the summer heat drifting in through the open garage doors of Emma's house.

The creature inside me, my inner wolf, delighted in the series of strikes. She was the strength woven into my muscles and the fire that drove my pulse. We'd grown close over the past months. Never in the eight years since my werewolf gene triggered had I been so intertwined with her. I felt near invincible.

Thud, thud, thud.

Physically, at least. Although I'd found my place in Trish and Nate's pack, I'd lost others important to me. My friend Anne and I weren't on speaking terms since she'd stumbled across the secret I'd been keeping from her. It'd been a month since I'd heard from Ben. And crashing at Emma's place was becoming increasingly difficult.

Thud, thud. Thud.

A long belch echoed through the garage and broke my concentration. Roger lounged in a chair several feet away, his Chucks propped up on a battered stack of cardboard boxes labeled *Alex's Kitchen Stuff*. He'd been Nate's shadow since the Hunter attacked Hell's Bells. The teenager's eyes were fixed on his phone as his thumbs flew over the keys.

"Hey, Nate, the band for tonight wants to know if you can haul their gear," he said. "The drummer's mom needs the car or something." The downward tilt of his head hid most of the pink and puckered scar across his throat.

"Yeah, we can do that." Nate didn't turn his gaze away from me. "Let them know we'll stop by this afternoon."

Thud. Thud, thud.

Nate was forced to take a step back. He raised his eyebrows and grinned.

I returned the grin, lowered my gloves, and eased my stance. "Thanks for helping me squeeze in practice so early, but I should get ready for my interview."

Money was dwindling fast. Even though it was yet another minimum wage job, I sorely needed it. Otherwise I'd be stuck at Emma's, relying on my best friend to keep me afloat financially as well as emotionally.

The light scent of vanilla permeated the sweaty funk surrounding me. Roger and Nate looked toward the door leading from the garage into the house. Roger lowered his feet so fast that the stack of boxes almost tipped over into his lap. He reached forward to prevent the avalanche and turned a smile back in the direction of the door.

"Hey, Emma," he said. A flush of color crept up from his neckline through his face.

Emma stepped down from the doorway, holding a slim brief-case and wearing a pinstripe knee-length skirt and ruffle-back blazer. Her smile was bright and warm. "Hello, Roger." She shifted her attention to Nate. "Good morning."

Nate nodded and lowered the punching mitts.

My chest still rising and falling from the workout, I wiped the sweat from my brow with the back of my forearm. "Everything okay?" I asked Emma.

"I wanted to talk to you before I left for work," she said. "I'm sorry, guys, could Alex and I have a few minutes alone?"

"Not a problem," Nate said. He took off the mitts and tossed them aside. His gaze moved to Roger. The scruffy teen pocketed his phone, stood, and followed Nate out the garage doors into the sunlit front yard.

Emma watched them leave before she walked across the garage to me. Her designer heels added a few inches to her 5'3" height. "What time is your interview today?"

"At 9:30."

"It's already 8:30," she said.

"I know. I'm watching the clock."

"It's best if you arrive a little early," she said.

Didn't she think I could function as an adult? "I have it handled."

"Do you have an outfit picked out?" she asked.

"It's a retail gig. I don't need to dress up like Office Sex Favors Barbie." I regretted the words as soon as they left my mouth. Insecurity could make me a genuine asshole.

Hurt flickered in Emma's blue eyes, and the corners of her bow of a mouth turned down.

"I'm sorry, Em. I didn't mean that." I shifted my weight. "If my staying here is getting to be too much, I can go back to Ben's until I find another place." It's where she'd found me several weeks earlier, steeping in a toxic mix of anger and self-pity. Now that I'd left his apartment, I realized how awful it'd been there without him.

"No, it's fine. I asked you to stay with me." She squared her shoulders and lifted her chin. "Some colleagues are visiting today at one for a working lunch. Could you make sure there aren't any dishes in the sink? And please take the boxes up to your room if we can't store them in the garage?"

"Yeah, sure." When I'd abandoned ship at Ben's, I moved his extensive vinyl collection with me so the records wouldn't be ruined by the heat. It'd be a waste of money to pay for AC in an empty apartment. I'd lost track of the number of times Emma had asked me to move them from her living room.

Her frown deepened. "It's important, Alex. We're finalizing our annual donor event for Another Chance. It's the first one I'm coordinating as director, and the first time my coworkers are visiting my home. I want everything to be perfect."

My jaw tightened. This time I managed to remain quiet and only nod.

"Thank you." She turned and walked to her Vespa, a pearlescent moped with fuchsia and violet flames brushed across the flanks. "Good luck on the interview. I'll be thinking of you."

"Thanks."

A shadow of her previous smile appeared. She got onto the bike, placed the briefcase between her ankles, fastened her helmet, and started the Vespa. I followed her to where the garage's shadow reached the baking driveway. Roger waited at the edge of the drive and sent her off with a wave as Nate walked back up to me.

"If it doesn't work out here, Trish and I always have a cot for you at our place," he said. With a heightened sense of hearing, being a werewolf often made one an unintentional eavesdropper. "I know she's your best friend, but she's a wizard. Wolves do better when we stick together."

I shook my head. "Thanks, but I'll be all right. I have that interview today. Once I have the job, I'll swallow my pride and ask my parents to wire me money for an apartment deposit. I love Em like a sister, but this living arrangement could really mess up our friendship." I'd already lost Anne. Losing Emma too would destroy me.

"Any word from Ben?" he asked.

A sharp ache twisted in my chest. I shook my head again and lowered my eyes. I didn't want Nate to see how close I was to tears.

Nate grinned and punched me in the shoulder. "They'll get it sorted. He's too hooked on you to stay away."

I rubbed my shoulder. "I'm going to ask Reginald to cover Ben's apartment expenses. Ben won't be happy about it, but I can't afford rent on two places."

"Speaking of affording things, the repairs on his motorcycle are done. Trish and I can float you some cash—"

"No, I've had the money set aside for the repairs," I said. It'd been the last bit of money I'd acquired from Emma's evil ex . . . Well, after purchasing the boxing gloves, punching mitts, and the heavy bag that hung a few feet from us. Now Ben's rent on his empty apartment would quickly eat through my meager savings account if I couldn't get his grandfather's help.

"Should the bike be dropped off at Rear Window?" Nate asked.

I nodded and bit my lip. Hard. It came in waves like this. I'd be fine one moment and then be ambushed by hurt when something reminded me of Ben. His sister, Joan, convinced us it wasn't safe to exchange text messages. She refused to give me his location because of my closeness to Trish, and Trish with the Committee. The situation made me feel helpless.

I despised feeling helpless.

The guys left, and I went inside to get ready for my interview. Walking through Emma's beautiful, sizable home made me feel like a filthy stray. I didn't touch anything on my way to the second-floor guest bedroom and bath.

I lingered in the shower, briefly entertaining the idea of not going to the interview. If I got the job, I'd eventually run into rude customers—the standard prelude to me being fired.

Maybe I could bridge the income gap with a ride-share gig. I'd done it plenty of times before. But my car, having barely survived an encounter with an angry werewolf last winter, erred on the side of unreliable.

The hot water cascaded over me, easing my sore muscles. I closed my eyes and reached out to my wolf. She filled my chest, belly, and limbs with an intimate warmth, causing me to smile. "We can do this," I said.

A black denim skirt and one of Ben's band t-shirts seemed appropriate for the interview. I wrangled my soggy curls back into a ponytail. There wasn't enough time for my hair to dry, so it dampened my shirt collar as I applied lipstick and charcoal-colored eyeliner. I tried to squeeze more water from my hair with a towel as I made my way down to the kitchen for a bite to eat.

I tossed the towel aside on a chair back at the kitchen island and brought a bowl of cereal and a cup of coffee out onto the back patio. The scents of chlorine, flowers, and warm stone filled Emma's well-kept backyard. A modest, pretty garden surrounded the pool.

My phone buzzed and rattled on the glass top of the patio table. The noise no longer prompted an instant thudding of my heart. I didn't pounce on the device to see who sent the message. Munching on my cereal, I turned the phone so I could read the screen. It was Emma.

I forgot. Please be sure the trash goes out this morning. Thank you.

I'd stayed too long in the shower to take care of any clean-up before I left, so I added the chore to my *shit-to-do-later* list for when I got back.

EMMA LIVED IN a neighborhood on the east side of Hopewell, surrounded by an invisible social bubble. I'd joked with her that my thrift-store clothing might get me ticketed while I went for runs. She'd suggested renting a purebred dog and a blue-eyed blond guy to jog with me.

"Oh, and you'll have to wear matching running outfits, you and the guy," she'd said. "If all three of you match, you're golden. No one will bother you."

As I drove closer to the city center, the cracks in the sidewalks grew larger and the houses grew smaller. Every other yard had a sign for the upcoming city election. I couldn't help scowling at a familiar face on an especially large banner.

The man beamed a grin of bleached teeth from an unnaturally tanned face. A flag flew unfurled behind him in case anyone doubted his loyalties. The block lettering read *Joe Stone for Mayor: Putting Your City First*.

"Jackass," I muttered. Joe Stone recently joined the Committee that governed the supernatural citizens in Hopewell. He promptly made them feel unwelcome by bringing in a Hunter. The justification? To protect the Commoners, non-supernatural citizens, from the monsters he said had infiltrated their city.

Monsters like me.

His blatant dislike for us should have made him ineligible for the Committee, but men like him are rarely the best option—or even qualified—for the positions of power they hold.

Trish, Joan, and I had disabled the Hunter, but not before he killed a young activist werewolf, Isaac, and gave Roger the gruesome scar on his throat. The Hunter had made an attempt on my life, and Ben's as well. Ben used magic to protect us, but in doing so, he'd further damaged the tether that limited his abilities. Now the Committee wanted him for breaking his criminal sentence.

I threw 2-D Joe a parting glare. He'd denied ever ordering Isaac's death or the attack on Hell's Bells that nearly took Roger's life, but my gut told me otherwise. Stone hadn't lost anything. He was still in the running for mayor and even ahead of the other candidates by a large margin.

I tried to turn my focus to my interview at Rear Window Records. Before I could look further into Stone, I needed to find an apartment and be able to feed myself.

Damn Maslow and his hierarchy.

2

WHEN I ARRIVED downtown at Rear Window Records for the interview, I parked at the back of the building out of habit. I glanced up at Ben's apartment on the second floor, where I'd lived for the past six months. It was like worrying at a split lip with your teeth. It hurt, but I couldn't help it. I turned off my phone for the interview and entered the old building. A door off the left of the stairwell led into the shop.

The shop wasn't open to customers this early, but the back door had been unlocked for my interview. The bell sounded above the door, and the Arctic Monkeys played on the overhead speakers. The music made me smile.

A young woman with short platinum blonde and blue hair looked up from a magazine behind a U-shaped counter with a single cash register. She grinned when she saw me and called out. "Good morning. Can you flip that lock for me, please?"

I did so, then walked past rows and rows of bins, each housing albums for sale. Old concert posters, photographs, and t-shirts were posted along the exposed blond brick walls.

"Morning, Sara." I stopped at the counter. She was the manager and Ben's superior, so I'd gotten to know her through him. I gave her coffee mug a hungry glance.

"Caffeine?" she asked.

"Please."

Sara nodded and started back toward an employee-only room sectioned off with a heavy curtain. She called over her shoulder, "I'm sorry we have to do this, but the boss wants all the paperwork filled out and in place." She returned and set the chipped mug of steaming coffee beside her own. "Come on over here."

I walked around the counter to join her.

She pulled a barstool over beside her before she sat down. From underneath the counter, she retrieved a manila folder. A job application and tax forms were set in front of me.

"No interview then?" I asked.

"I already know you have a passion for music." She gave the papers a wave. "Have a seat and start filling this stuff out. We can chat while you do so."

I made it as far as the second field on the application before I faltered.

The address. I didn't know where I'd be living.

"Have you worked in retail before?" Sara asked.

I nodded and wrote in Emma's address for the time being. "I've worked in record stores before." During the five years I bounced around the country, it'd been my fallback job. I knew I excelled at it—the knowledge of music part, anyway. But minimum wage barely covered expenses, depending on where I lived.

Sara watched me write, taking a sip of her coffee. Her black lipstick had stained the mug's rim. "How are you with customers?"

Shit.

"Um," I glanced up. "I'm okay."

"'Okay'? If you've worked in a record store, make that retail in general, you know there are plenty of rude customers. A lot are going to assume you know nothing, and you're only here to fetch things for them while they leer at your ass." One side of her mouth turned upward. "Are you going to be able to deal with that?"

Ben must have told her about my impatience with such customers. I swallowed and set down the pen. "Aren't there things I can do that won't require too much face-to-face with customers?"

Accepting and working with my wolf had improved my temper, but I preferred avoiding a risky situation in the first place. "Can I help with inventory? I don't mind answering a question here and there, but maybe—"

"What?" Sara leaned back and laughed. "You're the newbie! You have to serve your time before you get to call shifts."

"But you must need someone to fill Ben's place while he's out," I said.

"Well, you *are* a walking music catalog, like Ben. And cuter." She winked. "How long is he planning to be gone? The boss said it's a family thing, but ordering and stocking is a bitch without him."

This is where I, as Ben's significant other, someone he'd share important life details with, was expected to know the answer.

I didn't. I'd asked, but he and his sister didn't answer. Maybe they didn't know, or maybe he didn't consider me as significant as I'd thought.

I picked up the pen and continued filling in the blanks on the application. "He's not sure how long it will be." I didn't look up but felt Sara's gaze on my bent head.

She paused before she spoke again. "I'll see what I can do." She sipped her coffee. "About shifts with lighter customer traffic."

"Thanks."

The bell over the back door sounded. Sara frowned to herself and set her coffee mug down. "Didn't you lock that?"

"Yeah. I thought I did." I looked up from the application.

She stood and called out. "Good morning! I'm sorry, but we're not actually open yet."

A faint metallic odor wafted toward me. Wisps of energy were drawn from around us, and the hair on my arms and the nape of my neck rose. My body could sense a wizard preparing to cast a spell.

"You're not?" A man around my age rested his hip against the counter and gestured back over his shoulder. "The door was open."

The guy could have walked off a runway with the designer clothes he wore, a sheer, long-sleeved shirt and fitted black denim.

He had that high couture look of a living skeleton: hawk nose, sharp cheekbones, and smears of dark makeup on his hooded eyelids—all bolstered by light curls topping a black fade.

Sara smiled. "I'm sorry. My mistake. You're welcome to come back at eleven."

The man's long-fingered hand slid a show flier across the counter. "Can you tell me about this performer?"

As he spoke, his voice dropped an octave and echoed back on itself in a way that made my skin crawl. I bit my lip to contain a growl. Wizards, like any other supernatural creature, were forbidden from blatant use of their gift in front of Commoners. Either this guy didn't know or he didn't care. Eyes wide, I looked at Sara.

"Yeah." Her pupils dilated and spots of color appeared in her cheeks. Her voice turned soft and dream-like. "That's Ben Sharpe. He played a few months ago at Hell's Bells."

I couldn't disrupt his spell without alerting Sara. But why would the stranger ask about Ben? I frowned and glanced at the flier beneath his black polished nails. "Who's asking?"

Sara stiffened beside me.

The guy's gaze slipped to me, and he smiled. The scent of cherries mixed with the metallic odor that clung to him. When his eyes met mine, my Shield burned on my breastbone. Whatever spell he used on Sara, he tried to use on me. It wasn't going to make it past the protective symbol tattooed on my chest.

"Sebastian," he said. "I'm an old schoolmate of Ben's and wanted to reconnect with him."

Ben never spoke about other wizards he knew. Since he'd been tethered at sixteen, he'd been shunned by the majority of them. Emma, his grandfather, and his sister were the only wizards I knew who even talked to him.

"That's odd. He's never mentioned you," I said. *Dammit.* Functioning Shield or not, today my mouth wasn't interested in checking with my brain before opening.

"Alex, don't be rude." Eyes bright, Sara smiled at Sebastian. She didn't smile like that at strangers, especially men. "I'm sorry, Sebastian, but he's out of town. He works here, though. If you leave your name and number, I can pass it on to him."

Sebastian answered Sara, but he hadn't looked away from me. "That would be great. Thank you." As Sara rustled around the register for a scrap of paper and pencil, he asked me, "You must know Ben, too?"

I narrowed my eyes. Jealousy and I weren't strangers, and my intense protection of Ben verged on territorial. My inner wolf's first reads on people were reliable. But this guy? Uncertain, she paced inside my chest, flipping between suspicion and curiosity. *Who was this guy and was he a threat to Ben?*

"Intimately," I said.

Sebastian's eyebrows lifted into his blonde, almost white, curls. He straightened to place distance between us, and the burning sensation of my Shield faded. "Noted."

Sara set a piece of paper and pencil in front of him. Sebastian glanced at her nametag and scribbled something down. "Do you happen to know where Ben lives nowadays, Sara?"

Before I could interrupt, she said, "He has an apartment upstairs." Sara leaned toward Sebastian. "Anything else you were looking for?"

Sebastian scanned the store once. "No, but I'm sure I'll be back soon. I've always enjoyed this place. Thanks for your help." He gave me a parting glance before he left.

When the door closed, Sara turned to me. Her pupils had returned to normal, and the schoolgirl blush faded from her cheeks. "And that is how you handle a customer."

I blinked. "Don't you think it's an invasion of Ben's privacy to tell some random person where he lives?"

"What's the harm in saying he's renting?" She shrugged. "Everyone rents around here."

"Except you told him where to find Ben's apartment," I said.

"What? No, I didn't. *That* would be an invasion of Ben's privacy." Her penciled brows drew together. "Are you going to make me regret hiring you? I can't have you snapping at customers."

I hesitated, not knowing how to tell her what had happened without mentioning the whole magic thing. And I needed the job. "I'm sorry. He threw me off when he asked about Ben," I said. "I'll do better."

She picked up the piece of paper and read it. Her eyebrows rose. "Oh shit. I didn't know Ben was friends with a Visser. Did you?" She handed me the paper.

I looked down at it. "No." At the mention of the surname, I thought of Isaac again. He'd been dating a Visser at the time of his murder. The family was well-known in Hopewell because of its size and wealth. The Vissers were prominent in the supernatural community because the family was, as Nate liked to say, *lousy with wizards*.

"Could you get that note to Ben for me?" Sara said.

I nodded, even though I wasn't sure when that would be. I folded the piece of paper over and stuffed it in the small purse I'd brought along.

After I completed the employment form in an attempt to validate my worth, Sara gave me a quick insider's tour around the shop. She went over the pay and how many hours she'd be able to give me. "Can you start in a few days?" she asked.

I nodded. "Yes. The sooner the better." If I wanted to protect my friendship with Emma, I had to get out of her place asap.

Exiting via the back of the building, I walked to the steps leading up to Ben's apartment. I wanted to grab the last few things I'd left there. Then I could ask Reginald to take the keys and the responsibility for rent.

I retrieved the keys from my purse and slowed when the strange scent from earlier, a chemical odor with traces of metal, reached me. Sebastian sat waiting on the stairs to the apartment.

3

SEBASTIAN WITHDREW A red sucker from his mouth and pointed it at me. "Alex, right?"

My nose flooded with the sticky sweet aroma of artificial cherries. A growl rumbled in my chest, and my fingers tightened on the keys.

"A lupine?" He chuckled and shook his head. "Ben always found your kind interesting." His teeth split the candy with a cracking noise.

I narrowed my eyes. Nate found elitist wizards like Sebastian irritating. I understood why. "What do you want? Sara told you he's out of town."

"Since you're *intimately* familiar with him, I thought you could tell me where he is," he said.

"No, I can't." Even if I knew, I wouldn't have told him. This didn't seem the type of person Ben would consider a friend.

Sebastian sat crunching on the candy as he studied me. He glanced at the keys. "When do you expect him back?"

"I don't know," I said. "He didn't say."

"You have keys to his apartment, but he didn't tell you where he went or when he'd return?" He arched an eyebrow. "That's odd, don't you think?"

His words hurt, but I clenched my jaw and remained silent.

Something beeped and he checked a small device clipped beneath his shirt at his waistband. "Alex, I can tell you're suspicious of me. Since we only met minutes ago, I'm not sure what I've done to—"

"You messed with Sara's head without giving it a second thought," I said. "You think the rules and people's boundaries don't apply to you."

Sebastian paused, his lips still parted mid-sentence, and turned his gaze back on me. "Wait." His head tilted. "You're being serious right now."

I stared him down.

"A harmless charm like that wouldn't hurt her," he said. "They don't even remember it."

My inner wolf paced, wanting so badly to bring him down a few pegs. I inhaled deeply, unfortunately getting another noseful of the cherry candy. When I exhaled, my tone remained even. "That's not the point," I said. "She didn't consent."

"Okay, okay." He chuckled, but broke eye contact to look at the stained cardboard stick he twirled between his fingers. "Point taken. No need for a lecture on morals." Sebastian stood, pitched the sucker stick aside, and descended the few stairs to stand in front of me.

His movement brought us eye-to-eye and way too close. The hair on the nape of my neck rose, but I didn't concede any space to him. The brown color of his eyes reminded me of dried blood.

Sebastian slowly smiled. "Let's not waste time arguing. You don't have to worry about any nefarious plan I have for Ben." His thin shoulders lifted. "Like I said, he and I are close friends, and I haven't seen him in years. I'm in town, so I thought I'd look him up. If you're in contact with him, please have him text me."

As Sebastian spoke, I caught another scent under the sweet scent of the cherry candy. Blood. Another low growl escaped me before I could stop it.

Sebastian stepped back and blew a sigh through his lips. "I'll find him eventually, with or without your help." He withdrew a set of car keys. "I'm sure you and I will be seeing each other again." He touched his fingers briefly to his forehead, tipping an invisible hat brim to me.

I watched him walk across the parking lot and get into a spotless, sleek coupe. After he left, I climbed the stairs to the apartment, unlocked the door, and gave it the required nudge with my knee to open it. Sebastian made me all the more anxious to hear from Ben.

I'd drawn the blinds in the studio apartment to keep the place cool, but it grew toasty anyway. The heat magnified the familiar scents in the small space. Memories associated with them, of my time with Ben, caused a sudden tightness in my throat.

More growling vibrated in my chest. When Joan first hid him away, he'd stolen her phone and texted me so I knew he was safe. Why hadn't he found another way since then to get in touch?

I walked to the kitchenette table, probably the most expensive piece of furniture in the apartment. It had been a gift from Ben's grandfather, Reginald. And, as such, Ben had despised it from the minute Joan brought it into our space. Fifteen years ago, because of his position on the Committee, Reginald tethered Ben. For me, the table symbolized the day Ben fled with Joan to avoid arrest by the Committee.

Spread across the table's surface were haphazard piles of papers, sticky notes, and folders. Everything remained exactly as I'd left it when Emma extracted me from the apartment. "You're going to drive yourself crazy, Alex," she'd said to me. "Please, come stay at my house. Step away from this for a bit."

I shook my head and gathered the papers. If Stone got away with coordinating Isaac's murder, he'd sail across the election finish line. He'd have even more power at his disposal, which would elevate his status in the Committee. The Commoner representatives were already jittery, thanks to his efforts to cast the supernatural community as monsters.

If Stone got more sway with the Committee, there would be more unjust regulations. He'd make our lives a living hell. I wasn't going to let Stone get away with harming the community I'd grown so close to.

The large duffle bag Ben used for touring served as a perfect container for my amateur sleuthing notes. I nosed around the apartment, retrieving an item here and there, erasing my presence from the space. Neither Ben or I was much of a material person, so by the time I finished, the place looked empty.

I paused at the mattress we'd used as a bed. His scent would be strongest here. If I laid down and wrapped myself in the sheets, I could surround myself with it. Another ache twisted in my chest.

Instead, I took a seat at the cleared table. I withdrew my phone, turned it on, opened the message thread with Joan, and sent yet another note off to her.

Please answer me. How close are you to getting his warrant dismissed? Is he okay? Can I see him?

The message posted to the thread beneath multiple unanswered messages I'd sent to Joan over the past weeks. I scrolled up to the last message I'd received from Ben when he stole his sister's phone.

I miss you, too.

I frowned, closed the message thread, and noticed I missed a call from my mother during the interview. My parents and I had a strict call schedule of once a month. It wasn't our family call day, but that didn't keep my mother from butt-dialing me. It happened a lot. I dismissed the missed call notification.

Next, I brought up a phone number from my contacts list but hesitated before dialing it. The idea of having Reginald cover Ben's rent sounded more plausible when I wasn't seconds from ringing up the older wizard.

Becoming housemates already stressed our friendship, so asking Emma to pay my absentee boyfriend's rent was out of the question. Nate and Trish barely kept enough to keep Hell's Bells running from one day to the next. My parents didn't even know I chanced dating someone. Plus, I planned to ask them for a deposit on a place for myself.

Reginald attempted to help Ben with expenses before, but Ben refused, just as he did anything his grandfather offered. In fact, Ben would be pissed about this, but I didn't know what else to do. Rent downtown had skyrocketed over the past few years. If Ben lost this apartment, he wouldn't find another affordable place within walking distance of work.

I sighed and sent the call through, ignoring the stab of guilt.

"Yes? Hello?"

"Hey, Reginald. It's Alex." A moment of dead air filled the line, and I wondered if a face-to-face conversation with the older wizard would have been better. I held my breath and hoped he wouldn't hang up.

"Miss Alex." His greeting sounded terse.

"I realize you're angry at me for helping Ben, but please hear me out," I said.

"If you believe you helped him by enabling him to avoid consequences for his actions, you're mistaken," he said.

"He was terrified, Reginald, and it wasn't fair," I said. "He did nothing wrong by protecting us."

Reginald raised his voice. "He's a tethered wizard who broke the law when he chose to cast magic. He acted recklessly."

Heat burned in my chest, causing my inner wolf to stir. I attempted to keep the anger from my tone, but it sounded strained. "I don't have anyone else to turn to for help with this."

Another pause. "Go on."

"Ben's apartment—"

"I'd hardly call that rundown space an apartment," he said.

I closed my eyes, clenched my teeth, and exhaled through my nose. "I want to find my own place, but I can't afford to pay rent on two." My stomach turned. "Could you please help Ben with rent while he's gone?"

There was a longer pause. "Very well, Miss Alex. If you feel he wants to keep his lease on that apartment rather than find more suitable living conditions, I would be pleased to help."

Relief washed over me. "Thank you. Really."

"Please send me the landlord's information so I can ensure payment reaches the correct person on time," Reginald said.

"Yeah, all right. When do you want to pick up the keys?" My fingers were clenched around them again, sweating.

"You may keep the keys," he said. "I have no need for them."

"Okay." I swallowed back the lump in my throat. "Have you heard from him?"

Reginald's tone stiffened. "I've excused myself from those Committee proceedings due to a conflict of interest."

"What? Why aren't you helping him? He's your family!" I didn't usually involve myself in the relationship between Reginald and Ben, believing two grown-ass men should deal with it on their own, but this was different. Ben's safety was on the line.

"Exactly. Anything I said in his defense would hold no value," he said. "It would be viewed as favoritism."

I thought of what got Ben into the mess in the first place—Isaac's murder. The Hunter. Stone. "I know a way you could help him."

"Miss Alex, I—"

"It wouldn't involve the Committee," I said. When he didn't object, I continued, "You could help me. I need info about the Visser family and Isaac." I held my breath again.

"Go on," he said.

"Isaac was dating Julia Visser, a wizard, when he was murdered. I asked Julia if her family was upset about her seeing Isaac. She got dodgy about it." I avoided telling Reginald about Isaac's involvement in Joan's local *Overthrow the Committee* club. "Trish said the Vissers bitch to you because you're the wizards' Committee representative. Did you hear any complaints from Julia's family about their daughter snuggling with a werewolf?"

Reginald cleared his throat. It signaled his intentional choice of words for discussions he considered delicate. "There was concern at first, especially from her father, but the Vissers are reasonable people. Her mother encouraged the family to put aside any reservations and allow Isaac to visit their home."

I growled. There had to be some connection. "Are the Vissers financial supporters of Stone's mayoral campaign?"

"I couldn't say if they are or not," Reginald said. "They are a more traditional wizarding family, but their views of the world are nuanced, even between the elder generation's siblings."

"How nuanced?" I asked.

"I recall when Julia's parents married, it caused a rift among some in the Visser family," he said. "Julia's mother, Tabitha, is a wizard, but her father, Franklin, is a Commoner. Franklin asked Tabitha to cease practicing magic."

"What the hell? She agreed to that?" It reminded me of Emma's Commoner mother. Susan despised the fact her daughter practiced "witchcraft." I couldn't see myself spending life with someone who wouldn't accept me for who I am—fur, fangs, and all.

"Yes, under the condition her children are allowed to practice as they wish," Reginald said.

"So Tabitha is the Visser," I said. "Why does Julia have her mother's last name, then?"

"The Visser name carries prestige," Reginald said.

I snorted. "Wizards wielding their privilege. Imagine that."

"Tabitha's parents insisted," he said.

"What's Franklin's last name?" I grabbed a scrap of paper and a pencil from the bag.

Reginald paused. "Teuling. Franklin Teuling."

I tapped the pencil on the paper. "Wait. Isn't he on the Committee?" I couldn't keep all the old men in the group straight.

"Yes."

Thoughts raced in my mind. I scribbled down the name. "And he had a problem with Isaac seeing Julia—"

"Miss Alex, I—"

"Stone needed his Hunter to take out a well-loved member of the wolf community, and Teuling knew one interested in his daughter," I said. "Do you think we could use this to tie the Hunter's contract to Stone?"

"The accusation requires evidence. There is none that I am aware of," Reginald said.

"What about a confession from Teuling or Stone?" I asked.

An awkward pause. "I feel this may be a larger discussion we should have in the company of Father Aiden."

Aiden, the Committee Chair, kept order at the meetings and made sure everyone followed the proper procedures. He and I didn't have the most pleasant relationship. I swear he only tolerated me because Trish often invited me along to meetings.

"I get it," I said. "No secret plotting outside Committee business hours."

"I admire your determination, but please take care," Reginald said. "Joe Stone's influence within the Committee is strengthening. It worries me. We are currently not at our best for the supernatural community's interests. Don't draw Joe's attention to yourself more than you already have."

"Yeah, yeah." I didn't want to hear it. Whether it seemed wise or not, I couldn't shy away from bullies like Stone. "Hey Reginald, how many other wizard kids does Tabitha have?"

"One. She has a son, Sebastian, from before her marriage to Franklin," he said.

My heartbeat skipped. "Was he a friend of Ben's?"

He cleared his throat again. "Yes. The two were very close. They studied together under me for their apprenticeships."

Like Sebastian told me—close friends. "Thanks, Reginald," I said. "For the info and for taking care of Ben's place for him."

"Of course, Miss Alex. My pleasure," he said. "I'll see you at the meeting."

My pulse lurched. "Meeting?"

"The Committee meeting today. I was on my way out when you rang."

Dammit. My stomach sank. I vaguely recalled a text reminder from Trish, sent to me several days earlier, asking me to attend. She pulled me into Committee business when wanting another voice there for the lupine. "Right. Um, yeah. I'll see you there."

I ended the call and checked the time. If I didn't get something to eat beforehand, my stomach would be growling more than I did at those meetings. I grabbed the large duffle bag, took one last glance around, and locked the door to the apartment behind me.

4

I DISLIKED ATTENDING the Committee meetings. They were supposed to address challenges coming from the cohabitation of Commoner and supernatural citizens. The collection of representatives included nine Commoners—the majority of whom were old guys—but only one wizard and two werewolves.

I was a woman *and* a werewolf. It proved difficult to have faith in a system to speak for me when the majority of representatives were nothing like me.

Union Street Church, the Romanesque building where the Committee met, was still undergoing renovations from the riot that happened the previous month. What started as a peaceful protest had turned violent. Most of the stained-glass windows in the entryway were destroyed. Small bits of broken glass still glittered in the sidewalk cracks. Memories of angry screams, burning metal, and tear gas surfaced when I passed through the doors.

In the entry hall, I spotted a stout, middle-aged man in a rumpled suit. "Detective Grey?"

The man stopped and turned. There were as many wrinkles in his forehead as his suit. "Hello, Alex."

Only two people on the Hopewell police force, beyond Anne, were clued into the existence of supernatural citizens. Jakob DeBoer, Anne's partner, and Detective Sam Grey.

"Hi." I glanced at the three doors to our left leading into the sanctuary. "Do you have a minute?"

He checked his watch. "If it's quick. What'd you need?"

"How's Anne?" Numerous phone calls and texts I'd sent her went unanswered. At Emma's urging, I backed off and hoped Anne would reach out to me when ready.

"As her boss, I don't meddle in her personal business," Grey said, his voice gruff.

"But how is she adjusting to . . ." I shifted my weight and gestured broadly around us.

He hesitated, scanning my features not unlike Anne would, before launching into his answer. "Listen, the transition from Commoner to Commoner-in-the-know is rough on anyone. What I can tell you about Officer Reid is that she's a great cop. Officer DeBoer and I are lucky to have her onboard to help with Committee work."

I swallowed. "She's okay then?"

He frowned. "She's getting there." Grey gave his watch a glance and motioned to the sanctuary doors. "We should go inside."

We took one of the three doors into the cavernous sanctuary. Row after row of pews led down the main aisle to the front of the room. The stone walls and stained-glass windows rose up around us, past the wings of a balcony, and met far above in a vaulted ceiling. Multiple conversations echoed through the space as Committee members waited at a circular table on a raised platform.

I climbed the stairs, wishing the meeting could be on a different day. My current mood didn't bode well for the needed diplomatic behavior.

My friend and mentor, Trish, turned in her seat. She looked a bit out of place with her sleek, dark bob and fitted, contemporary clothing. Her red lips curved into a smile when she saw me. She was a werewolf, a leader and caretaker of our community, and the person who'd drawn me into the politics of the Committee.

"You made it," she said.

"Of course." I blushed, but I wasn't going to admit I forgot about her invitation to sit at the table during the meeting. Any supernatural citizen could attend by sitting in the pews but being a guest at the table had to be cleared through Aiden, the Committee chair.

Reginald already waited at the table as well, seated to Trish's left. He gave me a nod as I took the seat to her right. The other werewolf and a member of Hopewell's police force, Jakob DeBoer, sat opposite us with Detective Grey beside him. To Jakob's left sat Joe Stone, looking every bit the crooked jackass he was.

"Seems like we'll be allowing any violent and dangerous person a seat at our table," Stone said to no one in particular.

Trish's smile cooled. "Alex's suspension has expired, and she is here as my guest."

I'd lost my temper with Stone at a previous meeting and cleared the table to attack him. Reginald stopped me with a spell. I didn't appreciate the gesture at the time but understood now what a disaster it would have been for the wolves if I'd gotten my claws into Stone. Being seated at the table meant I spoke and behaved on behalf of my community.

I kept my voice low as I spoke to Trish. "Have you heard anything about the priority of Ben's case?"

She shook her head. "That hasn't hit the agenda."

Someone cleared their throat. Everyone present quieted and turned their attention to a dark-haired man with gray at his temples and hawkish features. Father Aiden wore a traditional priest's collar with a black, short-sleeved button-up. He looked around the table, his gaze pausing on each of us. "Are we ready to begin?"

A general murmur of agreement and several nods came from the group. Aiden opened a folder, one of several, in front of him. "We're starting today with an update on David Eastman."

The name caused me to shift in my seat. Among the wolves, Eastman had been referred to simply as the Hunter. I looked across the table at Stone. There wasn't even a flicker of a reaction on his features.

"David Eastman has recovered from his injuries in the Northwestern University medical ward," Aiden said. "He is in custody for the murder of Isaac Laska, a supernatural citizen of Hopewell, and an attack on Hell's Bells, a city nightclub."

I wanted to add *at the order of Joe Stone* but stopped myself. I even managed to lower my gaze to the table instead of sending Stone an accusatory glare.

"Detective Grey, can you please update everyone on the criminal investigation and trial?" Aiden said.

Grey nodded and referenced a notepad. "Eastman will be facing one count of first-degree murder of Isaac Laska. Because of the shooting at the club Hell's Bells, Eastman will also face twenty-six counts of attempted murder. If he's found guilty, Eastman will face life in prison without the possibility of parole."

"He'll serve his time as a Commoner then?" Trish asked.

Grey flipped the notepad closed and nodded. "Yes. Without his key, he no longer has any supernatural abilities. No special measures will be taken to contain him."

My stomach gave an involuntary lurch. I'd used my claws and increased strength to cut the key, a type of arcane charm, out of Eastman's body. I could still hear the snapping of sinew. And I'd done so in front of Anne, against the rules. That's how she found out I was a werewolf.

Grey looked over at Aiden. "Since the Chicago Delegation took a special interest in this case and pulled rank, I'll be traveling there next week for the trial."

I allowed myself to glance up from the table at Stone. He'd gone so far as to bring Eastman to one of the Committee meetings before we'd dug up the evidence to charge the Hunter. Stone relaxed in his chair, scribbling down some notes. How could someone so easily excuse themselves from doing something so awful?

"Thank you, Detective Grey." Aiden glanced around the table. "Are there any other questions?" When no one spoke up, Aiden shuffled his pages. "Mr. Stone, you have the floor."

I frowned and glanced at Trish. She pushed some stapled papers toward me and tapped a fingernail on the top of the page.

Proposal for Revised Safety Rules and Procedures, prepared by Joseph Stone—Mayoral Candidate, Putting Your City First

What the hell was this?

"Fellow Committee members," Stone said. "I hope that you have been able to review my proposal." He looked across the table at Trish and me. "Let me assure you when I drafted it, I had the best interests of *all* citizens in mind."

I glanced at Trish again. Her jawline twitched as she sat tall with her chin slightly lifted, staring down Stone.

"Our citizens deserve to feel safe in their city, their homes." Stone pointed to the sanctuary's entrance. "No citizen should have to worry about the violence that took place outside those doors."

Fear had been leveraged as a weapon by Stone, sparking the riots. Now he wanted to reframe the story. Anger burned in my gut, agitating the beast inside me. My jaw clenched, and I exhaled slowly through my nose to help calm her. A person like him shouldn't be on the Committee.

"What I'd like to do is open the floor to any questions or concerns about the proposal before we hold the vote," Stone said.

My heart skipped, and I gave Trish a panicked glance.

Trish leaned toward me, her voice low. "I sent your copy with Nate last week. Didn't he give it to you?"

I remembered then. Nate had handed me a folder, saying Trish wanted me to review the contents. I'd set the folder aside and forgotten about it. Chances were the folder still lay atop a box in Emma's garage.

Trish frowned. "You didn't read it."

My face flushed. *Nope.*

Aiden's voice cut into our conversation. "Ms. Drake, do you have a question for Mr. Stone?"

"Yes, I have several." She turned her gaze on Stone. "First, Mr. Stone, I'd like to say this proposal is quite the accomplishment.

I've never read anything that twists the English language so thoroughly." Trish smiled. "You'd think a wizard helped with this."

Stone frowned. "You had an actual question, Ms. Drake?"

"Can you explain your thoughts behind the proposed citywide curfew in your proposal?" Trish said.

I flipped through the pages in front of me, trying to scan the contents as quickly as possible. Ben, who'd grown up in Hopewell, mentioned a previous curfew passed when he was in his teens. It'd been opposed by the supernatural citizens.

Stone rested his fingertips on the table and leaned forward. "The curfew is meant to ensure citizens are home, safe, before nightfall when more violent crimes tend to occur."

Trish arched her eyebrow. "But, as written, the curfew only applies to Hopewell's supernatural citizens."

Reginald nodded. "Yes, I can foresee resistance from the wizarding community regarding this."

"Ms. Drake and Mr. Sharpe," Stone said. "Hopewell's supernatural citizens deserve the same amount of protection as any other citizen. With reports of hate groups threatening them, they will be kept from harm's way."

"So your solution is to lock us up at night in our homes while everyone else goes about their lives?" I asked. "If we don't go outside, we won't suffer bodily harm?"

"That's not—"

"Is there anything in here about addressing the hate groups themselves?" I flipped back toward the front of the proposal. "Because I don't see anything."

Stone paced his answer like he spoke to a child. "We cannot deny the citizens of Hopewell their right to free speech."

My wolf twisted, trying to force a growl from me. She disliked men like Stone. Arrogant in their privilege. Manipulative. I took a moment to inhale and exhale. "So we don't want to infringe on the rights of those who threaten harm, but we're fine making prisons out of homes of those who could be harmed?"

Trish nodded. "Locking away supernatural citizens at night only supports the baseless propaganda pushed by this Committee. This group regards us as monsters to fear, not equal citizens."

Another Committee member spoke. "They instigated a riot. There is no doubt they can be dangerous."

"That wasn't meant to happen," I said. "The gathering was a protest to speak out against tethering. They'd exhausted all other ways to communicate their frustrations to the Committee. They were tired of being ignored."

The man turned to face me. "And you didn't mean to attack Mr. Stone?"

My face heated, and I clenched my jaw to halt my less-than-helpful retort. An attempted attack on Stone had been a horrible mistake, and one that would be following me for a while.

Aiden's voice carried a stern edge. "Let's stay focused on the content of Mr. Stone's proposal. Personal accusations don't result in constructive discourse."

"There is also a part of this proposal that requests tethering be utilized retroactively." Trish cocked her head to the side. "After a riot caused by the objection to tethering, why do you believe digging through people's past and punishing them with tethers is a good idea?"

The blood drained from my face. Tethered for past acts? How *far* into the past?

Stone's smile was all show. His tone tight and low, he said, "Ms. Drake, if a supernatural citizen hasn't committed unpunished crimes in the past, there's nothing for them to worry about."

The room seemed suddenly too small and stiflingly hot. I lowered my gaze to where my hands rested on the table.

"*Twenty* years, Mr. Stone?" Trish's tone hardened. "You propose tethering supernatural citizens who've had infractions within the past *twenty* years." She looked around the table. "Can any of us here say we are the same person we were twenty years ago? And then to be punished for it?"

I swallowed against a surge of nausea. I'd nearly killed a man before fleeing from my childhood home and any possible punishment. Memories of that day, when I'd met my inner wolf, were foggy.

"We can't allow criminals to walk free here." Stone jabbed a finger down onto the stack of papers in front of him. "This ensures criminals will be made examples of to deter future crime."

"The only thing this ensures is that more wolves will die," Trish growled, "and you know that, so stop wasting our time." She waved her hand at the papers. "This whole proposal is a thinly veiled effort to exercise even more control over us."

Reginald cleared his throat. "The period of twenty years does seem a bit extreme, Mr. Stone."

Stone slammed his hand down on the table, causing me to jump. "Listen, people, if we want a safe city, we have to be willing to make some hard choices." Stone turned his gaze on Trish. "Let me repeat: if you haven't broken the law and weaseled through the system, you have nothing to worry about."

I gave a sideward glance at Trish.

Her body tensed, and her brown eyes shifted to a liquid gold color. "This feels a bit personal, Mr. Stone."

Because of their connections through the city, Trish and Nate had on more than one occasion slipped through the Commoner and supernatural community law systems.

"Focus, everyone," Aiden said.

I raised a shaking hand. Aiden's gaze, and everyone else's at the table, shifted to me. Aiden nodded. I stood, my palms leaving sweaty prints on the tabletop. "I wanted to say a few things about tethering. Trish is right. Tethering a werewolf is a death sentence."

Stone scoffed, looking around the table. "I think you're being a bit dramatic, Alexis."

"It's Alex," I growled. I paused to fight back the surge of irritation. "And no, I'm not being dramatic. Most Hopewell wolves I've met have lost a friend or family member to tethering."

"The wizards do just fine with tethers, don't they, Reginald?" someone asked.

I frowned at Reginald. Did he realize how his grandson struggled every day with his tether? How it affected his mental health? Ben missed his connection with magic to the point of illegally weakening his tether. His attempt only restored a fraction of his voice silenced by the punishment.

"Ah, they . . . A wizard's experience with a tether is different from a werewolf's," he said. "The tether silences the wizard's voice. To cast a spell, a vocal component is required."

"For werewolves, a tether creates a magical barrier between ourselves and our inner wolves," I said. "The emotion we harness into our gifts has nowhere to go. Instead, it floods our minds." The thought of containing all that raw emotion in my head with no way to act on it terrified me. I swallowed, but my voice still sounded hoarse. "We can try to manage it, but eventually the pain becomes overwhelming. Most wolves will take their life to find peace from that feedback loop."

Murmurs traveled around the table. I looked at Stone. His face had reddened. He'd conveniently left the repercussions of tethering out of his report.

"There is no standardized system for tethering, and it ruins lives." I shook my head. "Stone's . . . Mr. Stone's proposal of enforcing these new rules with tethering won't keep anyone safer. It'll only harm relations between Commoners and the rest of us. Instead of preventing riots, this may cause more. I don't think the Committee should approve this proposal." I gave an awkward glance around the table. "Thanks." I sat down, my heart hammering at my ribcage.

Trish's hand covered my own. The murmuring around the table renewed, and Aiden's voice broke into the noise. "Please, everyone." The individual conversations subsided. "Thank you for your insight, Miss Steward. Does anyone else have questions or thoughts on this proposal?"

I looked at Jakob, but he avoided my gaze. It didn't seem like Reginald planned to speak either. Why weren't they sharing their thoughts on what a terrible idea this proposal was?

No one else spoke up, so Aiden turned his attention back to Stone. "It seems there are no other questions or concerns. Any final words before we vote, Mr. Stone?"

The man across the table from me was a barely contained ball of rage. His stance, hands planted firmly on the table and leaning toward me, caused my inner wolf to attempt to push her way to the surface. Low growls slipped from between my clenched teeth as I returned his glare.

Stone looked down at the table, exhaled, and then straightened both his posture and tie. His smile and tone were pleasant as he addressed everyone. "Yes, thank you, Miss Steward."

I blinked.

Stone's voice raised to a more formal *I'm-addressing-you* tone and volume. "Thank you for reminding us all what we *Commoners* are dealing with." He gave the word air quotes before he glared across the table at me. "Manipulative and lying monsters."

His words caused me to bare my teeth, and my growling became more pronounced.

"Mr. Stone," Aiden warned. "Show some respect."

Stone pointed across the table at me. "Let me remind you all that she was at the riot. She was with the pack of criminals smashing the historic windows of this sacred building!"

Aiden's voice grew sharp. "Mr. Stone! That's enough."

Trish snarled, and I rose to my feet. "I wasn't smashing anything! I wanted to make sure my friend was safe!"

Stone gave a short, abrupt laugh, looking around at the Committee members. "I'm sure you were, just as you leapt over this table with the intent to shake my hand."

My heart sank. Again with the goddamn leaping-at-him thing. I hadn't planned on killing him, just giving him a black eye. And maybe a broken nose.

Aiden rose to his feet with a scowl, his brows drawn together. "Mr. Stone, this is your last warning or you will be excused from the table."

Stone raised his hands, palms facing forward. He nodded. "Yes, Father. Of course." He took his seat again amidst a rumble of sudden conversation.

Trembling from the adrenaline, I lowered myself back in my seat. Trish sat with her elbows on the table, eyes closed, pressing her fingers to her temples. Reginald's hand rested on her shoulder.

Aiden remained standing. "Each representative here carries the responsibility of striving toward a Hopewell in which both Commoners and supernatural beings peacefully cohabitate. Both types of citizens enrich our city. As you vote on this proposal, I hope this is kept close to your minds and hearts."

As a guest, I was excused while the official representatives held the vote. Chewing at my thumbnail, I paced outside the closed sanctuary doors. If those rules were passed, people weren't going to be happy. The capture of the Hunter had relieved tension between the Commoners, wolves, and wizards. Stone's awful proposal would only build it up again.

Footsteps sounded from inside the sanctuary. I stepped back out of the way of the doors. They opened, and various Committee members filed out. Serenity, a young woman wearing glasses and a priest's collar, saw me and briefly embraced me in a hug. When we parted, her eyes were sad. My heart fell. She gave my shoulder a squeeze and left out the front doors.

The scent of a fellow wolf reached me. Jakob emerged from the sanctuary, uniform hat in hand, and started toward the front door.

"Jakob, wait."

He paused and looked back at me. With a slight frown, he walked over and nodded. "Good afternoon, Miss Steward."

"You can drop the formalities." I jerked a thumb toward the sanctuary. "How'd it turn out?"

"Seven to five in favor of the proposal."

"You were one of the five, right?"

Instead of answering, he glanced toward the doors.

I fought to keep the snarl from my voice. "Right? Jakob?"

His frown deepened. "I don't need to discuss that with you."

I stepped closer, into his space, and lowered my voice. This time I allowed my irritation to color my tone. "Is Nate right about you? Does Stone have you on a leash, doing whatever he asks?"

Jakob's face flushed, and his eyes narrowed.

"Alex."

Trish's voice caused me to turn from Jakob. She stood with Reginald between the sanctuary doors and the front doors of the church. Her features were grim, and she waved me over. I gave Jakob a parting frown before following Trish and Reginald outside.

Trish lit a cigarette with trembling hands, her entire posture rigid. She exhaled a stream of smoke and lowered her sunglasses over her golden eyes. "From this point forward, keep your interactions with Jakob to a minimum."

"He said the proposal passed." I looked between Trish and Reginald. "What does that mean for us?"

"Well," Reginald said, "we'll all need to be a bit more careful—"

"—It means we're all in danger," Trish interrupted, exhaling another stream of smoke.

Walking to my car, I tried to remain calm, but a lingering dread wouldn't release my mind. Was there any way the Committee would find out why I'd left my parents' home? What my inner wolf had done to that man? Trish promised to contact me after she spoke to Nate.

My phone vibrated in my pocket. I got into my car and checked it. Another missed call from my parents. Again, no voicemail. Was this an accidental dial too?

I began to call them back but noticed the time. Everything around me faded away, and an icy realization gripped my gut.

Emma's meeting at her house.

An hour ago.

5

I SCRAMBLED TO start the car and almost backed into someone in my rush to leave the parking spot. A horn blare announced my rolling stop before I turned onto the main street and sped back to Emma's. My mind whirled with excuses for why I hadn't prepped the house like she'd asked.

Emma's driveway appeared empty except for her moped. I slipped in the front door like a kid arriving home past curfew. In the living room, I paused to scent the air and listen. There were no sounds of movement or conversation.

I padded through the living room and picked up faded, unfamiliar scents that must have been Emma's coworkers. Then I smashed my toe on the corner of a box. One of the many boxes of records cluttering the room. Cursing, I limped into the kitchen and dining room.

Alone on the patio, facing away from the sliding door, sat Emma. A half-empty glass of wine rested on the table beside her.

I slid open the door and stepped onto the patio. "Hey there."

Emma glanced over her shoulder and turned back without a word. She picked up her glass of wine.

I took a deep breath and sat beside her at the table. It was covered with dirty dishes and the remains of what must have been the business lunch. I turned my chair to face her. "I'm really, really, *really* sorry, Em."

Emma took a sip of wine, not looking at me.

"After the interview, I took longer at Ben's apartment than expected," I said. "Then there was the Committee meeting I'd forgotten about. Those take forever. I lost track—"

"I understand." She shrugged. "It wasn't important to you."

I frowned. "What?"

"You were busy with other things." Emma finally looked at me. Her perfect brows furrowed, and the corners of her mouth turned down. "It was important to *me*, Alex. Really important. I trusted my best friend to do this one favor, pick up after herself, and then I get home minutes before my coworkers arrive and your shit is all over the—" She waved her hand, and wine sloshed out of the glass into her lap. "Dammit!"

I grabbed a napkin from the table. "Let me help."

"No!" Emma swatted my hand away, set her glass on the table, and blotted at her clothes with her own napkin. "I have it." She began to sniffle.

"Em, I'm so sorry."

She looked up, her face flushed and her eyes shimmering with tears. "I broke three nails trying to move those boxes so my guests could walk through the living room!"

I shrunk back in my chair. Emma had been raised to appear perfect in every way, at all times, no matter what. This luncheon with her coworkers was no exception. "I'll move the boxes upstairs as soon as we're done talking. Tell me what else I can do to fix this."

"I think you need to stay somewhere else."

It wasn't a surprise and would be better for our friendship, but being asked to leave made my chest ache anyway. I looked down and scratched at my chipped nail polish. "Okay." I'd crash with Trish and Nate until I could get into a place of my own. We sat in silence a moment longer before I asked. "Did the meeting itself go okay?"

Emma gave a pained smile and shook her head. "I don't know." She pressed her napkin to the corners of her eyes. "I think so?" She glanced over at me. "How did your interview go?"

"I got the job."

"Congratulations."

"Thanks."

My phone rang, the ringtone belonging to my parents. "Sorry Em, it's my mom. I need to take this."

She waved me away. "I have to clean up and get back to work."

I walked inside the house and answered the call. "Hey, Mom."

Her voice was tight. "Hello, sweetie. I've been trying to reach you. What are you doing right now?"

"Not much," I said. "You sound worried. Is Grandma okay?"

"Yes, of course. Grandma is fine," she said. "We're all okay. We were wondering if we could come for a visit."

"What? Why?" They very rarely visited. We didn't think it was safe in case they drew attention to me. I'd gone years at a time without seeing my family as I moved around the country to remain hidden.

Dad's voice sounded muffled in the background. My mother must have covered the receiver.

I frowned. "Mom, what's going on?"

A rustling noise came across the phone, and then my mother's voice was clear again. "Alex, we're already on our way. We left New York last night and stayed at a hotel to make the trip easier for your grandmother. We should be in Hopewell within an hour."

"What!" My heart leapt, and my skin went cold.

"It's important," she said. "We wouldn't surprise you like this otherwise."

"Please tell me what's happening," I said.

"We will as soon as we see you," she said. "What address are you at now?"

My pulse thudded in my ears as my mind raced for an answer. I hadn't told them about living with Ben or with Emma. And now was I technically homeless until I called Trish and Nate. "I . . . um—" I looked quickly around me, as if an answer would present itself.

"You probably aren't prepared for visitors. Let's meet at a park in an hour and a half. We'll bring along a late lunch, early dinner. Then you can go to your apartment and clean it up while we get settled into our hotel. We'll be staying at a Holiday Inn right downtown."

"Your hotel? What the hell, Mom!"

"Language, sweetie," she said. I could envision the tightness in her jawline. "Please text me the address of a nice park where we can meet you. Make sure there are trees so your grandma can be out of the sun. We love you. See you soon."

The line went dead, and I lowered my phone to stare at it. I searched for a park close to Emma's place and sent the address to my mother. I checked the time so I wouldn't be late.

Cursing, I rushed up the stairs to change into something nicer to wear. Why the hell were they ambushing me for a family picnic? Anxiety churned in my stomach as a million horrible reasons sprung out of my imagination. Most involved the man on the university track team who triggered my werewolf gene.

I emptied the small dresser of my entire wardrobe trying to find something to wear. In my panic, everything seemed unsuitable. A low growl rumbled within my chest as I tossed aside one piece of clothing after another.

I spun toward the empty dresser, nearly panting, and caught sight of myself in the mirror. Golden eyes stared back at me from a flushed face wreathed in curly hair. I closed my eyes and took a slow, deep breath.

"It's okay," I whispered. "We're okay."

The creature inside of me receded, responding to my efforts to settle my body. I looked toward the bedroom door and thought of Emma's large walk-in closet. She was petite but bustier than me, so I bet I could at least find a shirt that would fit.

I ran out of my bedroom to the top of the stairs. "Emma, I need your help!" No response. I walked down another step and tried again. "Em!"

The patio door swished open on its track, and Emma appeared at the bottom of the stairs. She held onto the railing, frowning up at me. "Are you really asking for my help right now?"

An animal-like whine slipped from my lips. My eyes widened, and I covered my mouth.

Emma rolled her eyes. "What do you need?"

I lowered my hands. "Can I borrow a shirt? My parents are here for a surprise visit. I don't have anything to wear that says, 'Your adult daughter totally has her shit together.'"

Emma turned away. "Take whatever you need."

"Thanks, Em." I spun and dashed for her closet.

I PULLED INTO the gravel lot of the city park five minutes late. It made me uneasy to see the family car. Even with eight years of wear, it reminded me of my old life in New York. The vehicle looked out of place in this city that felt more and more like my new home.

The cicadas' late-summer song droned beneath rambunctious shouts of the children. I walked toward an expansive green space with a soccer field, playground equipment, and picnic tables. Stands of mature trees provided pools of shade through the park.

Beneath a huge tree's canopy were my parents and my grandmother. I smiled, and my heart expanded within my ribcage. I'd missed them so much. My mom was busy ordering my father to move a picnic table deeper into the shade. She held a restaurant to-go bag. From her seat in a folding lawn chair, my grandmother saw me first.

I could already smell her, the soothing fragrance of lavender reaching me on the warm breeze. It loosened the tension between my shoulder blades.

She stood and beamed as she held her arms open. "Alex."

I hugged her small body and inhaled her scent. It brought a flood of childhood memories, most linked to being safe and comforted in her arms. "Hi, Grandma." I started to cry, but they were happy tears.

My parents stood beside my grandmother, waiting their turn to greet me. My mother's eyes shimmered as she hugged me, wrapping me in the gentle aromas of hand lotion and shampoo. "Oh sweetie, we've missed you." She released me into my father's embrace, the only other gentle touch I'd known from a man until I'd met Ben. I hugged him tight too, relishing the smells of shaving cream and Irish Spring soap.

"I hope I remembered correctly, Alex. No onions, right?" My mom unpacked the sandwiches from the bag onto the picnic table, already down to the business of filling her family with food.

I nodded and helped my grandmother move her chair to the end of the table. "You guys scared me earlier when you called."

My mother glanced at my father. His brow creased, and he sat down. "Alex, we've had odd things happening at home that made us nervous. There have been people asking about you."

"Me?" I didn't keep in touch with anyone from my life in New York other than my family. "Who's asking?"

"It happens every now and then," my mother said, "usually when the university track season starts." Her words caused me to frown, and she placed her hand over mine.

The man I attacked—no, who attacked me—had been a star athlete on the university's team. The creature inside me stirred. Even now, she bristled at any glimpse of him in my memories. Damp leaves, bright blood, even the scents of spring from that day lingered in my nightmares.

"But this time it's different," my father said. "Someone is interested in the settlement we made through the young man's attorney." The payment took every penny Grandpa had left us.

I exhaled sharply through my nose, and my fingers curled against the wood surface of the picnic table. "I thought his parents knew the judge and had those court records sealed." Even though we paid damages for the man's injuries, his family didn't want details of what happened traced back to their son. We didn't argue the point since it kept me safe from prying eyes as well.

"We think someone outside the usual court system is asking," my grandmother said. She was referring to a system that existed for the supernatural community. A Committee for upstate New York.

"What?" My eyes widened and my pulse sped up. "Why now after so many years?"

"We don't know," my dad said. "We can't think of anything we did to trigger an investigation. We're always so careful."

My mother's fingers squeezed mine. "Our trip here took twice as long because of all the detours your father insisted on taking."

"Alex, did something happen here that you haven't told us about?" My father leaned forward. "Something that could've drawn their attention?"

I dropped my gaze to my sandwich. Heat rose up my neck and through my face. Tangling with a rogue wizard and wolf, almost losing my best friend to a secret brainwashing organization, getting arrested, shutting down a hate group, being caught in the middle of a riot, punching a cop and getting arrested again, losing my other friend because she discovered I was a werewolf, and taking out a Hunter intent on murdering me and my found family? They were all possibilities.

Somehow I'd also found my home away from home, befriended the most influential wolves in Hopewell, and taken a chance on a serious relationship with a guy I liked—all while trying to grow closer to this beast inside of me so she doesn't kill anyone, plus hold a job, pay rent, *and* afford to eat . . . Honestly, what *hadn't* happened over the past eight months?

"Alexandria?" My mother's tone sharpened. She frowned and removed her hand from mine. Apparently, my tells haven't changed since my teens.

"I may have gotten into a bit of trouble here," I said. "But it should've been cleared up." Trish said my record with the Hopewell Police Department had been wiped.

"What kind of trouble?" My father's tone was all business too. My parents were here to get to the bottom of why people were asking about their daughter, and they did not have time for my shit.

I pushed the sandwich away. The previously appealing smell turned my stomach. "I . . . um . . . There were . . . So, someone hired a pretty nasty guy to hunt people like me, and I helped to stop him." I glanced up.

My father sat pale and silent while my mother's widened eyes threatened to spill tears again. These weren't the happy ones.

"Why didn't you say something to us?" Mom reached for my hand again, and I pulled it away.

A snarl of irritation began inside me. I suddenly didn't want them here. They weren't allowed to drop into my life with no frame of reference and judge my actions. "I had to help. He'd already killed one of us, and I wasn't going to let him do it again."

"Were you helping your friends? The woman and man who own the music club?" my grandmother said.

"Trish and Nate. Yes." I looked at my parents again. "I don't understand how that made it back to New York. I've been to Hopewell Committee meetings and learned how they operate. These governing bodies are local." The Hunter we'd put away had carried a contract to find and kill me. Could it have been from someone in New York state?

"Why would you endanger yourself like that?" my mother asked. "You have to be smart. Think of your safety."

"We look out for each other. That's how it works here." I frowned. "The Committee is a pain in the ass, but at least I can speak up on behalf of the others."

"Language," my mother said.

My father shook his head. "It may be time for you to move again. It's nice you were able to make friends with other people like yourself, but your mother is right. You have to do what's right for you . . . what keeps you safe."

I chewed at my thumbnail. Who would be poking around in my past? And why? I'd made a lot of new friends, but I'd also pissed off a few powerful people.

My first guess was Stone. Trish, Joan, and I had broken his Hunter, taking away Stone's ability to target and remove supernatural citizens. He'd pivoted to pushing his new safety laws through the Committee, hoping to accomplish his original goal.

"Alex, what are you thinking?" My grandmother watched me, her food untouched.

"I think I know who is asking about the settlement. He lives here." If I remained in Hopewell and Stone knew I'd almost killed a man, he'd have me tried, sentenced, and tethered under his new laws. Panic tightened my chest. I couldn't stay.

Run.

"It's settled then. You're leaving," my mother said. She pointed at my sandwich. "Now quit fidgeting and eat."

Run.

My inner wolf pressed upward through my consciousness. I squeezed my eyes shut and hid my shifting hands in my lap. It wasn't her first choice to run away from what threatened me. That's why I found myself in the current situation. But we wouldn't survive being separated from each other.

The aroma of lavender surrounded me, and my grandmother's small hand rubbed my back. She'd left her seat to comfort me. I leaned back into her embrace. "I don't want to leave," I said. "I don't want to be alone again."

"I know, sweetie," Grandma said. "I'm sorry."

When I'd settled my nerves enough to not flash glowing eyes or gnarly claws, I promised I'd immediately get my things and put Hopewell in the rearview mirror. My family would stay the night at the hotel and head in the opposite direction tomorrow morning. We weren't sure when we'd see each other again. I hugged my parents and grandmother, telling them how much I loved them, before returning to Emma's house.

Nate and Trish had worked with me over the past several months to understand my inner wolf. I'd grown to love her and cherish her presence. I already couldn't imagine life without her. She and I had become more in sync than we'd ever been.

But right now, I was scared.

And she was pissed.

6

AT EMMA'S HOUSE, I rushed up the stairs to the spare room. My skirt and the top Emma let me borrow were ditched for something more practical: a t-shirt and pair of jeans. I dropped to my knees beside the bed and reached underneath it for my go-bag. It was always packed just in case I had to . . . *run*.

I stood, set the bag on the bed, and stuffed several more items of clothing into it. Footsteps on the stairs made me freeze, and my attention jerked toward the hallway. All my nerves were firing. A low growl rumbled up from my chest.

The scent of vanilla caused the sound to die in my throat, and my best friend appeared in the doorway. Emma took a step back when she saw me, her blue eyes wide. "Alex?"

"Weren't you going back to work?" I yanked at the zipper of the bulging bag. It got stuck.

"I decided to finish my workday here." Emma paused. "Are you going somewhere? When I asked you to find another place, I didn't mean you had to leave today."

No, no, no. The pain began in my chest. How did I think I could take off without saying goodbye to Emma? I wrenched on the stubborn zipper. "I need to go."

"Go where?" She entered the room. Cautiously. "What's wrong? Is it Ben?"

Ben. Another stab of pain in my chest. I bit my lip, and my vision blurred. How in the *hell* was I going to tell Ben what had happened? Joan hadn't allowed me access to him. I didn't even know where I was going yet.

Emma's fingers settled on my shoulder. "Please talk to me."

I pushed the bag aside, squeezed my eyes shut, and tried again to calm the beast pacing inside me. She wanted to fight, but I was signaling we should run. Deep breath. Inhale. Exhale. "My parents said someone is asking about the settlement from back home, the one where I attacked that college athlete."

Emma's tone turned icy and her fingers tightened on my shoulder. "What you mean to say is the college athlete who assaulted and attempted to rape you."

My stomach twisted. I opened my eyes and nodded. "We think someone from here has been nosing around in my past, trying to find any screw-up to charge me with in a Committee trial. Trish had my Hopewell records expunged, so there's nothing from my time here to use."

"But that attack happened years ago," she said. "It's so far in the past, I don't see how—"

"Stone created a package of laws passed today in the Committee meeting." I frowned. "It allows the Committee to retroactively punish us for crimes within the past twenty years."

Emma's eyes widened again, and her hand covered her mouth.

"So I have to leave." I looked at Emma, who'd put up with my shit with an endless supply of patience. Well, maybe I'd maxed it out a few times. I'd never felt I had to be anyone but myself with her. As an only child, I'd never had a sister, but she came close.

She shook her head. "How can Stone do that?"

"He has people scared of monsters living in their city," I said.

"We have to be able to do something," she said. "That guy *attacked* you."

I sat on the edge of the bed and threw my hands in the air. "You know that's not how it works here. Under no circumstances are we to harm the Commoners. I nearly killed him." I wiped away a tear that slipped. "I don't want to go, Em."

Emma sat down beside me and hugged me. That's when the waterworks really kicked in. "Have you talked to Trish and Nate about this?"

"No, I only recently made the decision," I said. "Plus, they have other things to worry about. They have criminal records of their own. I'm sure Stone is eager to punish Trish, too. She helped take out his Hunter." I shook my head. "Everything is such a mess."

"You should tell them anyway, Alex." Emma released me. "You don't want Trish to be blindsided if she reaches out and you're gone."

She was right. I should give Trish the courtesy of knowing what I'd decided. As a matriarch of the wolf community, Trish had invested a ton of time into me. I nodded. "Okay, yeah. I'll stop over there before I leave town."

The doorbell sounded downstairs.

My pulse skipped. All the muscles in my body seized up again.

"I'll get it. I'm sure it's nothing." Emma stood. "If it's okay, I'd like to go with you to Hell's Bells." She left the room. Her footsteps receded down the stairs and toward the front door.

I grabbed my bag and slunk to the bedroom door. I invited the beast inside me to share more space. She immediately filled it, and my senses magnified. My sharpened hearing picked up the opening creak of the front door.

Emma's tone tensed. "Can I help you, Officer?"

"Yes. I'm Officer DeBoer. May I speak to Miss Steward?"

The familiar voice caused the hair at the nape of my neck to stand on end.

"Your Anne's partner, right? I'm Emma Arztin. Anne's a good friend of mine," Emma said. "It's nice to finally meet you."

My heartbeat thudded in my ears. The Committee had sent Jakob to arrest Ben. Was he here to do the same with me?

Jakob paused before he spoke again. "It's nice to meet you as well, Miss Arztin, but—"

"You can call me Emma."

She was stalling. I rushed to the bedroom window facing the backyard. The guest bedroom was on the second floor, so the jump should be easy. I slid up the frame of the window, popped loose the screen, and pulled it back into the room.

"Emma. I'm sorry, but I need to speak to Miss Steward as soon as possible. I noticed her car in the drive," Jakob said.

The window was going to be a squeeze. I passed my bag through and let it drop to the lawn below. Backing through the window worked, and after I got my waist through, I braced my shoes against the siding before pushing off. I landed on the grass and froze. Only faint traces of Emma's and Jakob's voices carried through the house and the screened slider.

Lowering myself so I wouldn't be visible through the first-floor window, I crept toward the backyard's gate. I passed through, headed down a brick walkway alongside the house, and peered around the corner. Jakob's cruiser was parked between me and my car. He stood at the front door, his back to me as he talked to Emma. She beamed her smile, but her fingers fidgeted with a strand of her hair.

"Please, Emma, a lot of trouble could be avoided if you called her to the door," Jakob said.

I crouched back around the corner again and dug for my keys. I wouldn't have much time to get into my car before Jakob noticed me. When I shifted my weight to get the keys, my phone dropped out of my pocket. It clattered onto the walkway, jarring my amped-up hearing. I froze again, my heart pounding. Footsteps sounded from the front of the house and across the driveway.

"Officer DeBoer, wait, I'll call her down for you," Emma said.

So much for this exit route. I snatched up my phone, grabbed my bag, and ran toward the backyard. The footsteps quickened, and Jakob's voice called out. "Alex, stop!"

Was he crazy? Why would I stop for him? He obviously wasn't concerned about my well-being if he was here to arrest me for the Committee. Instead of opening the gate, I leapt the fence into the backyard. I dashed across the lawn for the patio. I'd go through the house and out the front, right to my car.

The gate door slammed. Jakob's footsteps drew closer behind me. His scent strengthened with every passing second.

Emma waited at the patio, having thrown the screen door open. I barely passed her into the house before Jakob's weight struck my lower body.

We fell forward into the dining room chairs with a horrendous crash and the sound of splintering wood. Both my bag and phone flew from my grasp. I twisted and turned onto my back. Snarling, I drove the heel of my shoe into Jakob's shoulder. "Get away from me, you traitor!"

He gritted his teeth and grabbed at my ankle, but I scuttled backward until I ran into the wall. I pushed my back upward along the wall until I stood, panting, my hackles raised. I couldn't turn and run now. He was too close.

Jakob rose to his feet, his gaze locked with mine.

I reached down inside of myself and invited my wolf forward. My knuckles popped and enlarged as my hands shifted shape. My fingers lengthened, and claws formed from my chewed fingernails. I bared my teeth and growled.

"Why do you make everything so hard?" Jakob's eyes hadn't even changed color. Only a rigid jawline and pinched brow gave any hint of emotion. "You consistently make things more complicated for yourself and everyone around you."

"Why do you have to be an asshole?" I snarled.

"I'm doing my job," Jakob said. "You have to come with me."

Frustration boiled inside me, threatening to give in to anger. I glanced at Emma. It wasn't the first time I'd wished her wizard abilities would lean more toward fireballs than healing. She'd pushed herself back, pale and trembling, against the kitchen island.

I took a deep inhale, then exhaled. My voice lost a bit of its bite. "You know what's going to happen if you hand me over to the Committee, right? They'll have me tethered."

Jakob frowned. "That's not guaranteed. You'll be put on trial."

"For defending myself. Eight years ago," I said.

"You'll have a chance to argue your case," he said. "But right now, you have to come with me." He took a step forward.

"A man attacked me! He triggered my wolf gene." Maybe if Jakob knew what happened, he'd understand the injustice of the situation. "If it weren't for him, I wouldn't be a werewolf."

"I'm sorry that happened to you," Jakob said.

"Why do you agree to round us up for the Committee? You, of all people, should understand what tethering does to wolves," I said.

Jakob inhaled sharply through his nose.

"What happened that you hate us all so much?" I frowned. "What awoke your wolf?"

"That has nothing to do with this." His eyes narrowed. "And quit making assumptions. I'm where I am to help us."

I tried to recall everything I'd learned about Jakob. He'd grown up in Hopewell. There was an older brother, Nate's friend, they'd lost. My stomach clenched, making me nauseous. "It was your brother, wasn't it? You would've been younger when—"

Jakob frowned and his features hardened. "My brother knew the consequences, and he chose to break the law anyway."

"Trish said your brother was tethered for carjacking," I said. "Commoners don't get the death sentence for carjacking! Why should we?"

His face reddened, and his voice grew hoarse. Gold surfaced through the brown in his eyes. "We wolves are gifted, but it doesn't change the fact we have to follow the rules."

"The rules are bullshit, Jakob," I shouted. "The trial is bullshit. The Committee. All of it!"

"Then why waste Trish's time?" he said. "Why get involved with the Committee?"

"To protect people from it!" The realization occurred to me after months of asking myself the same thing. "Don't *you* want to protect us?"

Jakob's frown deepened. "I'm a representative for the supernatural citizens, but I'm also a Hopewell police officer. It requires me to protect *everyone*, not just the wolves."

"You're doing shit for the wolves by enforcing these laws," I growled.

"Let her go," Emma interrupted. "She was leaving Hopewell anyway. No one will know. I won't say a thing, I promise."

"She's not leaving unless it's with me." Jakob took another step toward me. "Please, Miss Steward."

There seemed to be no reasoning with Jakob, and my patience with him was running out. Shoulders sagging, I pushed away from the wall. I held my hands aloft so he could see them and crouched to retrieve my phone. "Can I take my bag?" I returned my phone to my pocket.

Jakob hesitated, but then nodded. "I don't know how long you'll be held. You may need a change of clothes or two."

I took a hold of the bag's handles and stood. One last chance to get out of here.

Emma started to cry and rushed over to hug me. "I'll talk to Reginald and Trish right away. They can fix this."

She still believed Reginald would stand by Trish before the Committee's laws. He wouldn't. If he'd chosen the rules over his own grandson's well-being, there was no hope for me.

I wrapped my arms around Emma and inhaled deeply. My nose filled with her vanilla scent. "Please tell Trish and Nate what happened . . . And my family. They're at the downtown Holiday Inn."

Emma nodded and released me, wiping away tears. "I'll see you again soon."

I already felt the guilt. "I'm really sorry, Em." I turned toward Jakob. "I'm ready."

"Alexandria Steward," Jakob said, "I have with me a warrant for your arrest in relation to violating Committee Safety Guideline 21A. I ask that you come with me. If you resist arrest, I have permission to use whatever force is necessary."

Jakob followed me into Emma's pristine living room. We wove around the boxes of Ben's records toward the front door. My gaze frantically combed the room and landed on a crystal bowl of truffles.

I snatched up the bowl from the table, dropped my bag, and spun on Jakob, using the heavy dish as a bludgeoning weapon. His eyes widened, and his arm flew up to block the dish from striking his head. The dish glanced off his arm and knocked his hat to the floor.

Without pause, I swung the dish again. This time he caught my forearm. He seized my wrist and gave it a sharp twist. The pain shot up my arm all the way to my shoulder. I yelped. The dish fell from my hand.

With my free hand, I swiped at his face, my claws extended. He attempted to lean out of my reach. The movement backed him into a box of records. When he leaned forward to correct his balance, I yanked him toward me. I turned and tucked my body beneath him, hauling him over top of me. He fell onto his back through Emma's glass coffee table with a tremendous crash.

My arm free, I grabbed my bag and dashed toward the door. The tinkling of glass and growling behind me assured Jakob would be on his feet soon. I shot out the front door to my car. My chest heaving, I tried to retrieve car keys from my pocket. The shifted form of my hands, larger than normal, made it nearly impossible.

Goddamn skinny jeans!

Something bashed into me from behind, and my body slammed against my car hard enough to knock the wind from my lungs. Jakob's scent overwhelmed me. He wrenched one of my arms up behind my back and held me against the car. "Don't move," he growled near my ear.

I stood gasping for breath as the metallic clicking noise signaled he'd cuffed one of my wrists and then the other. The pressure behind my body eased, and he hauled me back from the car by my upper arm.

As soon as my breathing allowed, I tried to twist away from him. "Let go of me!" Unlike the cuffs he'd used on me before, I couldn't snap the chain link on this set.

We struggled the entire ten feet to his cruiser. I used every inch to tell him what I thought of him arresting a fellow werewolf, inventing several words along the way.

Jakob tossed me into the backseat and slammed the door. I sat shaking with fury, unable to contain my growling and snarling.

"Office DeBoer, you're bleeding," The car window muffled Emma's voice. "Let me help you." She stood outside the front door, holding my bag and Jakob's hat, her features strained.

A growl lingered in Jakob's voice. "I'll be fine." He walked over to her and accepted both the bag and his hat. "Thank you." The back of his uniform, especially his sleeves, were torn and stained with blood.

He got into the cruiser and tossed my bag over to the passenger seat. Jakob put on his hat and clasped the steering wheel. When he looked at me in the rearview mirror, his eyes were their usual brown.

I took the opportunity to narrow my eyes at him and release a fresh bout of growling.

He stared at me a moment before he looked away, shook his head, and started the cruiser.

I turned and watched in the rearview mirror. Hands clasped, Emma stood in the front doorway and watched us back out of the drive.

The view of my friend, her house, and my car in the drive receded. Fear returned with a vengeance. How could Jakob betray me like this? I was furious he'd uphold and enforce rules that harmed our community. And I was terrified of what awaited me at the hands of the Committee.

7

I DIDN'T KNOW where the Committee held supernatural beings while we awaited trial. I would have preferred not to find out firsthand. By the time Jakob drove me downtown, most of the fight had left me. We pulled into the drive behind St. Anthony's Cathedral, Aiden's place.

Jakob looked up in the rearview mirror again. "We're going to walk into the church and straight to your room. Please, don't make a scene."

Meeting his gaze would only renew my anger, so I scowled and looked away.

He exited the cruiser and helped me out of the back seat. His grip on my forearm caused my fingers to tingle. We walked to a set of double doors that served as a back entrance to the cathedral. Jakob rang a buzzer, and one of the doors clicked and opened.

Inside the cathedral, the air was cooler and laced with the aromas of incense and age. The back halls were unfamiliar to me, since whenever I visited Aiden, I entered through the grandiose front doors. Jakob guided me down some stairs and rang another buzzer. We gained access to another set of stairs, this one older and hewn from stone. The air chilled further, and the scent of dampness crept up my nose. At the bottom of the stairs, we followed a low-ceilinged and narrow corridor.

"What is this place? Are we beneath the cathedral?" I asked.

Jakob didn't answer right away, as though unsure he should. "The entrance is under the cathedral. We're beneath the streets."

I'd only recently learned from Fillip, a local vampire, that a whole network of tunnels existed beneath Hopewell. We arrived at a wider hallway, and Jakob paused at a metal door. He turned me away and punched numbers into a keypad. The door's lock released. We entered an empty room with dim lighting, a crude toilet, and a cheap cot. The walls, ceiling, and floor were stone.

"Don't try to break through the door. It's built with us in mind." Jakob fetched a key from his pocket and unfastened the handcuffs. "I'll need your phone and any other devices." He stepped back and placed his body between me and the open door. Behind him, hanging above the door, a basic clock ticked. He waited with an outstretched arm and open hand.

"I want to see Trish," I said.

Jakob shook his head. "Your phone, please."

"Don't I get a phone call or something?"

He frowned. "Your charge is with the Committee. It's a different legal system. No phone call." When I returned his frown, he added, "I'm sure Trish will be here soon."

I got my phone from my pocket, sick with the knowledge that it was my last link to anyone. Clenching my jaw and lifting my chin, I tossed him the phone.

"Thank you," he said. "Do you have any other electronic—"

"No," I growled. "Where's my bag?"

"It has to be searched first. Then someone will bring it to you." He stepped back to leave the small room. "I'm sorry, Alex."

The door closed, and I was trapped in the stone box to wait.

The steady ticking of the clock became a repetitive tapping in my head. I considered taking it down and smashing it, both to vent my anger and silence the noise. But then I wouldn't have any idea of how much time passed.

Had Emma found my family at the hotel? Would I see them before the trial?

I paced, my wolf refusing to allow me to settle. The space surrounding me seemed to grow smaller by the moment. Despite Jakob's warning, I checked every part of the door to see if I could get around the locking system or simply wrench the door from its hinges. Long, jagged scratches in its surface were the only reward for my efforts. The reinforced door completely cut me off from any sound or smell beyond the stone room.

Finally, I sat on the cot, closed my eyes, and attempted to calm the creature inside me. I inhaled slowly through my nose.

Tick, tick, tick.

Exhale.

Tick, tick, tick.

Growling, I lay down on the cot and covered my ears with my hands.

I DIDN'T REALIZE someone stood at the door until the mechanical lock released with a dull clank. I leapt to my feet. The clock read 10:00 p.m., so I must have passed out into a fitful sleep on the cot. The hair on the back of my neck and arms rose as I waited, my entire body tense, for someone to enter.

Trish walked into the room carrying my bag. The door closed behind her. A surge of fear for what was to come hit me, and I rushed to hug her. She held me tight, and I began to cry. Trish allowed me to soak her shoulder with tears. She parted from me and brushed my cheekbones dry with her thumb. "Emma told me what happened. She's taken your family into her home and is waiting with them."

My chest hitched again with a sob as I thought how worried they would be. "When is the trial?"

"Tomorrow afternoon," she said.

"They're going to have me tethered, aren't they?"

Trish nodded. "They will try."

"What can I do?"

She shook her head.

A chill ran through me. "Is there anything?"

"Alex, we will do everything we can, but I want you to prepare yourself for the worst," she said.

I lowered myself to sit on the edge of the cot. Trish set my bag down at my feet.

"It was Stone, wasn't it?" I asked.

She nodded again.

"Do I even get a say in this whole thing?"

"Yes, but Stone will try to bring your wolf forward," she said. "He'll want to show the other members you are out of control and pose a threat to the Commoners."

Even now the beast inside me filled my head with horrific ideas of how to dispatch Stone, most of them being painful and messy. I squeezed my eyes shut and clenched my fists, trying to calm her bloodlust. "Will I be alone?"

"Unlike the Commoner's law system, all Committee trials are closed. The trial will involve the Committee members, so Reginald and I will be there. Nate, Emma, and your family will be waiting for you at the conclusion of the trial."

I shook my head, and somehow my body found more tears. I covered my face, embarrassed to appear fragile in front of Trish. She was always so stoic.

Her hand settled on my shoulder. "No matter what happens, Nate and I will not abandon you. You are a wolf, Alex, a cherished member of our family, regardless of what they take from you."

Trish didn't think I would make it through the trial without being convicted. Either her confidence in me and my control had finally found its limit, or she believed the Committee was more corrupt than she'd let on. It only made me more determined to win against Stone during the trial.

I wiped at the tears with the heel of my hand. "Okay." I cleared my throat and sat up straighter. "I can make it through this." I'd argue my case and show the Committee werewolves could be legit Hopewell citizens, the same as Commoners. I had to. The only other option was to lose and serve a sentence tethered, something I wasn't sure I'd survive.

I GOT LITTLE sleep that night, and the few hours I managed were filled with nightmares. When Jakob opened the cell door the next afternoon, I was tired but awake and ready. I avoided looking at him, remained silent, and didn't put up a fight when he guided me outside to his patrol car. We rode to Union Street Church in complete silence.

Unlike other times I'd sat in on a meeting, the Committee members were eerily silent, as if they were attending a funeral. They were seated at a long table on a raised platform. Aiden sat at the middle of the table, with six representatives flanking either side of him.

Jakob led me to a chair positioned on the floor in front of and slightly to the right of the raised table.

Reginald waited beside the chair, his features grim. "Good afternoon, Miss Alex." His fingertips were dusty from the chalk he held.

Strange glyphs, drawn in chalk on the floor, encircled the chair. Unease made my skin prickle. "What's this?"

"A precaution," Reginald said. "Officer DeBoer will remove your restraints for the duration of the trial. This will ensure you remain within your allotted space."

Jakob unfastened the handcuffs and stepped back. Reginald crouched and pressed his fingertips to the drawn border. His eyelids lowered and he whispered, in the cadence of poetry, words I didn't understand.

A strong and fluid draw of energy brushed past me as Reginald prepared to cast his spell. Goosebumps appeared along my arms. Reginald spoke some final words, and the energy around us released. It smoothly eased back into place. He stood and wiped his fingertips on a handkerchief from his front suit pocket. "Miss Alex, can you please raise your hand and attempt to step forward?"

I lifted my hand in front of me and took a tentative step toward the outline. My fingertips met resistance, like a semi-pliable invisible wall. The glyphs on the floor pulsed with a blue light. I frowned and poked at it but couldn't extend my fingertip beyond the border.

Reginald nodded. "Thank you." He turned from me and spoke to Aiden as he climbed the stairs. "She is ready." He took a seat at the long table.

Was I? How could they possibly know? No one on the Committee, except for Trish, had spoken to me since I was taken to that horrible cell. The details of the charges against me, other than the soup of rule numbers Jakob spewed during my arrest, weren't communicated to me.

The doors of the room boomed as they slammed open. Joe Stone strode in carrying a briefcase. He didn't join the other Committee members, but approached a table set up to my left, also facing the long table of representatives.

"Apologies for the tardiness, Father, but I had a previous event." Stone set the briefcase on the table. He opened it and withdrew some files. "Let's get on with this. I have an interview at two thirty."

It made me want to nail the guy right between the eyes.

"Mr. Stone, the trial will take as much time as needed," Aiden said. He looked down at Stone over the top edge of his reading glasses. "You can reschedule your interview." He addressed us both. "Please, have a seat."

I sat down on my lone chair. I wasn't sure what to do with my hands and settled on clasping them in my lap. Why didn't I get a table like Stone? I felt exposed sitting in front of the Committee without some sort of barrier between us. My wolf shared in my anxiety. She tried to push a growl forward, but I bit my lip to hold it back.

"Committee members, we are here today to consider the case of Alexandria Steward. She has been charged with—" Aiden paused and looked at Stone. "Mr. Stone, these are not the charges or sentencing the Committee has agreed to hear."

"They've been updated since some new information has surfaced," Stone said.

A cold lump of dread congealed in my stomach. What was he trying to pull?

"No." Trish looked down the length of the table at Aiden. "This is not acceptable."

Stone gave a short laugh. "Well, we all know why *you* don't want it to go through. One fewer soldier for your army, right?"

"Mr. Stone, Ms. Drake is correct. This charge and proposed sentencing will be dismissed, and we will hold the trial on your previous, approved brief. Procedures are in place for a reason."

Stone's reply was tense. "Of course, Father." He shuffled the papers in his briefcase and walked to the table with a stack of folders. Stone handed them over to Aiden, who distributed them to the other Committee members.

As Stone returned to his seat, Aiden opened his folder and read aloud, "Alexandria Steward has been charged with Assault with Intent to Do Great Bodily Harm. The proposed sentencing is twenty years to be served under a tether."

I clasped the edges of my chair, suddenly lightheaded. Twenty? Years? Panic hit me, and I looked up at Trish. Her gaze rested, unblinking, on Stone.

"Mr. Stone, you may begin," Aiden said.

"Thank you, Father." Stone stepped from behind the table to address the Committee. "On a spring morning, eight years ago, Miss Steward left her parents' home alone to go for a jog. She was finishing her fourth year at NYU on a track scholarship."

Eyes wide, my gaze whipped to Stone. My breath caught in my throat. The beast inside of me lurched forward, pushing at my consciousness. *No, no, no, this wasn't happening.*

"On that same morning," Stone continued, "a young man by the name of Brock Wheeler, a member of the NYU university track team and an Olympic hopeful, was out for a run to prepare for an upcoming meet."

At the mention of the man's name, a violent twisting pain erupted inside me. I bent forward and pressed a hand to my chest, as if expecting my inner wolf to claw her way out. I clenched my teeth to contain sudden snarling noises. Someday, somehow, I might move beyond my hate of the man that attacked me.

But this creature nestled inside my breast? She would never forget or forgive him.

"He met Miss Steward along a public trailway and greeted her. He recognized a fellow athlete and extended a hand to begin a conversation with her." Stone looked over at me, his features darkening. "That's when the monster that is Miss Steward attacked the Commoner."

Another bout of pain sliced through me. The edge of the seat I clasped cracked under the pressure of my grip. My breathing was more akin to hyperventilating. I looked from Stone quickly back to the floor. If I kept looking at him, she'd surely attack. Sweat slipped off the end of my nose and dropped between my shoes.

I had to stay in control.

"Brock suffered traumatic injuries throughout his body," Stone said. "A broken jaw, shattered teeth, punctured lung, and damage to his kidney, just to name a few. Snapped in half, his tibia protruded through the skin of his leg." Stone paused. "In a matter of seconds, this young man's future was stolen from him by the creature sitting just to my right. His life's dream of becoming a professional athlete ended before it began."

I squeezed my eyes shut, trying to focus on my breathing instead of Stone's words.

Inhale. *It's okay.* Exhale. *You're safe.*

Instead of being in the sanctuary of Union Street Church, my mind's eye brought me back to that place. The odors of damp leaves and mud flooded my nostrils along with the stink of the man's fear. And that other scent, the one that I could taste. Metallic . . . warm and delicious.

"Miss Steward?"

I jerked my head up and blinked against the sweat that stung my eyes. Twelve people stared down at me from the table, waiting. I wiped at my eyes and cleared my throat. "Yes?"

Aiden frowned. "I said, we are ready to hear your defense. Or do you need a moment?"

"No!" A growl punctuated my answer. I cringed and cleared my throat again. "No, thank you." I stood on trembling legs and wiped my damp palms on the front of my shirt.

My gaze sought Trish's. She watched me with golden eyes and gave me a slight nod. I straightened and lifted my chin, addressing the people seated at the table. "I went out for my run that morning, and the man approached me. I felt nervous and uncomfortable. When I didn't speak with him, he seized me . . ."

I paused, panting, to keep the snarling wolf contained.

". . . He pulled me from the trail, and . . ."

My inner wolf thrashed against my hold, tearing at my insides. I couldn't stop my body from shaking. Sweat trickled from my hairline and ran down my back.

". . . He attacked me."

Stone scoffed from beside me. "Attacked you?"

I grew disoriented. Horrid memories I tried years to forget replayed anew in my mind's eye. My screams hot against the hand covering my mouth. "He wouldn't let me go. I tried everything to get away." Fingers pressed into the skin of my throat to quiet me. "I couldn't breathe."

"I don't think—" Stone began.

"Mr. Stone! You've had your opportunity to speak," Aiden said.

"I thought he might kill me," I said. "And then . . ." My mind fumbled to recall the details. I could never fully recall the moment my wolf emerged. ". . . I escaped him."

An alarm beeping on my watch. Garbled cries for help. That savory, copper scent.

Inhale. *It's okay.* Exhale. *You're safe.*

"I walked home."

Would the Committee members see the change in my eyes, from hazel to gold? I took my seat and buried my claws into the chair. My hands, the joints throbbing, must have shifted while I'd been speaking.

Please. Stop.

My inner wolf hated the request. Intermittent waves of pain spasmed through my body. She'd spent twenty-two years repressed inside me. She wasn't going back to being muzzled without a fight.

Aiden turned his gaze on the others. "Does anyone have questions for either Mr. Stone or Miss Steward."

Trish spoke up. "Mr. Stone, did Brock Wheeler have a history of assaulting young women when they didn't return his greetings?"

Stone scoffed. "We're not here to judge Mr. Wheeler's character, but Miss Steward's. If you must know, he has an outstanding community record. He didn't hesitate when I asked him to share his story. His testimony was powerful, honest, and riveting."

"I have a question, Father Aiden." One of the men at the table looked from Aiden to me. "Miss Steward, *if* this man attacked you as you said he did, why didn't you report it years ago, when it happened?"

I gaped at the man, unsure I'd correctly heard the question.

A growl sounded from Trish's end of the table. "I ask such a foolish question to be removed from—"

Aiden held up his hand. "Please, Ms. Drake."

My gaze darted from the questioner, to Trish, to Aiden, and back. Another bead of sweat rolled down my back.

My mother is crying. The pretty floral print of her bathrobe is marred by the ruined, filthy clothing she peels away from my shaking body. My grandmother washes the blood and mud from my numb skin . . . skin I'm not sure is mine. My teeth won't stop chattering, no matter how hard I clench them to keep the sound locked away inside.

I'd been so confused. And so frightened. "I . . . I was scared."

The man nodded. "Scared to lose control and harm someone else?"

She sensed him, this man trying to pin me with his questions. I stared at my feet so she couldn't see him. Pain ripped through me, and a long whine escaped. I clutched at my chest. My canines started to lengthen, along with my ears. I couldn't trust what would come out of my mouth, so I shook my head.

Trish's voice was like a balm. "Miss Steward, had your wolf already been awakened *before* your assault?"

I focused on my shoelaces and shook my head again.

"But after he attacked you, you had these abilities?" she asked.

I nodded and chanced a verbal answer. "I didn't understand what happened."

"How old were you?"

"Twenty-two."

Stone snorted and made a show of shuffling his papers. "I don't see how this is relevant."

Trish addressed the Committee. "Most werewolves are familiar with their abilities by twenty-two because the gene has already presented itself. They've received guidance in how to live as a wolf. However, unless triggered, the gene can lay dormant for someone's entire life. It's possible Miss Steward never would have become a werewolf if not for Brock Wheeler attacking her that morning."

"Ms. Drake." Aiden's voice carried a tone of warning. "You are only allowed questions you may have to clarify the case, please."

I split my attention between who was speaking and my effort to stop my body from shifting further. A deep inhale through my nose and slow exhale through my mouth helped. *You're okay.* My gums ached as my canines retracted. *We're okay.*

"Mr. Stone, when was Brock Wheeler found?" someone asked.

Stone referenced his papers. "Twenty minutes after the attack."

The Committee member leaned back in his seat and grimaced. "Those injuries for that long? Horrific. The pain must have been unbearable." He frowned and shook his head. "And a possible Olympic runner. What a loss for our country."

"Mr. Stone, I have a question." Serenity, a younger female pastor, raised her hand. "The attack on Miss Steward—"

"Mr. Wheeler," Stone said.

Serenity held a tight-lipped smile. "This happened in Miss Steward's home state of New York. Why are we trying Miss Steward for a supposed crime that took place outside the Hopewell Committee's jurisdiction?"

I chanced looking up from my shoes and glanced between Serenity and Stone. These Committees set and enforced rules at a local level. A glimmer of hope fluttered in my chest. I'd fled home before learning what a Committee was, let alone which one watched over the New York suburbs where I grew up.

Stone's gaze darkened as he stared up at Serenity. "Are you questioning the integrity of this case?"

"Mr. Stone, please answer the question," Aiden said.

"Is it because the New York City Delegation recognizes the concept of self-defense?" Serenity asked.

"Order," Aiden said, throwing Serenity a frown. "Please, allow Mr. Stone to answer the original question."

"Thank you, Father." Stone cleared his throat. "The location of the crime falls *outside* the New York City Delegation's ward."

My pulse stuttered. "But my parents live right outside the city."

Stone's smile appeared smug when he turned toward me. "I simply referenced the districting lines, Miss Steward."

My wolf lashed out, and the sudden pain made me gasp. Dark spots danced in the perimeter of my vision. I clutched at my sides and leaned forward to rest my head on my knees. *We're okay. I'm okay.*

"There is no Committee assigned to the area where Scott and Kimberly Steward's house is located," Stone said. "It is one of the many areas outside the cities that is either forgotten or overlooked, allowing these monsters to run free."

"Mr. Stone," Aiden warned. "Language like that is not tolerated here."

"In fact," Stone said, "If Miss Steward had remained, it's possible she'd still be endangering good citizens like Brock Wheeler."

Was it possible I could have stayed with my family? No wandering from place to place, working shitty temp jobs so I could eat, and trying to find somewhere safe to hide?

"Instead she is in *our* city as a threat to *our* citizens," Stone said. "All of you witnessed her attempted attack on me."

"A Hunter you invited provoked her!" Trish said.

Stone slammed his fist on the table, causing me to jump. "She's not in control!"

"Order!" Aiden was on his feet.

The room fell silent except for my labored breathing.

"Does anyone have further questions?" When no one at the table spoke up, Aiden nodded. "Then we'll put this to a vote."

Aiden read through the names of all present, asking for their vote. The vote fell exactly the same as Stone's safety proposal.

Five not guilty. Seven guilty.

"Miss Steward, the Committee of Hopewell has found you guilty of Assault with the intent to Do Great Bodily Harm," Aiden said. "For your crime, you will serve twenty years from this day under a tether. If during that term you cause any other harm upon another . . ."

Aiden's voice faded as icy dread filled my swiftly rising and falling chest. Claws sunk into my chair, I turned to Trish. Her eyes gold and her jaw clenched, she stared straight ahead. I glanced over my shoulder at the door. With one last look up at the table, I leapt from my chair to run.

I collided with the invisible magical barrier. A blue shimmer vibrated into being in front of me. Snarling, I swiped at it with clawed hands, but it held.

Reginald descended the stairs, his bushy eyebrows drawn together. He spoke to me, but I couldn't hear it over the roaring in my ears. My consciousness waned as the beast inside me claimed control. It was a relief, in a way, from all the pain she'd been inflicting on me.

Reginald lifted his hand. He seemed smaller and less significant than before. My jaws and teeth could easily sever the muscles and tendons holding his frail body together. I would destroy all of them. But first I needed to find my way out of the prison he'd trapped me in.

The unmistakable prickling of magic ran along my skin. My Shield, tattooed over my breastbone, flared hotter than ever before. Suddenly it snapped, as if my entire chest had been cracked open.

I lost consciousness.

8

I AWOKE TO the sound of arguing.

"This cannot go on." Trish's voice seethed. "He will have every last one of us killed. Do something!"

Aiden's voice quietly replied. "Patricia, please, I'm not able to. You know that."

The cool, damp air carried the scent of St. Anthony's. My eyes opened to a roughly hewn stone ceiling.

"Patricia." Reginald's voice. "As moderator, he is forbidden to interfere."

"He's a coward," Trish growled.

My hand flew to my throat where I'd seen the cross-like tether branded on Ben. Nothing felt different. I abruptly sat up, drawing the attention of the other three in the small room. I'd been placed on some sort of stone table. My chest ached as if I'd caught an oncoming train with my sternum.

"What happened?" I looked at Trish. "Did I hurt anyone?"

Trish strode to my side and embraced me. "No one was injured."

The legs of my jeans were torn, along with the shoulder seams of my shirt. "How far did I shift?"

Trish released me. "Further than you're comfortable with. You will need your Shield repaired. Reginald had to break through it to lull you to sleep."

Only twice before had I fully shifted into the canid monster most people think of when they hear "werewolf." It had happened over six months ago, when Emma's evil ex strapped me to a lab chair for his crazy mind experiments. The other time was when she protected me from the man who assaulted me, and why I'd been brought to trial.

I always strove to hold back my shifting before reaching full-on werewolf. In that form, so much of myself was given to my inner wolf that I had little to no control. I was pissed about my broken Shield, but thankfully Reginald stopped her . . . me . . . from harming anyone. I looked over Trish's shoulder at him. "Thank you."

He gave a curt nod and looked away.

"Patricia," Aiden said.

Trish met my gaze with a wavering smile and eyes threatening tears. She brushed some curls back from my forehead and gave it a kiss. "We will all be here for you afterward, Alex. Be brave." She stepped back to turn away from me.

My eyes widened and I seized her wrist. "Wait. Trish? Where are you going?"

Trish shook her head and pried my fingers from around her wrist. She left the small room.

"No, wait!" I jumped down from the stone table. My knees buckled and my vision swam. I grabbed the edge of the table. "What's happening?" I tried to focus on Reginald and Aiden. "What've you done to me?"

"They're merely lingering effects of the sleep spell," Reginald said. "Miss Alex, please rest back. We don't want to restrain you against your will. We will try to be as swift as we can."

It must be the stage in the sentencing when they burned the tether onto me. My pulse raced. I shook my head and stumbled back along the edge of the table. "No. I'll leave right away. I won't come back to Hopewell. I promise. You'll never see me again. Please, don't do this."

Aiden silently waited, his sharp gaze watching me as Reginald spoke. "This is what the Committee has ruled. This is what shall be done. The same tether is dealt to everyone. No one is an exception." His next words I didn't comprehend, but the effects of his magic surrounded me.

The room seemed to tip. I grasped at the table to remain upright. Someone lifted me from my feet. The scent of incense enveloped me. The hard surface of the table was beneath my back. Once again, the stone ceiling filled my field of vision. Aiden's and Reginald's faces appeared in and out of focus above me.

My inner wolf pitched and turned, confused. We couldn't orient ourselves to our surroundings. Shallow pants left my lungs, and I started to cry. "He was going to kill me."

Aiden stood beside the table near my head. With his thumb covered in an oily substance, he traced a mark on my throat. It was cold on my skin. He stepped back out of view. I tried to lift my arms, to wipe the mark away, but no longer had control of them. I barely felt the energy Reginald drew for his spell. His fingertips touched the skin of my throat, and it felt as if a hot iron had been pressed to my skin.

I screamed.

No. I howled.

A white-hot pain cleaved through my throat to shoot along the length of my spine. I couldn't breathe, the pressure of the tethering spell not unlike the man who nearly crushed my windpipe. My unreliable vision narrowed to a tunnel before finally, and blessedly, it vanished altogether, and I lost consciousness yet again.

THE THIRD TIME I awoke that day, it was in a cold sweat. The room appeared dark even though I'd opened my eyes. Hair stuck to my forehead, my whole body trembled, and my throat burned. I rested on a bed, but not one I recognized. When I tried to scent the place, to orient myself, nothing happened.

I pushed myself up into a seated position and rubbed at my aching temples. My mind was foggy. All my senses were dampened, as if I'd been wrapped in cotton gauze, sealed away from the world. I tried to pop my ears, to clear my hearing, but couldn't. Tentatively, I reached down within myself, inviting the creature inside me forward.

Silence.

Alone in the dark, my eyes filled with tears and my pulse quickened. I felt for the edge of the bed, swung my legs over, and stood. Reaching ahead of me, I blindly groped around the space. My toe caught something on the floor, and I tripped. I fell to my knees and, with a crash, took the contents of a bedside table with me.

"Dammit!" I again reached for my inner wolf, this time to improve my vision. She didn't respond. The heavy darkness remained draped around me. I fell back to sit on the floor and began to cry.

The door opened, and a sliver of light sliced through the dark. A silhouette stood in the doorway. "You okay in here?"

My racing thoughts couldn't place the man's vaguely familiar voice. He crossed the room. I pushed myself back against the side of the mattress as he crouched in front of me. He reached out for my arm. I yanked it away and shouted. "Don't touch me!"

"Right. Sorry. Hold on." He rustled in the mess, and a switch clicked. A bedside lamp, now on the floor, lit up the room with a soft glow.

For a brief moment, I still didn't recognize the man in front of me. I scanned his features, taking in the tousled mohawk and piercings. Then everything snapped into place. "Nate?"

He nodded, stood, and extended a hand to help me to my feet. "How do you feel?"

I accepted his hand and stood, looking around at what must have been Trish's and Nate's bedroom. We were in their apartment at their club, Hell's Bells. Somewhere safe.

My fingers came into contact with the hot skin of my throat, and I winced. It radiated heat and stung like a terrible sunburn.

"Alex?" Nate frowned and looked from my fingers to me.

I latched my arms around his waist and buried my face into his shoulder. He smelled faintly of cigarettes and sweat. I started to sob.

Nate's arms wrapped around me and tightened.

"I can't feel her." My crying made my words a garbled, snotty mess against his shirt. An enormous sense of loss overtook me.

His hand moved over my back as he hugged me. "Shh, I'm here. We're here for you."

"Alex?" A female's voice sounded in the room.

I pulled back from Nate to see the newcomer and experienced the same moment of disconnect as before. Sleek dark bob. Lips as red as her sundress. It clicked. Trish.

She embraced Nate and me as one. "You're safe. We have you."

I might be safe, but I was incomplete. "Trish, what did Stone try to change at the trial?"

She inhaled sharply through her nose. "It doesn't matter."

"What did he try to do?" My voice pitched upward, making the interior of my throat burn. A faint buzzing sounded in my ears.

"Medical records listed Brock Wheeler as clinically dead before being revived," Trish said. "Stone wanted attempted murder added to the charges. If found guilty, he requested you be executed."

Lightheaded, I grasped tighter onto Nate.

"Look at me, Alex." Trish's gaze held mine. "That doesn't matter. He didn't succeed. This is what we focus on . . . how we react to this. You are here with us, and we will help you through this."

A tremendous wave of anger threatened to drown me. "Those people." I envisioned them lined up behind the table and looking down at me. Passing judgment on me. "I hate them." I squirmed to free myself from Nate and Trish.

Neither of my friends loosened their hold.

"They can't do this. I hate them!" My voice rose to an angry scream. I threw my body against their embrace. "I'll kill them for this!" My throat and the area behind my eyes throbbed with pain. I imagined the Committee members' bodies strewn about the sanctuary floor, taken apart because of what they'd done to me.

The buzzing sound, a whining and thick static, spiked in volume until it became deafening. I cried out and clasped my hands over my ears, but the noise originated from *inside* my head. The tremendous pressure behind it threatened to crush my mind.

Feedback from the tether.

I wilted and dissolved into more sobbing. I'd been so close to making peace with the beast inside me, my constant and intimate companion. Instead of running from her in fear or muzzling her with control, I learned to open my heart to her. We'd grown intertwined. Stronger together than apart.

Now she was gone. I didn't protect her as she did me, and they'd taken her.

I was alone.

Empty.

After I'd expended my body's allotment of tears, and the anger had subsided to numbness, I sat red-eyed with Nate and Trish at their kitchen table.

"You might be scared right now. Confused. Angry," Trish said. "That's all completely normal."

I watched the steam rise from my barely touched tea. "There's nothing normal about this."

"Do you have any questions for us?" Nate said.

"Why didn't I know you?" I asked. "You came into the room, and I didn't recognize you. My brain short-circuited."

"Werewolves rely on scent to identify people," Trish said. "You can't do that now, so your mind waited for visual cues to register."

"The fact your nose is wrecked is also going to mess with your eating." Nate frowned. "It's going to taste like shit, but be sure you get food in you anyway. There've been tethered wolves that end up wasting away because they don't eat."

"What about my ears?" I asked. "Am I always going to feel like they're stuffed full of cotton?"

Trish shook her head. "The sensation will fade as you reacclimate to the Commoner's range of sound."

A Commoner. For a period of years I'd wanted to be a Commoner again. I didn't want to deal with the supernatural and all the bullshit that came packaged with it. But I wasn't that person anymore. I was a proud werewolf. Or at least I had been.

"How long will it take to feel like myself again?" My sore throat made my eyes water.

"We can't answer that," Trish said. "We can help you through general side effects but can't say how long it will take you to adjust."

"What about this noise looping in my head?" The buzzing in my mind, for now at least, had dimmed. "Is that going to fade away with time, too?"

"No," Trish said. "The channel from your mind to your body, what you use to shift, has been blocked by the tethering spell. The emotions used for drawing on your gifts as a werewolf will be trapped in your mind. The stronger the emotion, the louder and more painful the feedback. That will last for the duration of the sentence."

Twenty years.

Nausea threatened to bring up the little bit of tea I'd managed. I had no release valve for the rage and loss I was experiencing. I couldn't take action. Those dark feelings would remain inside me to fester. "I get it now ... Why most tethered wolves don't make it."

"You'll make it," Nate said.

"Emma would like you to live with her, but Nate and I feel you should spend the first few weeks with us," Trish said.

"At least until you get a feeling for how things will be different," Nate said.

I shook my head. "I don't want to be at Hell's Bells right now."

Nate's jaw twitched. "Emma isn't a wolf. What you're going to face isn't easy, and we'll be able to explain what's happening. A wizard can't do that for you."

"No," I said. "I don't want to be reminded of how I'm different from the rest of you." I had no idea what life would look like now, but I didn't want to be the object of the wolves' pity.

Trish placed her hand over mine. "You're still a part of this community. The wolves may have questions, especially the young ones, but they won't mock or reject you."

"We don't shun our tethered like the wizards do," Nate said.

And I'll have to explain to numerous people, multiple times a day, what was taken from me. I pulled my hand away. "You didn't help me when they did this to me, and I don't need your help now." I scowled at my teacup. "I'm not staying here."

A growl rumbled out of Nate. His voice lowered. "She's fought hard for you—"

"Nathan, love. Patience. Please." Trish lifted her chin. "Alex, we won't keep you with us against your will. But please, stay in Hopewell and check in with Nate or me each day. Call or text us. Don't run away and face this alone."

Run.

It'd been such a large part of my life—first a hobby that brought me peace, then a skill that got me into college, and finally a survival instinct. But what difference would running make now?

I stood. "Can I see my family?"

"Yes, of course," Trish said. "Waking from a tethering can be difficult and frightening, so Nate and I wanted to be with you. It also would have been upsetting for them. But I can take you to Emma's home now."

I nodded. My head pounded and my eyelids were swollen from all the crying. My parents and grandmother would be upset anyway, seeing me this way, but I wanted to be with them. "I'm ready."

Trish drove me from Hell's Bells to Emma's. She didn't fill the ride with unnecessary conversation. Instead, she left the radio volume low and occasionally reached over to rest her fingers on my shoulder.

Only when we were leaving the car to walk up to Emma's house did Trish speak. "Alex, when you make the decision on where to live, please let Nate and me know."

The thought of moving away from Hopewell, leaving Emma and the wolves behind, still caused a clenching ache in my chest. I nodded. "I will."

Before I could knock, the door to Emma's home opened. A petite and curvy blonde woman regarded me with widened blue eyes. She immediately threw her arms around me and started crying. The faint traces of her vanilla-scented perfume reached my nose.

Click. Emma.

"Let her through the doorway, dear." My grandmother motioned me inside. Emma walked with me, clasping my hand between both of her own.

I sat between her and my grandmother on the couch. Four faint impressions in the carpet marked the absence of the coffee table. My voice burned in my throat. "Sorry about the furniture, Em."

Wiping at tears, Emma giggled. "It's okay. I didn't like that thing anyway, and I've been wanting a new dining room set."

I leaned into my grandma's hug to enclose myself in her lavender fragrance. Like Emma's, her scent was a pale ghost of what it had been.

My grandma rocked me gently as she spoke over me to Trish, who hovered at the front door. "Please, have a seat."

"Thank you for the offer," Trish said, "but I have to get back."

Two figures were suddenly standing beside us. I quickly sat up and almost cried out, startled. My parents had entered the room without me hearing them. Emma gave her seat to my mother.

"Alex, we were so worried about you." My mom hugged me. "I can't believe they wouldn't let us be there for the trial."

"I'm glad you weren't," I said. "I wasn't at my best."

"Thank goodness you're okay now, though." Mom rubbed my arm and searched my features. "You're okay, aren't you?"

I wiped at my damp eyes. "No, I'm not. But I will be." I wasn't confident of that. However, if I didn't give her something, she wouldn't stop asking for answers I didn't have.

My dad reached out and squeezed my shoulder. "It's good to see you here, safe." He spoke to Trish. "Thank you for taking care of our daughter when we couldn't."

Trish gave him a slight smile. "She's part of our family, too."

My throat tightened with guilt over how I'd treated her earlier at Hell's Bells. Trish and Nate had never been anything but welcoming to me. I managed a weak, "Thank you, Trish."

"At least now you can come home with us," my mother said. "There's no need for you to hide away anymore."

I'd missed having my family in my life without worrying about my safety. But the time I'd spent in Hopewell was the longest I'd remained anywhere. It was my home now. I looked to each of my family members in turn. "I'd like to stay here with my friends. I want to try to make it work."

My parents frowned, glancing at each other.

"Of course, dear." Grandma smiled. "We understand, and you can visit us now anytime you'd like."

"Maybe we can stay for a little bit," Mom said, "if it's okay with you, Alex. I don't want to leave you so soon after those awful people—" She bit her lip, but her eyes filled with tears.

"Would you mind, Alex?" Dad asked.

"No, I don't mind." I did, but I couldn't say that because they'd wonder why. If they stayed for several days, and I could convince them I didn't need their support, they'd pack up and head home. They'd be safe.

"You're all welcome to stay here." Emma smiled. "There's plenty of room."

"Thank you, dear," my grandmother said. "Your home is lovely."

Being surrounded and supported by those I loved should've brought me comfort, but it didn't. I was too busy thinking ahead to what I wanted to do next.

Moving forward, I could attempt to keep my head down like Ben had—before I met him, anyway—and commit to a quiet life in Hopewell. But twenty years without my wolf wasn't a realistic option for me. We'd grown so intertwined, half of me was missing.

I couldn't live without her.

My head throbbed with pain and anger. I was nauseous with it. As a result, the buzzing noise caused by the tether skewed my thoughts dark. I was scared for the other werewolves and what would happen to them. But I also couldn't stop thinking of the people who'd done this to me.

I planned to repay every last one of the seven votes. Who would be first was an easy choice.

I would end Joe Stone.

9

MY PARENTS AND grandmother accepted Emma's offer to stay at her house. She graciously put them up in two of her three remaining guest rooms. When I told them Emma and I were meeting a friend for lunch, my family left for the Hopewell Botanical Gardens.

I pulled at the lightweight scarf Emma lent me for our lunch date with Anne, arranging it for the umpteenth time in the visor mirror of her Prius.

"Stop fretting," she said. "It'll be okay."

"Maybe this was a bad idea. She hates me." My tone flat, I tugged at the scarf's edge to hide more of the inflamed skin on my throat. "I haven't heard from her since she found me yanking the Hunter's key out of his body with my monster claws."

"She doesn't hate you. She found out her friend is a werewolf," Emma said. "She's . . . struggling with the concept."

"Her partner, the guy she has to trust with her life on a daily basis, is a werewolf!" I motioned to the absurdity of the situation. "Don't you think she'd struggle with that?"

"Her friend of *three* years. It's different." Emma glanced at me. "And you're making assumptions. Anne is still adjusting to Jakob, too."

"Wait." I narrowed my eyes. "How would *you* know that?" When Anne discovered I was a werewolf, Emma wasn't sure if she'd tell Anne she was a wizard.

Emma's cheeks reddened.

"You told her?" I frowned. Emma and I rarely kept anything from each other. "When?"

"Shortly after she found out about you," Emma said. "After she accepted Detective Grey's offer to help with Committee work instead of getting her memory wiped. I thought it'd be better to tell her sooner rather than later."

My chest tightened and a low buzz began in my head. I muttered a few choice curses and looked away out the passenger window.

"You're mad," Emma said.

"It's fine. I'm glad you can still be friends with her." It wasn't fine. Being able to choose how and when to tell Anne about myself would've been preferable to being forcefully outed and not having a chance to explain. "Our friendship existed on life support, anyway. I had to bend a few rules to get at the Hunter."

"Laws," Emma said. "They were laws."

"I had to bend a few laws—"

"Break," Emma said.

"Okay, I had to break a few laws." Laws Anne swore to uphold.

We parked in the lot for Anne's favorite brewery. Emma offered her own patio for the lunch meeting, but Anne wanted to meet somewhere public. I read the request as another sign of her shattered trust in me.

I grabbed the briefcase Emma lent me with my notes on Stone, and we walked toward the brewery. "I hope she agrees to this. I need all the help I can get to put this guy away." With Stone off the Committee and behind bars, I hoped his safety laws would go down in flames. Then my tether would be removed, and I could become whole again.

The late summer sun caused heat to radiate up from the sidewalk. The hot breeze of the day felt great on my bare legs, shoulders, and arms.

Emma smiled at me. "That sundress is so pretty. You should get a few more."

"Em, focus." I returned her smile anyway and ran a hand down the fabric. I'd scored the dress at the resale shop for $12.

"I know, I know." She gave a wave of her hand. "Though I'm a bit worried by the choices you're making. The day after you received a criminal sentence, you're doubling down on trying to topple a favored mayoral candidate."

"If I don't go after him, others are going to end up like this, too." I motioned at my throat.

Emma paused outside the entrance of the beer garden, stopping me with a hand on my arm. "You have another option. Give your information on Joe Stone to Anne, and then forget him and live your life. Twenty years is a long time, but Trish and Nate said they'd be your support group. I'm not leaving you anytime soon. You can see your family again."

"I'm not sure that *is* an option." I shook my head and dropped my gaze. "I can't bide my time living like this. Wolves don't usually make it through to the other side. Why would I be an exception?"

"Alex?"

I looked up at her with a frown.

A crease appeared between Emma's eyebrows. "It's not just about the other werewolves, is it?"

The buzzing in my head spiked. Those bastards sealed my wolf away from me, and I wasn't going to stand for it, sanity be damned. I clenched my jaw but didn't answer.

"Okay, I'm sorry." Emma took my hand. "This isn't a decision you have to make before we go into a meeting you're stressed about. I have plenty of time to talk you into seeking a simplified and happy life." She gave my hand a squeeze and led me through the gate of the beer garden. We crossed the brick patio, past community tables, and toward the back wall covered in climbing hops plants.

A woman sat at a four-top, the sun making her auburn hair glow. She wore a Hopewell PD t-shirt, aviator sunglasses propped up on her head, and an analytical gaze as she studied the menu. Her name snapped into place in my mind. Anne Reid.

She looked up at us and lowered her sunglasses.

"Hi." I tried for a smile. Anne probably picked up on my nerves the moment I spoke. I sat down across from her and set the briefcase on the ground near my feet.

"What a beautiful day for your day off!" Emma beamed. She sat down between us.

Anne's expression softened, and she smiled at Emma. "I've been enjoying it so far. I think I'll drive out to the lake after this."

Emma's smile turned mischievous, and she lifted a finely shaped brow. "Will you be taking Carolyn along?"

Anne's cheeks turned rosy, and she fidgeted with the menu. Cloth bandaging wrapped her left hand from the base of her fingers to her wrist. "Maybe."

Emma squealed with giddiness.

Anne chuckled and shook her head.

I watched them, realizing even though it'd been two months since I'd spoken to Anne, their friendship hadn't been disrupted. Emma and Anne were friends before I arrived in Hopewell, and now their friendship continued without me. But why wasn't Anne upset with Emma like she was with me? I stared down at my hands, folding a cocktail napkin over.

"Alex, you should see the two of them together." Emma grasped my wrist, her eyes bright. "They. Are. Adorable."

I gave Emma a weak smile and looked at Anne.

Anne's smile faded, and she handed the menu to Emma. "Pick out your drinks and food. I've already ordered."

A waiter took our drink and lunch orders. After he left, Anne studied me from across the table. "How've you been?"

Assuming Anne wouldn't be interested in casual conversation with me, I was unprepared. "I've been better." I shrugged. "Found a new job at Rear Window Records." I gave Emma a sideward glance. "In the process of looking for an apartment."

Anne's eyebrows rose above her sunglasses. "Things didn't work out with Ben?"

"No, we're okay." I swallowed back the sudden lump in my throat. "He's busy with family stuff, and I wanted a place of my own." She should've known about Ben and me through her partner Jakob.

"Huh. Is he with his sister, Joan?" Anne asked.

I paused. This is what she really wanted to know, why she asked about me. I'd never talked to Anne about Joan, and I wasn't going to start now. "I'm not sure."

"You're not sure who Ben is spending time with?" Anne's default *interrogation mode* was entertaining, except when I was its focus. She gave me a moment to struggle for an answer before commenting, "We're still investigating why and how Joan's protest devolved into a riot. Hopefully she'll be smart and stick around in case we have more questions."

I frowned and the low buzz in my mind returned. "I'm not sure where she is now. We haven't spoken in months." In an attempt to divert the focus from me, I threw a few questions back at her. "How's work? Get hurt again?" I pointed to her bandaged hand. The last time we'd had a civil conversation, she favored an injured knee.

"Yeah. A minor outpatient surgery to correct it." Anne leaned back in her chair with her pint glass and lowered the bandaged hand to her lap. "My job has been rough these past few months with all the changes because of my new position. Jakob and I are now working directly with Detective Grey on both standard Hopewell PD stuff and any unique cases that come up."

I hesitated. "Are you okay though? I mean, are you feeling—"

"I'm getting closer to the role I want, faster than planned, but not in the way I expected." Anne smirked. "Life is full of surprises, right?"

My cheeks warmed.

Emma's abrupt laugh cut the tension. "It is, isn't it?" She smiled at Anne. "Thanks again for agreeing to talk to us about Isaac Laska, especially since you already have so much stress with work."

"There were no personal connections I could find connecting the Hunter to Laska," Anne said, "Because of that, and what I've researched on Hunters, I agree with you two. My gut says contract job. There's another person involved who hired Eastman."

"I'm telling you, it's Stone that hired the Hunter," I said. "Can you keep me in the loop on what you find?"

"I don't think that's a good idea," Anne said. "I need to be more careful about sharing details of open investigations. I never should have told you our progress on Laska's case."

"But it's important to me to nail Stone," I said. "He wants to harm people I care about."

"Leave the police work to us," Anne said, turning back to me. "What do you have on Joe Stone I can use?"

I reached down and retrieved the briefcase. "I tried to gather and organize my notes the best I could for you." I set it on the table.

Anne held up her hand. "Don't open it here. I'll look at the notes back at my desk."

I nodded. "Yeah, okay. I wrote down everything I could recall on Stone since meeting him."

"You don't have evidence? Just your opinions?" Anne asked.

"They're not my opinions. It's what I recalled from actual events." I frowned. "I had a recording from the fundraising event Emma's mom hosted for Stone, but the Hunter destroyed it. There's a copy of some Committee meeting notes since they're archived and available to any supernatural citizen in its jurisdiction. You'll read Stone's obvious slant on how we should be governed."

Anne gave Emma a quick sideward glance, as if to double-check the truth of what I'd said.

Emma wasn't even paying attention to the conversation anymore. She used her phone to take a picture of herself holding the pint of rose-colored beer she'd ordered. Usually I'd be able to tell which beer it was by aroma alone, but now . . .

"The problem is how you and your friends at that club came across some of this information," Anne said. She knew Trish's and

Nate's names but had cultivated a strong dislike for them because they seemed to squirm out of any legal repercussions for their criminal behavior. Anne wasn't as straight-laced as Jakob, but still struggled parsing out nuances when it came to breaking the law.

But my trial hadn't followed the same Commoner law structure. "I'm sure you've noticed how this case is different from others you've worked on."

Anne frowned again.

I held up my hands to ward off any lecture of how I wasn't a police officer. "I'm not saying I know more about this investigation than you, but I don't think you'll be working within the same guidelines you're used to."

She shook her head. "We'll see. I'm not making any promises. Hand over the notes, please."

I slid the small briefcase toward her. "Thank you."

Anne set the briefcase beside her and took a sip of beer. "If Stone is the crooked bastard you say he is and he wins the election, I realize he'll have the clout to hurt a lot more people. Legally. I don't want to see that happen."

My reminder . . . Her investigation was for the greater good, not for me. I nodded and made another crease in a cocktail napkin in front of me. "I don't want to see that, either."

"When is our food coming? I'm starving." Emma collapsed back in her chair and blew a strand of pink hair from in front of her eyes. A kitchen staff member brought a large tray to our table. Emma brightened and sat up.

We had lunch, but the food didn't taste good. I disassembled my sandwich to find something within it to eat, and finally discarded the bland pieces back into the serving basket. Even my beer seemed watered down.

"Don't like the food?" Anne asked. "You were always the first to finish when we'd eat here. Well, most places."

I smiled and shook my head. "The food is fine. I'm just not that hungry."

Anne paused, sandwich held halfway to her mouth.

"Can I have your pickle?" Emma asked. I nodded and she snagged it from among the sandwich parts.

I sat silent through the majority of the conversation between Emma and Anne. Emma made a few attempts to include me, but I finally gave her a nudge under the table to make her stop. Anne would see right through the thinly veiled attempts to make us a happy trio again.

That's never going to happen. The buzzing whine started in my head. *She has Emma. She doesn't need or want your friendship.* I squeezed my eyes shut and pinched the bridge of my nose. *She probably wouldn't even notice if you were gone.*

"Alex?" Emma's voice cut through the noise. "Are you okay?"

I opened my watering eyes to see Anne and Emma staring at me. "I'm sorry. I'm getting a bit of a headache. Must be the sun. I forgot my sunglasses in the car."

The three of us paid our tab. Emma and I left for the car. Despite my hunch that Anne wouldn't be able to resist diving into my notes on Stone, my heart weighed heavy. I missed her.

"I think that went well." Emma smiled as she drove. "She didn't yell at you once."

"Yelling at me in a public space? That's a pretty low bar to clear," I said. Plus, calm and collected Anne would never lose it like that.

"And she didn't get up and walk out on you," Emma said. "That's what I was afraid of."

I frowned. "Thanks for the vote of confidence, Em."

Emma shrugged. "It was a possibility."

"And yet Anne doesn't have any problem with you keeping secrets from her." I draped my arm along the open window. "Must be nice being a wizard."

"I shouldn't have told you." Emma frowned. "I knew you'd be pissed."

I snorted. "I would've found out."

"She would have, too . . . about me," Emma said. "I'm sorry you were forced to tell her instead of having the choice like I did. I don't know what I can do about that."

The tether's feedback started to hum in my mind. I closed my eyes, blowing out an exhale. "Did you explain to her why I kept my secret from her? The rules we have to follow?"

"No." Emma's fingers fidgeted at her steering wheel. "I'm sure someone explained everything to her when she agreed to take the position."

I shook my head and looked out the passenger window. We rode in silence for several minutes.

"Alex?"

"What."

She hesitated. "Does this mean you aren't coming with me to the fundraising event at the gallery tonight? Because if not—"

"Em, why do you insist I go to these fancy events with you? They never end well."

Emma waved aside my concern. "This one will be different. What are you wearing?"

"I haven't decided." She'd asked me to be her plus one to the event, the proceeds of which would go to Another Chance Ministries. I suspected the invite was an attempt to keep me busy so I couldn't spend time secluded. "Can't I wear this? You said it looks nice."

"No, you can't," Emma said. "It's too casual."

"What about the skirt I wore to that campaign party where your mom called the police and had me thrown out?" I asked.

She ignored my snark. "No, you can't wear that again. Some of the same people will be at this event. Plus, I've already picked up a dress for you because you don't own black-tie event pieces."

I groaned. "I told you not to buy me any more clothes. They're all so expensive, and most of them get ruined."

"I rented the dress." She smiled, obviously pleased with herself. "So you can't be upset with me."

I shook my head. "What type of art is this anyway?"

"Photography."

"Can't I be a couch potato with my family tonight?"

"No. I know you. You're telling me you want to be with your family, but as soon as I leave the house, you'll hide away alone in your room and spiral." She glanced at me. "It's for one evening. Hopefully it'll help get your mind off what's happened, even for just a little bit."

"Fine." I owed it to Emma after wrecking her work luncheon, and she was saving my family money by putting them up at her place. The least I could do is stand around in some ridiculous dress for a few hours.

10

"OH, HELL NO." I stood with my arms crossed in the doorway of Emma's expansive walk-in closet.

"Please?" Emma shook the hanger, causing the dress to sparkle like a disco ball.

I mock-shielded my eyes. "If I wear that, I'll blind anyone trying to look at me."

"This cut is perfect for you," she said. "It even has a scarf so you won't feel self-conscious about the tether."

"The tether?" I motioned to the dress. "There are *other* bits of me I'll be more self-conscious about in that thing." Maybe I could make up for Emma's ruined luncheon some other way.

Emma lowered the hanger and stomped her foot. "Alex, you're being difficult."

"I don't care." I leaned back against the doorframe and shrugged. "I'm not wearing it. You'll have to go alone."

"Can you at least try it on? If you absolutely hate it, I'll stop bothering you. I'll go to this important event without my best friend who I'm really worried about." Emma waited, holding out the hanger to me.

I sighed, snatched the hanger from her, pushed her into the bedroom, and shut the closet doors. I changed in front of one of the several full-length mirrors in the closet. When I turned toward the mirror, my eyes widened.

Well, shit.

Emma was right, as she was about any piece of clothing she insisted I wear. The beautiful dress fit me like a glove. The sparkling fabric didn't appear gaudy, like on the hanger, but shimmered only along my figure's curves. The longer length fell right above the knee, which I liked. If I tried to run or jump in it, though, there'd be problems. The scarf shimmered a bit too much for my taste, but it covered the ugly brand on my throat without feeling like any fabric rested there.

"How does it look?" Emma's voice, from the other side of the closet door, caused me to jump. I imagined she already had a hold of the handle.

"You can come in," I said. "Just don't gloat, please."

The door opened and Emma stood by my side. I turned in front of the mirror, searching for something wrong with the dress.

"Perfect." She looked a bit too smug. "Any objections?"

I frowned at the mirror. "No."

She laughed, gave me a quick hug, and selected another hanger from the closet. "Great! I'll get ready."

Whenever Emma and I went out, I got ready in a fraction of the time it took her. While I waited, I opened the unanswered text thread to Joan. I grew more impatient by the day. I typed several thinly veiled, pissy messages to her before erasing each one. Did she know I'd been tethered? Did Ben? They had to know. When we last talked, Joan said she was negotiating Ben's tethering violation with the Committee.

My fingertips settled on my throat. The inflamed skin still made the mark tender to the touch. I reached out for her, the being I'd shared a body with for so long.

Nothing.

Just quiet emptiness.

Her absence hurt more than the tether's feedback. Those people had hollowed out my insides. Extracted the marrow from my bones.

"Alex?"

I jumped, my heart thudding.

"Are you okay?" Emma's brow wrinkled.

"Still adjusting to the shitty hearing. I'm all right." I wasn't, but this event was important to Emma. I stood. "Let's go before I change my mind about being seen in this thing."

After a round of oohs and aahs from my mother and grandmother, and embarrassed acknowledgment from my father, Emma and I were on our way.

Hopewell had a vibrant art scene with many galleries sprinkled across the city. Emma explained that the venue we were driving to only received customers by appointment. To me, that meant most of the art within its walls cost more than the combined value of my material possessions.

We entered the pleasantly lit space, and several volunteers immediately swarmed Emma to ask about the evening's itinerary. She deftly dealt out answers and assigned tasks. I wandered from her side, snagging a champagne flute from a passing tray, to look at the art installment on the gallery walls. The chilled drink didn't have much taste, but it soothed some pain from my sore throat.

Judging from the photography displayed, the artist favored black-and-white shots. I wasn't familiar with the ins and outs of the medium, but the pieces on the walls were beautiful. Even though they weren't in color, the photos used a full palette of grays and framed subjects in interesting ways. There weren't any people pictured. How could someone make a discarded child's toy look so compelling?

One specific photograph caught my eye, and I took a step closer, my nose a foot from the composition. I recognized the place. A large ceramic pipe, draped with moss and lichen, jutted out from a leaf-covered bank. The pipe's large opening faded into pure black—a void. The scent of raw sewage came to mind. Nate and I had met an informant there, a vampire named Fillip, when we were investigating Isaac's murder.

"What are your thoughts on this one?" The question was a burst of warm air on the back of my ear and neck.

I almost choked on my last sip of champagne as I spun to face the person. A sharply dressed man stood close behind me. Platinum blond and black hair. Lazy smile. Rust-colored eyes beneath half-lowered eyelids. His name snapped into my mind—Sebastian Visser.

To my horror, my face flushed. I jerked a thumb back at the photo. "Are these yours?"

His eyes narrowed ever so slightly as he studied me. "Yes." He glanced along the length of the gallery wall. "Commercial photography pays more, but I prefer to play." Sebastian's gaze returned to the drainage pipe photo and then to me. "Are you familiar with this location?"

"It's in Hopewell."

"All of these are from around Hopewell. Why did this one catch your attention?" The edges of his smile twitched.

Holy hell, it suddenly seemed hot in the room. I swallowed. "It . . . I . . ."

His head tilted to the side. "You're different from when we met at the record store." Sebastian's gaze dropped down the length of me and moved back up again. "The clothing choice is better, but it's something else."

Was it that obvious that she'd been taken from me? Even though I hid the tether's mark with the scarf, could he tell? Emma hadn't said I appeared any different, but maybe she didn't want to upset me. A low buzz spun up in my head along with a new sensation.

Shame.

"I need to find someone." Turning away, I almost collided with Emma. She stepped aside, caught my arm, and replaced my empty glass with one of the two cocktail glasses she held. Emma beamed her dazzling smile at Sebastian.

"Hello." She released my arm and extended her hand to Sebastian. "I'm Emma Arztin, director of Another Chance Ministries. I'm so glad to finally meet you in person, Mr. Visser. Speaking on the phone isn't the same."

"Sebastian." Instead of shaking her hand, he held it loosely in his. Smiling, he brushed the tops of her fingers with his thumb. "Thank you for entertaining my idea for the show."

Emma's cheeks turned rosy. "No, thank you for your generous offer. This will give our funds a welcome boost and allow us to reach more clients."

I frowned. Was he using the same sort of razzle-dazzle trick with Emma as he had with Sara? That was *not* okay. Unlike most of the wolves and wizards I knew, Emma hadn't bothered getting a Shield. I tugged on her elbow. "Em, can we talk?"

Her smile didn't falter, and she didn't break eye contact with Sebastian. "Just a moment, Alex."

He continued, "I wanted to express my appreciation. Another Chance helped a friend of mine when I couldn't." He arched an eyebrow. "You may know him. Ben Sharpe?"

My pulse skipped, and I glanced at Emma.

"What? Ben!" She looked at me and laughed before turning back to Sebastian. "Yes, he's a friend of ours, too. It seems like forever ago when I met him. I was still in college and volunteering at Another Chance. How do you know him?"

"We were friends in high school and afterward, before I left to pursue my career," he said. "Life happened, and we lost touch."

What was this guy up to? Could his donation be genuine, or was he using Emma to locate Ben? The buzzing in my mind grew louder.

"Ms. Arztin—" Sebastian began.

"Miss. And please, call me Emma."

He chuckled. "Emma, I'll leave you to enchanting the common folk and shaking as much as possible from their tight pockets." He lifted Emma's hand and admired her outfit. "It shouldn't be difficult for someone so stunning."

The pink in Emma's cheeks crept across her nose. "If you feel up to the challenge, I'm sure a well-placed word here and there from the artist will help."

"Challenge?" Sebastian's eyebrows rose, and a spark of something other than indifference lit his eyes. "I accept." He released Emma's hand and gave us each a nod and smile.

Emma watched him leave, her bottom lip caught between her teeth.

I continued to frown. "Em, no. Not him."

She fanned herself as she turned to me. "But he's *really* yummy. Do you think those shoes were Louis Vuitton?"

"What? I didn't even look—"

"Maybe Jimmy Choo."

"Em, I couldn't care less about his damn shoes. He came into Rear Window during my interview looking for Ben. There's something about him I don't trust."

"He's a Visser. Most of them are wizards," she said. "Did you sense him using magic at the shop?"

I shook my head. "No. Yes. I mean, it's more than him being a wizard."

Emma crossed her arms.

"I'm not trying to spoil your fun, but he cast some sort of charm on Sara, the store clerk," I said. "She turned into a blubbering mess. Wizards aren't supposed to mess with Commoners like that, right?"

"Of course we're not." She laughed. "But look at him, Alex. He doesn't need magic to get that type of reaction from people. The guy oozes charisma."

"But I felt it, Em," I said. "There's no doubt in my mind it was some sort of magic, and he used it to get info out of Sara about Ben."

Her smile faded, and she glanced after Sebastian. "Do you think he did the same to me?" Unlike werewolves, wizards couldn't sense the casting of magic unless it bumped up against their Shield.

"I don't know. Maybe?" I gestured to my throat. "I can't tell anymore with this thing. This is why you need to get a Shield—to protect yourself from people like him."

Emma looked at me. "With your Shield broken, wouldn't you be affected too?"

Sudden realization struck—maybe even backhanded—me. I scowled after Sebastian, my face blazing. "That. Asshole."

Emma's eyes widened, and she covered her mouth.

I glared at her. "It's not funny, Em."

"I'm sure Ben will understand. He's been gone for a while, and you've been alone."

"Emma!" Tears pricked the edges of my eyes.

She lowered her hand, the amusement gone. "I'm sorry. That wasn't kind." Emma hugged me. "Charms are harmless. You'll be okay."

I didn't return the hug. Emma and I had different opinions on how harmless men's uninvited advances could be. It bothered me, not knowing Sebastian's intent. And manipulating someone's emotions like that was wrong.

"Did you see the great spread of food?" She offered me a smile.

"Nothing tastes good, and I'm not that hungry." I took a sip of the cocktail she'd given me and scanned the crowd over the brim of my glass. The gallery filled, the event underway.

Raucous laughter caused goosebumps to rise on my arms. My gaze jerked toward the sound, and my mouth went dry. Spray tan, tailored suit, and a smile like a shark's . . . Joe Stone stood not twenty feet away. He held a cocktail in one hand and gestured with his other as he spoke to a couple standing with him. A well-put-together woman stood at his elbow, staring up at him and nodding occasionally. His wife, maybe?

My fingers tightened around my glass, and my stomach burned. "Why the hell is that bastard here?"

"What?" Emma caught sight of Stone. The blush of color left her face. "Shit." She looked back at me with a frown. "Alex, I'm sorry. Someone else on staff handled the guest list. I had to delegate tasks in the rush to pull this event off at the last minute. I meant to double-check it, but I—"

"Why would he be on the list in the first place?" I scowled. "He's a terrible person."

Her words sharpened. "Mayoral candidates are always on the list. It benefits Another Chance to build a relationship with them. I can't decide who stays and who goes depending on my or my friends' personal tastes. I have to think about the organization and our clients."

I blinked. For a brief moment, Emma's frosty mother had shone through her eyes.

"I said I'm sorry, but I can't ask him to leave now," Emma said. "Would you like me to have a volunteer drive you home? I understand if you do. I won't be upset."

I debated on taking her up on the offer. I could ditch the stupid dress and spend the evening cocooned in the dark and warmth of my bed covers. But I bristled at the idea of Stone's presence forcing me to leave. "No, I'll stay."

"Okay. Again, I'm sorry." Emma ran her shaking fingers through her hair. "You can do this! Drink your cocktail. Ignore him." She gestured to the walls. "Enjoy the pretty art."

A volunteer called Emma. She inhaled, and on her exhale a brilliant smile replaced her frown. "Coming!" Emma hurried away to help with whatever question or task the volunteer had for her.

Another bout of laughter erupted from Stone, and I clenched my teeth. I struggled to keep it together after he'd taken part of me. Because of his recent package of laws, my fellow wolves were scared and unsure of what their futures held. Meanwhile, Stone enjoyed a big-ticket event, not giving us a second thought.

I threw back the rest of my cocktail and shadowed Stone, taking care to keep my back to him. Instinctively, I reached out to my inner wolf, seeking a boost in my hearing. My anger magnified when, again, she didn't respond. Inside my head, the buzzing pitched upward into a whine. The bits of Stone's conversation I did catch were mind-numbingly boring, but the seething anger I carried motivated me to keep tabs on him.

I hoped Stone would somehow mess up. That he would give me what I needed to expose him for the awful criminal he was. When that happened, his new safety rules would go down with him. Then the cursed mark would be removed from my throat, and I'd be reunited with my inner wolf.

My stalking behavior was rewarded when Stone and his maybe-wife moved across the room to speak with a grey-haired older man and a tall young woman with long lavender hair. The sight of the young woman caused my pulse to quicken, and her identity clicked into place. Julia Visser, Isaac's girlfriend when he was killed. I recognized the man with her as one of the many old guys who sat as Commoner representatives on the Committee. So maybe the guy was her father, the man Reginald mentioned on the phone, Franklin Teuling.

I swapped my empty cocktail glass for a full one from a passing tray. Sipping my drink and feigning interest in the photography, I meandered close enough to eavesdrop. The proximity to Stone proved uncomfortable.

"Julia, if you don't mind keeping my lovely wife company, I have some uninteresting business to discuss with your father." Stone flashed his signature grin.

Her smile tight-lipped, Julia looked at the quiet woman beside Stone. "Of course not."

I waited to allow the two men to get ahead of me and then followed them toward one of the gallery's rear exit doors. My legs were a bit wobbly, and I almost ran into the doorframe on my way out. With little to eat for lunch and no dinner, maybe I should have tried the food Emma pointed out. Rotten timing for my blood sugar to crash.

Once outside, my only choice for cover was an aggressively manicured, waist-high hedge situated between the building and the adjoining courtyard. I tried to crouch behind it, but then realized I wore a ridiculously fitted dress and heels while holding a cocktail glass. Blinking my eyes, I impatiently waited for my vision to adjust to the dark. I reached out with my free hand to find the ground, finally made it into a crouched position, but then slowly tipped back onto my ass.

Thankfully, the self-absorbed nature of the men prevented them from noticing my less-than-subtle presence.

Stone chuckled. "The last thing I need from you right now, Frank, is a sudden fit of conscience."

Teuling's hands were in his jacket pockets, and he frowned up at Stone. "I was guaranteed that there would be nothing in that young man's death that led back to me."

I scrambled for my phone to record the conversation. Unfortunately, it was tucked away in a small purse Emma had lent me, the strap of which had somehow gotten twisted around my body.

"There won't be," Stone said.

"Jakob DeBoer and that woman cop have been asking questions," Teuling said. "I only did what was best for my daughter."

So Jakob and Anne were looking further into Isaac's murder together. But would they find anything before Stone crossed the election finish line?

"Of course, you were," Stone grinned. "Nobody can fault you for that. Any father would have done the same for their child."

"He was distracting her with his radical views. She was studying for her master's," Teuling said. "She didn't need someone filling her head with nonsense. I had no other choice."

"There's no need for guilt," Stone said. "And don't worry about Jakob. He and Grey are on my radar."

"I wanted him tethered, Joe. You didn't say anything about having him killed!"

"Careful, Frank." Stone glanced back at the building. He lowered his voice, and I barely heard his next words. "You asked me to take care of the creature, and I did. Your daughter is safe because of me."

I followed the chain purse strap slung over my shoulder to find the purse itself. The clasp challenged me, but I finally extracted my phone. The screen lit up and blinded me in the dark. "Shit!" I held the phone against my chest to cover the light from being seen by the two men.

"What was that?" Teuling's tone tightened.

Their footsteps crossed back over the courtyard toward me.

11

THE DOOR OF the gallery swung open behind me, and I almost shrieked. The light from inside spilled out to illuminate me sitting in the grass behind the hedge. Frustration surged as I again waited for my vision to adjust, holding up my hand to shield my eyes.

Sebastian stood there. His gaze dropped briefly to me before he called out. "Frank, your daughter is requesting you. Something about actually putting your money where your mouth is and buying some pieces at exorbitant prices in the name of charity."

"Not now, Sebastian," Teuling said. "Tell her I'll be there in a few minutes."

Sebastian gave a snort and shook his head. "I'm not telling Her Highness to wait. Face the consequences of what you've created, Frank."

"We're done here anyway," Stone said to Teuling. "Come back inside. Relax. Enjoy the evening." The men's footsteps continued toward the gallery door and my hiding spot.

Sebastian sipped from his martini glass, but I caught the edge of his smile. He stepped out of the doorway and in front of me, shielding me from Teuling and Stone's line of vision. They passed into the building, the door shutting behind them and plunging me into darkness again.

Sebastian turned to look down at me. "Do you usually eavesdrop on shady dealings at big-ticket events?" The lighting cast deep shadows over his eyes and cheeks, making his face a skull.

"It's none of your business." The words were clumsy in my mouth. I made it to my knees and stood, though not as gracefully as I would have liked. Then I dropped my phone. I cursed, reached over to pick it up, and pitched forward off balance.

Sebastian caught me by the upper arm to prevent me from falling into the shrubbery. His fingers were as cold as ice. He smiled, and the skull leered at me. "Alex, I believe you're drunk."

"Don't touch me." Scowling, I pulled my arm away. "I'm fine." My balance was all wrong. I checked in with my body.

I'd always been careful about what I drank, not only as a woman but as someone who could wolf out and turn someone else into a snack if I lost control. But a werewolf's boosted stamina and quickened healing neutralized alcohol as soon as it hit our bloodstream. I'd grown used to a stronger tolerance.

The tether would take that away as well. My balance wavered again, the sensation alien to me.

Dammit.

I was drunk. Where was Emma?

"Why is an intoxicated would-be spy shadowing Joe Stone, mayoral candidate, only possible savior of Hopewell, and Frank Teuling, stepfather, greatest mistake of my mother's life?" Sebastian took another sip of his martini.

My mind struggled to keep his words in order. I blinked at him. "Why do you care?"

Sebastian leaned toward me and lowered his voice. His breath carried the piney scent of gin. "Because I'm fucking bored out of my skull while I'm waiting for Ben, and whatever this situation is has the stink of a hot mess all over it." He slowly smiled as his gaze dropped down to my mouth. "I'm intrigued."

My traitorous body flushed with heat. "No. It's none of your business." I shook my head and then my finger at him. "And stop using your creepy charms on me. It's not working. Leave me alone." I stumbled past him and reached for the gallery door handle. It took a few tries. I needed water and some food.

"Is agitating Joe Stone how you got yourself tethered?"

My stomach clenched, and all that blood drained from my face. I raised my hand to my throat as I turned back toward him. "How did you—"

"You left this in the hedge." Sebastian held the scarf on the end of a finger, making the gesture appear lewd. He'd seen my tether.

I snatched the scarf from him and attempted to put it back on, to hide my tether, without strangling myself. My fingers wouldn't listen to me. Sudden tears sprung into my eyes. "Go away, whoever the hell you are." I pulled the door open and glared back over my shoulder. "And leave Ben alone, too."

Back inside the gallery, I found the spread of food. The whining, piercing noise in my head slowly subsided. Emma appeared by my side as I gnawed on my third tasteless bread roll. "There you are. Where did you disappear to? I began to worry."

I glanced around before I answered her around a mouthful of bread. "I followed Stone."

"You what?" She frowned. "Why are you fol—" Emma paused and reached out to pluck something from my hair. She held it between us for me to see. "Why are there little leaves in your hair?"

I brushed her hand away, leaned toward her, and focused on speaking slowly and clearly in a lowered voice. "I know who gave Isaac's name to Stone. It was Franklin Teuling."

Emma quickly glanced around before looking back at me. "And you're loud-whispering. Why are you . . . Wait. Alex, are you drunk?"

I popped the rest of the roll in my mouth and chewed. "I think so."

"Oh no," Emma shook her head. "I wasn't thinking. Usually you can handle a few cocktails. I'd forgotten about—" She frowned again. "You can't follow Stone around in this state. He'll see you, and then you'll be in more trouble." She pulled her phone from her purse and checked the time. "It's close enough to the end of the event. The volunteers can handle teardown. I'll take you home."

"No." I shook my head, which only made it hurt. My eyes closed, I tried to collect my scattered thoughts. I swayed, opened my eyes, and grabbed the edge of the table. "I can get the evidence Anne needs. They might talk in secret again."

Emma carefully took my hands in hers and looked up at me. "We're going home." She looped her arm through mine, led me out the front door, and propped me up against a lamppost. "Wait here. The fresh air should help. I'm going to thank Sebastian again and say goodbye." Emma backed away, holding an open palm toward me. "Stay." She turned and hurried back into the building.

The bread helped. My vision cleared and my teeth felt less fuzzy. Maintaining my balance was still a bit tricky. I held onto the lamppost and debated whether I should sit down on the lawn instead. But I didn't want to embarrass Emma any more than I possibly had already.

The front door opened, and Stone strolled out with his wife on his arm. He stopped short when our eyes met. His features moved through a series of emotions before settling on the friendly neighborhood politician. "Alexis! We seem to keep running into each other."

I glared at him. "Piss off, Joe."

Stone's wife frowned and tightened her grip on his arm. "Who is this?"

He patted her hand. "Go ahead and wait in the car, sweetheart. I'll be there shortly." She left his side, throwing me a disapproving glance as she passed. He watched her disappear down the walkway before he looked back at me. Stone dropped his smile. "What are you doing here? Are you following me?"

"Why would I follow you?" I asked. "Surely your shady dealings ended when you had Isaac killed."

Stone groaned. "When will you let that die? You have no evidence. Get over it." He smiled. "Everyone else has."

My mouth went dry at his disregard of the wolves' loss. Bile and rage boiled up in my throat. If Stone had his way, the future of

Hopewell wouldn't include a safe home for us. A distant whining noise vibrated in my ears. "You're wrong. I have the evidence I need to take you down just like we did with your Hunter."

Stone paused and searched my features. "You're lying."

"No, I'm not." I went for the lie, hoping to scare him. "I recorded your chat with Franklin Teuling tonight. You can say goodbye to your mayoral run."

He frowned and glanced at my purse.

I nodded and placed my hand over the purse's clasp. "Once Aiden listens to it, you'll be out on your ass. No more Committee. And you know how much influence those old men have on the city government. No future for you there, either."

"What do you want for the recording?" Stone's frown deepened. "Money? How much?"

"Throw out those awful laws that were passed and give up your seat on the Committee." I was queasy as I admitted, "Then I'll drop Isaac's case and leave you alone."

"How do I know you haven't duplicated the recording and will keep a copy?"

I smirked. "You don't."

"So if I have the safety plan repealed and resign from the Committee, you agree to keep your nose out of my business?" he asked.

I nodded.

Stone chuckled. "Ah Alexis, do you think I'm that naive?" His predatory grin, the one that seemed natural on him, appeared. "You can't do anything to me. You're harmless with that collar we gave you."

My eyes narrowed. The sound in my head intensified to the point of being painful.

He jabbed a finger at me. "And if you continue to harass me, I won't hesitate to suggest you be executed for violating the terms of your sentence. If Father Aiden wasn't such a stickler for rules, we'd already be rid of you."

The reminder of how close I'd come to a death sentence without being aware of it weakened my knees. My grip on the lamppost tightened. Would he try the same with other wolves arrested under the new laws? What about Trish? Nate?

Stone stepped toward me and lowered the volume of his voice. "See, the good people of Hopewell deserve a safe home to work and raise a family. They shouldn't be frightened of monsters roaming their streets, allowed to do so under the facade of equality."

Hate flared inside me, and my heartbeat hammered at my ribs. I redirected the intensity of my anger to my wolf but came up against a wall. My body started to tremble, and dark spots danced in my already unreliable vision. The terrible noise in my mind increased further. My eyes watered from the pressure.

You can't do anything to stop him. You're useless. Just give up.

Stone grinned. "Now if you'll excuse me, it's been a long day."

My fist swung out, aiming to catch Stone in the jaw. In my inebriated state, the punch was slow and clumsy.

He leaned back and caught my wrist. Stone shook his head and sneered. "You argue you should be allowed to stay, yet you never fail to resort to the violence of your kind." He shoved my wrist away from him.

It forced me to step back to maintain my balance.

Stone checked his watch. "You may want to get home so you aren't out past curfew." He winked. "Goodnight, Alexis." Stone strolled away, whistling to himself.

I wanted to leap after him and claw his eyes out. Rarely had I experienced such a visceral hate for another person. What would I have done if I'd had access to my wolf? Proven his point that werewolves were monsters and shouldn't be allowed in Hopewell? Left him broken and bloodied? The noise and dark thoughts in my head made me nauseous.

Emma returned moments later, chatting with Sebastian while they walked from the building. She rushed to my side. "Alex, what happened? You're shaking. Are you starting to feel sick?"

I pressed my fingertips to my sweaty temples, attempting to quell the raging fire inside my skull. "Stone."

"What did he do?" Emma rubbed my back. "He didn't hurt you, did he?"

I shook my head. "I want to go home, Em."

"I'm so sorry I left you out here alone. I tried to be quick." She frowned and spoke to Sebastian. "Could you please stay with her while I get the car? It'll only be a moment."

His tone was calm and unconcerned. "Of course."

"Is that all right, Alex?" Emma asked.

I waved my hand. "It's fine. Go."

When Emma disappeared from sight, I turned my attention to Sebastian. "I've changed my mind."

Arms crossed, he leaned toward me. "Pardon?"

"I'll tell you why I was listening in on Stone's conversation because I need your help getting to Franklin Teuling," I said.

"What do you need from him?" he asked. "Questions on your retirement account? Were there investments you were considering?"

"I'm going to find proof of his involvement, then make him confess to giving Joe Stone Isaac Laska's name." I paused, uncertain I wouldn't be sick. "And then Stone having Isaac murdered."

Sebastian's eyebrows rose. "Frank had Julia's boyfriend killed?" His thumbs hooked into his back pockets, he glanced back toward the gallery. "Maybe I've underestimated you, Frank."

The awful noise in my head receded to an angry buzz. "Does he have a study or office at home? Can you get me inside it?"

He chuckled. "Why would I do that? You haven't been the most helpful person in my search for Ben."

"You don't seem to like Franklin. 'My mother's biggest mistake,' if I recall." I shrugged. "Or maybe it was all show so I'd believe your whole 'dark and brooding artist' act?"

Sebastian's amused smile vanished. His voice cooled, losing any hint of its smug undertone. "I look forward to the day she's free from that pathetic creature."

"He could be convicted of being an accomplice to murder. You could help make that happen." I took a chance, banking on his dislike for Teuling, but these past months I'd witnessed how much power hate could hold over someone.

Sebastian's chin dipped and he studied his nails. "Frank expects the four of us to play family and eat dinner together while I'm here. He has a study in the upper level of the house. It's empty from six until eight, then he wanders back up there for a cocktail."

My pulse skipped. "Can you get me in the house without being noticed?"

"If you stop jerking me around when it comes to Ben." The edges of his mouth curled, and he looked up through his eyelashes at me.

Warmth bloomed in my cheeks. "Dammit!" I scowled. "Stop doing that."

"Those are the terms I'm interested in," he said.

"But I can't . . . I don't know where Ben—"

Emma rushed up the walkway toward us. "Okay, the car is at the curb." She smiled at Sebastian. "Thank you for keeping her company. And thank you again for suggesting this event."

"You're welcome." He gave Emma the lazy smile that seemed to be his default. "Let me know when I can see you."

Emma blushed. "I'll be in touch." She did her best to steady me as we walked to the passenger side of her car.

I sank into the seat and closed my eyes. My whole body felt like dead weight.

She buckled me in and gave my knee a pat. "You'll be in bed soon." Emma moved to close the car door but stopped. "Here, Sebastian gave me this."

"What?" I opened my eyes to see her holding out my phone to me. "How did he—"

"You must have dropped it outside," she said. "He found it near some hedges."

I took the phone from her, mumbling my thanks.

Sebastian said he was Ben's friend, but something about him caused me unease. Maybe I was simply jealous. Sebastian knew a part of Ben that had never been shared with me. It wasn't unusual to have to pry any part of Ben's past from him.

I'd been trying to contact Ben for months with no luck. If I messaged Sebastian's name to Joan, I almost feared Ben would show up. What would that mean?

When we got back to Emma's place, my grandmother had gone to bed, but my parents were still awake watching television in the living room. Emma graciously snuck me up to the spare bedroom so I wouldn't have to face them in my drunken state. She helped me out of my clothes, into a nightshirt, gave me water and a few pills, and tucked me in.

Emma sat at the edge of the bed. "Alex, I think it's best if you forget about Joe Stone."

I shook my head, mumbling. "No."

"You can't protect yourself from him while you're tethered," she said. "He could really hurt you."

If I started to argue with Emma, the noise would return and my head would ache even more. Pulling the covers over my head, I turned over, away from her.

"Thank you for coming with me tonight," she said. "I'm sorry about the cocktails."

I wanted to tell her it was okay, that I should have been more careful. But I also wanted her to leave so I could be alone in a quiet, dark room.

She sighed and gave the bedspread a pat. "Get some rest. I'll see you in the morning."

What seemed like only minutes later, someone gently shook my shoulder. I blinked open my eyes. The hall light fell across the covers in the dark room, and Emma stood beside the bed in her nightgown and robe. She spoke in a hushed voice. "Someone is here to see you."

"What? Who?" A dull headache lodged between my eyes, and I struggled up onto my elbows. The tall, thin silhouette of a man waited in the doorway. My heart lurched. "Ben?"

The silhouette raised his hand in greeting.

12

EMMA'S BROWS DREW together, and the edges of her mouth turned down. "Are you okay with this? I can ask him to come back tomorrow when you're feeling better."

My voice sounded distant. "Yeah. He can stay."

She gave me a brief hug, turned away, and spoke to Ben. "Her family is here, staying down the hall."

Ben nodded and signed, "Thank you," in ASL. He walked into the room, and Emma closed the door behind him. We were wrapped back in darkness. I sat up and fumbled to find the light beside the bed. The mattress shifted, and the light clicked on. He'd found it first. Sitting on the edge of the bed, Ben smiled and opened his long arms to me.

I'd thought often about the moment I'd see him again. There'd been a lot of time to imagine how it'd go. It changed with each passing week I didn't hear from Joan or him. I got up onto my knees and shoved him off the bed. "You bastard! Where the *hell* have you been?"

Ben took a few awkward and stumbling steps back to remain upright. A slight frown and downcast eyes replaced his smile. He said something, but his voice, hindered by the tether at his throat, came across as a weak whisper.

My chest tightened. "I can't hear you." I'd never had trouble before. My heightened hearing had ensured that. The whining buzz of my tether's feedback returned, like a tiny drill inside my head.

He cautiously approached the bed, sat down, and leaned toward me. His breath warmed my ear. "I said, 'I know. I'm sorry.'"

"I worried about you." My body leaned into his. I was pissed I'd been left in the dark but was relieved he was safe.

He put his arms around me and kissed the top of my head.

I swallowed my pride and returned his embrace. With my nose buried at the bend of his neck, I took a deep inhale. His warm and spicy scent, like everything else, seemed paler . . . farther from me than before.

I cried.

"I'm so sorry, Alex." Ben's voice was barely audible as he spoke against my hair. "I should've tried harder to reach you."

"You're goddamn right you should have tried! What were you thinking?" I sat back and punched his shoulder. Then I felt awful about it and hugged him again.

He held onto me as a whole span of emotions tore up my insides. The dreaded buzzing of the tether's feedback spun louder in my head. With Ben, I wasn't required to keep my wolf hidden, and he wasn't scared of us. I could be my whole self.

But I wasn't whole anymore. Part of me had been taken away.

My crying dwindled to occasional sobs, and I sat back. I'd broken my self-imposed rules and tentatively lowered my defenses. Allowed Ben in close. "I trusted you, and you shut me out."

I felt betrayed.

He shook his head and took my hand in his. "I'm sorry. I didn't intend for you to feel that way. Joan said—"

A surge of anger seared my gut. The buzzing in my head throbbed. "I don't give a damn about what Joan says."

Ben's brow furrowed. His blue eyes disappeared behind dark lashes as he looked down at our hands. "Alex, I understand why you're angry, and I'm sorry. But Joan said we have to be careful. Joe Stone wants to make an example of me, and he's using Committee resources to hunt down Joan's group. He knows the group's mission is to replace the Committee."

Anne mentioned the ongoing investigation around the riots. "Why is the Committee even negotiating with Joan, then?"

"Because Stone hasn't been able to prove anything beyond Joan helping to organize a legal protest against tethering." A small smile appeared on his lips, and he looked up at me. "He's also still pissed at you, Trish, and Joan for taking out his Hunter." Ben raised my hand to kiss my knuckles. "We're trying our best. Please be patient a bit longer."

I wiped my eyes. "It's difficult when I don't know what's happening . . . if you're safe or not." If caught, Ben faced possible execution for such a gross violation of his sentence.

He nodded. "Yeah, I know. I wish this all would be over so I could stay with you." His hand tightened briefly around mine.

I bit my lip to stop even more tears.

Ben's eyes darkened. "And I hate that I wasn't here for you during the trial. If I had known that was happening, I would've found a way to see you."

My chest hitched with a sob. "I can't feel her anymore, Ben."

Frowning, he brushed some stray curls away from my damp cheeks. "Everything probably feels like shit right now, but she's still there." His own tether, meant to silence his voice and therefore block his access to magic, was camouflaged by tattoos. Ben had less than two years left to serve unless Joan's possible settlement with the Committee on his behalf lengthened his sentence.

I raised my hand to my tether. The skin burned. "I have to get rid of this thing. I'm useless without my wolf."

"I don't think there's a way to do it," Ben said. "Not safely."

"Reginald had said something about the tether. . ." My mind spun to recall his words. "The same tether is dealt to everyone. No one is an exception."

Ben nodded. "It's the same spell."

"My tether is the same as yours." Hope flickered in my chest. "Who helped you? Who cast the spell you wrote to get rid of your tether?"

"Does it matter? It didn't work." He gestured to his throat with his free hand. "It's weakened, but I still don't have full access to magic."

He didn't want to tell me. Before the Committee was notified of Ben's compromised tether, someone close enough to him helped attempt to break it. "It was Joan, wasn't it? You wrote the spell and she cast it."

His lack of confirmation was answer enough. Joan wouldn't risk her brother's future by helping me, though. If the Committee found out, the negotiations would be over.

"Alex, trying to alter my tether is what got me into this mess," Ben said. "It's why I'm hiding and can't be with you. They found out."

I shook my head. "You were found out because you cast magic to defend us from the Hunter, not for messing with your tether. Until then, they didn't even know you weakened your tether."

The possibility of damaging my tether dominated my thoughts. "Even partially reunited with my wolf, I'll have a better chance of defeating Stone."

"Stone?" Ben frowned and released my hand. "What're you talking about?"

"I'll be more myself. I can prove Franklin Teuling gave Isaac's name to Stone, and Stone ordered the Hunter to kill Isaac. Stone will be kicked off the Committee—"

Ben scowled. "You were just tethered! What the *hell* are you thinking?"

I clenched my jaw, my temples aching from the pressure inside my head.

He jabbed his finger downward. "I am *not* helping the person I care about most endanger herself."

My pulse stuttered. Heat rushed up my neck into my cheeks. Dropping my gaze, I twisted the edge of the sheets in my hands.

Emma had blatantly stated before, "You're part of his plans."

An awkward silence grew between us. Why was I so bad at this?

I cleared my throat and looked up at him. "Did Joan tell you about the *public safety* laws Stone had passed? I don't think the Committee will be negotiating with her much longer, Ben. You said yourself Stone is gunning for you and your sister's group. And if they catch you . . ."

He looked away.

"When I first met Joan, she said the protest was to pressure the Committee into dropping tethering. I thought, like Trish, we could create change from within, but it's not looking good." I exhaled, clasping my fingers. "And then I learned from Hannah, Isaac's sister, and Julia, his girlfriend, that Joan's group had set higher goals. They plan to take the whole thing down. Maybe it's time we try it Joan's way, and I want to start with Stone."

Ben grimaced and shook his head.

"The sooner Stone is shut down, the fewer wolves will be punished," I said. "If he keeps his seat on the Committee and wins the election, which all signs are pointing to, it could get even worse. Then it won't be just the wolves who are hurting."

"I don't know, Alex," Ben said. "The last time I tried that complex of a spell, the backlash from the tether nearly destroyed my throat."

My mind raced for a solution that wouldn't endanger Ben. "I know Joan can't afford to be caught helping me, but could you guide another wizard through the spell? And that way you're not further violating your sentence."

Ben frowned at the floor. "Emma's magic isn't compatible with my spell. I don't know any other wizard that would help us."

"I do." With the possibility spoken aloud, I could only think of being reunited with my inner wolf. "Please? If he says no or his magic isn't the right type, I'll give up on the idea."

Ben hesitated.

"Please, Ben." I nearly shook with anticipation. "I need to be able to feel her again."

His shoulders sagged. "Who do you have in mind?"

"Sebastian Visser."

Ben's eyes widened, and he inhaled sharply. He turned away, but not quick enough to hide the color that flushed his pale features.

It wasn't the reaction I expected after he heard the name of a friend. Sebastian must have lied to me after all. "He came into Rear Window Records looking for you while I was there for a job interview," I said. "His stepfather is Franklin Teuling, the guy who passed Isaac's name to Stone because he didn't want a werewolf dating his daughter. Sebastian seems to really hate his stepfather and is willing to help me get inside Teuling's study, but he's demanding to see you in return."

Ben cursed, chuckled, and shook his head. He looked over his shoulder at me. "Alex, Sebastian is unreliable."

"He said he was your friend."

"Not anymore." A tremor appeared in Ben's voice. "I don't want to see him."

I closed my eyes and rubbed at my temples. My already achy head pounded. I hadn't expected the snag in my impromptu plan to be Ben refusing to work with Sebastian. "I don't understand."

Ben's light touch settled on my arm. "What about Anne? Emma told me she accepted a job with Detective Grey and is looking into Stone."

I shook my head. "She is, but Anne will be fighting an uphill battle with the Committee. I overheard Stone assuring Teuling he wouldn't let Anne and Jakob discover what happened." Frowning, I lowered my hands. "And if I don't have anything to keep my mind occupied, if I'm not doing something to help, all I'm going to feel is this rage and hate banging around inside my skull. There's no way I can survive twenty years of this."

Ben dropped his gaze to his hand on my arm. He knew what living with a tether was like—to be incomplete. He also knew the increased dangers of a tether to a werewolf. The same spell also had physical consequences, along with mental.

I lifted his chin so I could look into his eyes. "Please."

"There's no guarantee Sebastian is going to risk it," Ben said. "He's one of the most selfish people I've met."

Hope flickered inside me again as Ben's resolve began to deteriorate. "Then he won't do it, but let him decide that." I paused before adding, in case the point wasn't already clear. "I'm going after Stone either way."

"I was afraid of that." Ben finally nodded. "Okay, I'll teach him the spell."

I grinned and hugged him. "I'll call Sebastian tomorrow and set up a time we can meet him." It was a win-win. I would regain some, if not all, access to my gifts, and Ben wouldn't be caught casting magic. "How long can you stay?"

"Just tonight," he said. "Joan is picking me up tomorrow."

"How did you get away in the first place?" I asked. "Bribery?"

He gave me a weak smile. "She found out about your trial and sentencing, let me know about it, and offered to drop me off here so I could be with you."

I lifted an eyebrow. "Doesn't she think that you visiting in person is more dangerous than us exchanging a few texts once in a while?"

"Yeah," he said. "She does."

"Tell her thank you for me." Joan wasn't really the bad person I tried to cast her as. She did what she thought necessary to protect her little brother. That often placed her between Ben and me. "Can we see each other again tomorrow night?"

"I'm not sure." Ben brushed the back of his fingers against my cheek. The gesture made my face warm. "I'll ask her tomorrow." He leaned forward and kissed me.

I'd missed him so much—his whispered voice, his light touch, his comforting scent . . . how he tasted.

. . . *the person I care about most* . . .

Warmth spread throughout my chest. I returned his kiss and then some. All the nerves in my body lit up. And so did the awful feedback from the tether.

Determined not to have my time with Ben ruined, I tried to push through the discomfort. It wasn't long before I grasped at the hem of his shirt and helped him pull it off over his head.

He returned the favor.

I dropped back onto the bed. He followed and was warm skin and sharp shoulder blades beneath my fingertips.

His hand found the long scar along my side. He bent his head to press a kiss against the bad memory carved into my skin.

The noise in my mind buzzed and whined, even as I drew my fingers through his dark hair. "I've missed being with you."

His breath tickled the skin of my inner thigh. "I've missed being with you, too." He hooked his thumb beneath the waistband of my underwear and looked up at me.

A tingling heat flooded my body, competing with the cursed sound in my head. I held my breath and nodded.

His hand moved to pull my waistband over my hip, and all the air seemed to leave the room. Suddenly his body weighed too heavy upon mine, too close, and I couldn't breathe. I seized his wrist and shook my head.

Ben froze. "Alex?"

"No. Stop." The scent of decaying leaves filled my nose. I shook my head again and gasped for air, disoriented. "No, no, no—"

The man was crushing me beneath him. I writhed and shoved at him to free myself.

"Alex." Ben pushed himself up onto an elbow.

Released, I sat up, panting.

"Alex, what's wrong?"

A cold sweat broke out over my skin. The noise inside my head was a high, piercing whine. *He'll take what he wants from you and leave. Nothing you do can stop it. Give up. Let him smother the life from you.* I pressed my fingers to my temples and squeezed my eyes shut.

Something touched my back. I flinched, and it quickly withdrew. My gaze darted to Ben, beside me.

"What's happening?" He frowned. "Tell me what's wrong so I can help."

I yanked the sheet up around me to cover myself. The edges of my words were sharp. "It's the damn tether." The effort to hold back tears made my voice hoarse. Being so out of sync with my own body threw me back to the first year after my wolf and I met. I'd been a stranger in my own skin.

Ben sat up. He rubbed his hand over my back. "Is it something I did that set it off?"

I shook my head and blinked back tears. If I spoke my answer aloud, I'd start crying. Again. Is this how it would be now if I tried to share myself with him? Had the tether taken this from me as well?

"Can I hold you?" he asked.

I sniffled. "Can I hold you instead?"

"Yeah, of course."

We settled under the covers. I wrapped my arms around Ben and kissed the area between his shoulders. I pressed my body as close as I could against the warmth of his. The lingering fear from the panic attack faded. I fell asleep with the steady rhythm of his heartbeat against my chest.

THE NEXT MORNING, I woke to the sound of the bedroom door opening and my grandmother's voice. "Alex, dear, are you awake? Emma has made a lovely—oh my."

My eyelids flew open and I sat up, pulling the bedcovers around me. "Grandma!"

Ben startled awake. Bleary-eyed, he noticed my grandmother and froze.

"You can't walk into someone's bedroom without knocking!" My face burning, I waved a hand at her. "I'll be right down. Please go. Now."

"I'm sorry, dear." Smiling and eyes twinkling, she said, "Be sure to bring your friend to breakfast." She gently closed the door.

I shook my head and covered my hot face with my hands.

Ben kissed the slope of my shoulder. "I can slip out if you want."

"No. Grandma will make a fuss about it," I said. "You'll have to meet my family eventually, right? I apologize in advance for anything they might say."

He smiled. "I'm looking forward to it."

We dressed and went downstairs to the dining room. Always the amazing hostess, Emma had a spread of pastries, eggs, bacon, and toast laid out. She caught sight of us and halted, a pitcher of orange juice in hand. Both her eyes and mouth were rounded as she looked to the table where my family sat and back to Ben and me.

I gave her a helpless shrug.

My parents looked up from assembling their breakfasts. My mother immediately frowned, and my dad seemed confused.

My grandmother looked smug. "Good morning, dear. Have a seat."

We pulled out some chairs at the table and sat down. I cleared my throat. "Mom, Dad, Grandma, this is Ben Sharpe." I hadn't told my family about Ben because I didn't think they'd approve of me dating when I was supposed to be keeping a low profile. "Ben, these are my parents Scott and Kim, and my grandmother Lunella." I gestured to each.

Ben gave them all his easy smile and a single wave.

"Ah, hello Ben, it's nice to meet you," my dad said. I wasn't sure he realized Ben had stayed overnight.

My mother remained tight-lipped. Her stern gaze scanned over Ben, at the unkempt hair and numerous tattoos, and then turned on me. Like my own, her tells hadn't changed either.

I ignored her and reached for the pastries. "And before anyone asks, yes, he knows what I am."

"*Who* you are," my grandmother said as she spread jam on her toast.

Ben smiled and signed in response, punctuated by a gesture to Emma.

She translated. "Ben is a wizard like me."

"Another wizard," my father chuckled. "Fascinating. Dad would tell me bedtime stories of the fantastical people he knew, and I'm beginning to wonder how much of it wasn't fiction." He toasted me with his coffee mug. "Quite the circle of friends you have here, Alex."

My heart warmed. I patted Ben's thigh below the table, smiling at him and then Emma. "Yeah, they've kept me sane while I'm doing the whole hidden werewolf thing." I looked around the table at my family. "In fact, if you guys want to head home, go ahead. Thanks for staying a few days. I'm feeling better." I'd feel a lot better if I knew they were on their way home, a safe distance from Hopewell if any bit of my half-baked plan went sideways.

Dad glanced at my mother and looked back at me. "Are you sure—"

"What is it that you do, Ben?" Mom stabbed at her eggs with her fork.

My body tensed. "He mixes music as an EDM artist. When he isn't performing, he works at Rear Window Records and part-time at the Sound Refuge as a sound engineer for their shows."

Ben's hand settled on mine beneath the table. When I looked at him, he smiled and gave a slight shake of his head. He released my hand and signed a question directed at my mother.

Emma, at the ready, translated. "He's wondering what you do, Kim."

My mom paused, her coffee mug halfway to her mouth. "Me?"

Ben nodded.

"Oh . . . Well, it's not *that* interesting." She glanced around the table. "I manage and write grants for a food security program in New York."

"What?" Emma's eyes widened. "Why haven't we been chatting about grant writing?"

"I suppose we could." My mother's shoulders relaxed.

"Yes, please!" Emma said. "Let's talk and exchange numbers after breakfast."

Mom smiled. "We may bore everyone else."

"Pfft, are you kidding?" Dad's expression of excitement was as convincing as that of a stage performer's—a bad one. "Fundraising? Event planning? Riveting stuff."

Mom laughed and swatted him on the side of the arm.

I exhaled slowly as the conversation continued without further interrogation of Ben. He winked at me, picked up his fork, and began to eat.

After the meal, Ben and I helped clear the table. My family, believing I still needed their emotional support, attempted to talk me into some sightseeing in Hopewell. I passed since Sara expected me within the hour for my first shift at the record store.

It took some convincing, but Joan agreed to Ben seeing me again later that night. She asked him to stay with her during the day while I worked. He agreed, and I left for Rear Window.

I messaged Emma on my break for Sebastian's contact details. When I tried to copy the info into my contacts, it was already there. He must have added it when I lost my phone at the gallery. I frowned at his name on the phone's screen and dialed the number.

He picked up after the first ring. "Hello, Alex."

"You added my number to your phone, too?" I asked.

"Of course," he said. "Are you calling to schedule a visit?"

"I'm calling for another favor," I said. "I need a wizard's help to break my tether."

"Your tether?" He sighed. "Why are you wasting my time?"

I winced. "Please?"

"Oh. You're serious." Sebastian started laughing. It went on a bit longer than necessary.

"Ben has the spell. You would cast it," I said. "It didn't completely work for him, but I want to try it anyway."

That shut him up.

I continued, "We can meet you tonight after I get out of work."

"Unraveling complex spellwork with Ben Sharpe? I can't think of anything else I'd rather be doing," Sebastian said.

We agreed to meet within a half hour after my shift ended that evening. He sent me an address for somewhere off the highway, south of downtown. Dangling the promise of Ben being there left me with a sour stomach. Hopefully, the spell wouldn't be a disaster and I'd be reunited, even if partially, with my inner wolf.

And a small, insecure, and jealous bit of me craved to know why Sebastian was looking for Ben.

13

MY SHIFT AT Rear Window passed without incident. Sara charged me with some restocking tasks so I didn't have to interact with many customers. When I clocked out, I felt good about finally making my way toward a paycheck again.

Daylight faded as I waited in the parking lot behind the building for Ben. Joan dropped him off, but she didn't leave her car to speak to me. Instead, we exchanged a brief wave.

"She doesn't know what we're doing tonight, does she?" I asked.

"No." Ben shifted his weight beside me and watched Joan's car leave the lot. "I wish she did, then I wouldn't have to feel guilty about it."

My stomach twisted. "I'm sorry."

He glanced up at the apartment we used to share and looked back at me. "I thought a lot today about what you said last night . . . that it might be time to put an end to the Committee. I think you're right. They've thrown red tape up everywhere to complicate negotiations for Joan. I don't want her to go through that anymore for me." Ben reached for my hand and slid his fingers between mine. "She's exhausted, and all I want is to be where you are. I don't like that you and I are being kept apart."

My cheeks warmed, and my stomach did that flippy-thing it does around him. "I don't like that we're being kept apart, either. Do you think you'll talk to Joan about how you're feeling? I can be with you when you do. You know, fortification for facing the big sister."

He smiled. "I'll handle it, but thanks for offering."

A buzz in my pocket signaled a text message. I withdrew my phone, read the screen, and looked up at Ben. "It's Sebastian. He's on his way to meet us."

Ben's smile disappeared. Without comment, he got into my car. I followed and glanced over as he buckled his seatbelt. "Do you think this is going to work?" The prospect of putting a dent in my tether gave me goosebumps.

"I don't know for sure. Technically, if it's the same tethering spell, this should at least weaken the tether's effect on you." Ben's gaze shifted to the mark on my throat. "But when I altered mine, I was desperate. I didn't care if something went wrong."

"So you understand why I'm willing to take the risk," I said.

"Yeah. I do." He looked away from me.

We drove only five minutes down the expressway before exiting to the west and taking a neglected street toward a rash of abandoned warehouses. A prickling discomfort ran along my spine. The seemingly vacant and neglected structures reminded me of the hideout the Hunter chose when he'd been in Hopewell.

Ben leaned forward in his seat with a frown. He looked up at the decrepit buildings. "Wait. Why are we here?"

"I'm not sure," I said. "Sebastian gave me the address. I've never been over here before. Have you?"

He leaned back. Instead of answering, he muttered something under his breath I couldn't hear. Already curious about his reaction to meeting up with Sebastian, I now had more questions.

I pulled into an empty gravel parking lot overgrown with weeds and strewn with bits of trash blown over from the highway. I killed the headlights and engine. The repetitive hum of fast-moving traffic drifted in through the windows.

We stepped out of the car into the evening heat. It felt nice after spending the day at Rear Window in AC. The red brickwork of the warehouse appeared crumbling, and many of the tall windows had been broken by wayward rocks.

Ben waited, reclining against the car's side with his arms tightly crossed. His jawline twitched, and every once in a while his gaze darted toward the lot's entrance. It was too much for me.

I pulled his arms open and slipped myself between them to face him. "Before he gets here, can you tell me how you know Sebastian? He said you two were close friends who lost touch."

Ben's hands came to rest at my waist. "I've known him since my freshman year in high school. He and I were best friends." Ben swallowed and color rose in his cheeks. "After school . . . we were together. We shared a place."

I blinked. "Oh." Ben's abrupt discomfort at the mention of Sebastian's name last night finally made sense. "You two dated."

Ben grimaced. He looked past me to the drive. "Something like that."

"I'm sorry. I didn't know." No wonder he acted anxious. I'd set him up on a night out with me and his ex. I felt like an idiot. "He didn't say anything."

Ben shook his head. "I could have."

"Why didn't you?"

"It didn't end well, so it's a painful memory," he said. "And all that bullshit is in the past. You and I are what I want to focus on, you know?"

"If seeing Sebastian is too uncomfortable, you can back out," I said, though I hoped he wouldn't. I needed at least some access to my inner wolf, and Sebastian's help with Ben's direction seemed my current best shot at achieving that.

"You really want this," Ben said. "And nothing says I have to see him afterward."

I didn't know what else to say to put him at ease, so instead, I leaned forward and gave him a soft kiss. When we parted, his thick lashes were halfway lowered, and a slight smile played on his lips. His smile grew, and his hands drifted into my back pockets.

He pulled me tighter against him and kissed me in return, his not as innocent as mine.

Like before, the tether's feedback began to buzz between my ears. I pressed myself against Ben, wanting this tiny moment with him. But without the confidence of my inner wolf driving us, my body wasn't having it. The awful noise in my head grew louder until, frustrated, I pushed away from Ben.

"Alex?" His cheeks were flushed. "Are you okay?"

A car approached from down the street, and its headlights swung into the parking lot. I moved back another step from Ben to get some air. I nodded. "Sorry. Yeah. I'm fine."

Sebastian parked the coupe next to my car and got out. He saw Ben, slowed, and stopped several feet away. "Here we finally are. I've been looking everywhere for you." Sebastian spared me a glance. "I didn't think she'd ever let me see you."

Ben scowled at Sebastian, moved to my side, and took hold of my hand.

"Do you think you can help me or not?" I slipped my fingers between Ben's.

"What do you think, Ben?" A corner of Sebastian's mouth curled up. "Should we break a few Committee rules for old times' sake?"

"Is that a yes?" I tried to keep a tight hold on my irritation with Sebastian. I didn't want him to needle Ben, but also didn't want him to leave.

Sebastian sighed. "Of course I can help." The gravel crunched under his shoes as he walked closer to us. He gave Ben a once over from head to toe. "You look good. Healthy." The naked sincerity in his tone, absent of any ego, verged on intimate.

I suddenly needed to remind myself of Ben's words to me. *Person I care most about . . . all I want is to be where you are.* Sebastian was someone from the past, and Ben wanted to keep it that way.

"And slipping a tethering spell?" Sebastian gave a low whistle. "You should have called. Imagine the damage we could have done springing people from their tethers."

Ben's sour expression didn't change. He simply lifted his other hand and gave Sebastian the finger.

Sebastian, undeterred, cocked his head. "What did good ole granddad think of you getting so close to unraveling his work? Was he pissed? Proud? A bit of both?" He chuckled. "I would have killed to be a fly on the wall for that conversation."

Swallowing, Ben looked away.

I'd had enough. "Shouldn't we get started?"

Sebastian's gaze lowered to Ben's hand tightly clasping my own. His grin faded. He raised his chin and studied Ben from beneath his hooded eyelids. "Let's head inside. You can tell me about how the tether spell is built and how you got around it."

He turned and walked toward a metal door at the building's base. We followed in his shadow. Ben released my hand to wipe his sweating palms on the side of his shirt.

I rubbed the inside of his arm with my free hand, my voice lowered. "Thank you."

Sebastian pulled open the door, the hinges screeching and grinding from rust, and stepped aside. Ben and I passed through the doorway. Sebastian had left on his car's headlights, and the bright beams lit the otherwise dark space. The voluminous room spanned a good length of the building. The amount of dust on the various shipping crates and piles of broken boards and bricks could be accurately described as a blanket.

I walked further into the room and pulled up short. An elongated, jagged hole stretched across the floor into the shadows. It seemed the wood had rotted and collapsed, and something had fallen through. I took a cautious step and leaned forward to peek down into the hole, but someone caught my wrist. I looked back, and Ben shook his head at me. He drew me to him and spoke near my ear. "Please. I want to help you with this and leave as soon as possible."

Sebastian waited for us, hands in his pockets, watching Ben as we crossed back to him. "Ready to start?"

Ben withdrew paper and a pencil from his back pocket. He turned toward a stack of boxes to use as a table and unfolded the paper into a larger sheet, running his hand over it to flatten out the wrinkles. "The tether is constructed of a superfine mesh pattern."

Sebastian moved close to him and looked at the paper. Ben frowned and leaned back. Sebastian's smile turned crooked. "I can't hear you unless I'm right next to you. Do you want my help or not?"

From his other side, I rested my hand on the small of Ben's back. He glanced at me, and I gave him a smile. Swallowing, he looked back at the paper and repeated, "The tether is constructed of a superfine mesh pattern."

I scanned the page. Arcane symbols and numbers that reminded me of those never-ending equations from algebra class covered the sheet. None of it made sense. "Mesh doesn't seem like a great barrier."

Sebastian, his hip resting against the crate, pointed at some scrawled writing on the page. "But it constricts when the wizard reaches out for the energy to fuel their magic."

"Yeah. It does the same thing when lupine channel their emotions to power their abilities." Ben looked at me. "It's like one of those woven finger traps you get at carnivals."

"The more you struggle, the more it tightens," I said.

"And the barrier sort of solidifies," Ben said. "There are fewer holes in the mesh."

Sebastian looked up from the paper at Ben. "Why didn't you build a fortified path through it? Like a tunnel?"

Ben shook his head and tapped on a different grouping of symbols. "The tether is designed to react to direct tampering like that."

"That must be why it zapped Em when she tried to heal your throat," I said.

Sebastian straightened and held his hand out. Ben passed him the pencil, and he started to write on a blank area of the page. "Why'd Emma have to heal you?"

Ben rubbed the back of his neck. "I built a barrier to protect Alex and me. The backlash from the tether tore me up a bit inside."

"A barrier against what?" Sebastian continued scribbling.

"A truck," I said. "A Hunter tried to run us down with it."

The pencil stopped its scratching, and Sebastian looked up at Ben. His eyebrows rose to disappear behind his blond curls. "An oncoming truck? While tethered?"

Color crept up into Ben's face. "A compromised tether."

Sebastian chuckled and shook his head.

Ben dropped his gaze to the paper, and a small smile crept onto his lips.

A stab of jealousy nailed me in the chest, and I frowned. I didn't want such a petty emotion to get in the way when so much was at stake. "So if the tether reacts like that, how'd you get past it in the first place?" I asked.

"Right here." Sebastian pointed with the pencil to symbols near the bottom of the page.

"Yeah," Ben said. "I thought, instead of fighting to break through it, why not try going the other way."

"Like the finger trap," I said. "You loosened the mesh."

Ben nodded. "Sort of twisted it so the holes remain larger. It's still a barrier, but a less substantial one."

Sebastian tapped the fresh writing on the page and looked at Ben. "What do you think?"

Ben reviewed the symbols, plucked the pencil away from Sebastian, and added a few marks to the page. "You're still shit at showing your work."

A hip resting back against the crate, Sebastian crossed his arms. "It's unnecessary."

"It's how you find mistakes." Ben set down the pencil.

I slipped my arm around Ben's waist. "Are you changing it?"

They both looked up from the scribbled arcane symbols at me as if they'd forgotten I was there.

"Adjusting and translating it," Sebastian said.

"Are you sure you want to try this?" Ben asked me, his brows pinched together.

His hesitation gave me pause. "What is he planning to do?" I motioned to the paper. "I don't understand any of this."

"I'm going to paralyze and dissolve it." Sebastian backed away a few paces from the stack of crates. "Come on over, Alex."

Dissolve it. Break down the barrier keeping my wolf and me apart. I let go of Ben and walked to Sebastian. "What do you need me to do?"

"Hold still." His cold fingers lifted my chin so he could get a closer look at the tether. He nodded to himself, released my chin, and smiled. "This is probably going to hurt."

I attempted to remain motionless, but my body quivered. I couldn't wait to be reunited with her.

Sebastian withdrew a small plastic tube with a sliding lever from his pocket. He pulled the lever back, and something clicked into place. With the end of the tube pressed to his fingertip, he pushed a button at the opposite end. The device clicked again. A perfect bead of blood formed on the end of his fingertip.

I'd been so preoccupied with my plan to have Sebastian alter the tether that I didn't consider the type of magic he practiced may be different from Ben's. Shadows of doubt crept into my thoughts, but they weren't stronger than my need to break the tether.

Nothing was.

Sebastian pressed his bloody fingertip to my throat and drew it downward across the symbol burned into my skin. I couldn't sense Sebastian gather the energy around us, but I recognized the language he murmured. All the wizards spoke it when casting. Like at the record store, his voice dropped an octave and bent back on itself. The eerie effect, a type of multivoice chant, gave me goosebumps.

I squeezed my eyelids closed so I wouldn't have to meet his intense stare. At first, a pain reminiscent of the tether's burn stung my skin. But then an increasing force pressed against my throat.

An electric crackle sounded from the tether, and a sharp hiss from Sebastian. The pungent odor of burnt fingernails caused me to open my eyes. Sebastian clenched his teeth and glared at the mark on my throat.

He launched into another incantation. Immediate pressure. My airway narrowed, and I fought against the blind panic that rose in my mind. After another crackling noise, my airway collapsed. I choked and grasped for Sebastian's hand to pull it away. Large dots danced in my field of vision, and my knees weakened.

Garbled noise, maybe shouting, filled the area, and suddenly I could breathe again. The large gulps of air I took burned in my lungs. Sebastian's fingertips weren't in contact with my skin anymore. I eased myself to kneel on the floor so I wouldn't fall, my head pounding and spots vibrating in front of my eyes.

Ben crouched beside me, his words not audible yet above the thrumming in my ears. His fingers repeatedly brushed my hair from my face, and his other hand rested on my back between my shoulder blades.

I looked up to see Sebastian standing behind him, staring down at me. He wiped blood from beneath his nose with the back of his hand. His fingers were singed black up to the first knuckle.

"Alex?" Ben's faint voice came into focus.

"I'm okay." My voice sounded hoarse, and I immediately regretted speaking as my throat's interior surged with pain. I blinked my watering eyes.

Ben tried to embrace me, but I shook my head and pushed him away. "Give me some room."

On my knees in the dusty and forgotten room, I tentatively reached inside myself for her. No response. My search grew more frantic. The spell had to have worked. Where was she?

"Alex?" Ben's hand settled on my arm.

I shoved him this time. "No!" I lurched to my feet and staggered a few steps away, trying to create empty space around myself. My eyelids lowered, and panting, I tried again to focus and sense my inner wolf. Panic and anger flooded my mind, causing the deafening buzz I'd come to dread. I clasped my hands to my ears and screamed, desperate to somehow release the resulting pain.

A small shift moved beneath my breastbone, causing a bloom of warmth to spread beneath my skin. My heart leapt. Watery eyes widening, I looked at Ben. The words burned inside my throat. "She's there."

With his arms clasped tight around himself, he said something to me. His lips moved, but the volume of his voice didn't register in my ears.

I lifted my chin to scent the air. Nothing. "What's happening?" A sharpness edged my tone. I moved on unsteady legs back toward Ben and Sebastian. "I felt her, but my senses are still junk. Why didn't it work?"

"It did work." Sebastian returned a bloodied handkerchief to his pocket. "You're a fucking werewolf, not a wizard. It's only logical the results would play out differently for you."

What an arrogant jackass. I resisted the urge to snipe back at him. I had to remain in Sebastian's good graces because I still needed his help.

Ben held out his hand, giving me the choice to step forward and accept it. "How do you feel?"

I did so and took his hand in mine. "My throat hurts."

"It took a few tries," Ben said.

"Twice." Sebastian snorted. "It only took twice."

"The tether fought him," Ben said.

I looked at Sebastian's singed hand again. "Are you okay?"

He sneered. "Of course I am."

I realized how unrealistic my expectations had been. Ben had altered his tether, not destroyed it. If all the effects of a tethering spell could easily be removed, Reginald would have revised it by now. I swallowed, my throat and eyes stinging.

Ben opened his other arm to me, but I bit my lip and shook my head. If I stepped into his embrace, as soon as his arms closed around me, I'd cry. I wasn't going to do that in front of Sebastian. At least what everyone tried to reassure me of was confirmed.

She was still with me.

"Are we done here?" Sebastian studied his burnt nails. "I'm growing bored."

"Thank you," I said. "I know doing this put you at risk."

"No need to thank me." He gave me a lazy smile. "I didn't do it for you."

My free hand settled at my throat. "What time should I be at your place tomorrow?"

"You mean the Teuling residence?" Sebastian asked. "We eat at six. Frank retires to his study at eight. Depending on how much time you want to rummage around, sometime within that span."

"Are there any cameras or other security-system things I should worry about?" I asked.

"It will all be taken care of," he said.

Ben's fingers tightened around mine. He frowned. "What are you doing, Alex?"

"I told you I'm going after Stone either way. Sebastian is getting me into Teuling's study so I can look for something there tying him and Stone to Isaac's death."

Ben's frown deepened. "That sounds like a terrible idea. I thought you were going to talk to Teuling."

"You're not coming along?" Sebastian asked.

"I can't," Ben answered, but his gaze rested on me. "If I get caught, I'll jack up all Joan's efforts so far to help clear me."

I'd realized that, so I hadn't shared the details of my plans with Ben. I preferred there be no temptation for him to help me.

"I'll watch over her for you," Sebastian said.

"No one needs to watch anyone," I said. "I'll be fine."

Sebastian shrugged. "I'll see you tomorrow." He turned his attention to Ben. "It was great working with you again, my friend. Can I leave you my number? I'd like to set up a time to talk with you. Alone."

I tightened my hold on Ben's hand and looked up at him.

Ben's cheeks were flushed and his brow furrowed. He shifted his weight and swallowed. "No."

When I looked back at Sebastian, he stared at me. There was no self-satisfied smirk or lazy smile, only an uncomfortable intensity to his gaze. He backed away, turned, and exited the building to his car. The coupe rumbled to life outside.

Ben and I left the building before the lights of Sebastian's car swung away from the building and he left. I lifted Ben's hand and pressed the back of it to my cheek. "Thank you."

He glanced at me. "You're welcome." Ben freed his hand from mine and walked to my car.

We left for Emma's in an odd, awkward silence. I finally broke it. "Something on your mind?"

He hesitated before answering, but I couldn't hear his soft voice with the windows open.

I closed them. "Try again, please."

"I'd forgotten how well he and I work together. I build; he disassembles. It's been forever since I've been able to discuss the craft with someone. He's extremely intelligent when it comes to magic. Before I got tethered, we studied under Reginald together." Ben shook his head. "But he's such a selfish asshole."

I wrestled with the pang of jealousy Ben's words caused me. I'd never be able to connect with him on that level when it came to his passion for magic. "What type of magic is his focus?"

"Necromancy."

"What?" My stomach gave a sickening twist. "Em said wizards who practice necromancy are targeted by Hunters." Maybe I shouldn't be partnering up with him. The last thing I needed was a Hunter in the mix. "It's considered dark magic."

"The term 'dark magic' is used by those who think necromancy shouldn't be practiced. It's a messy and volatile area of magic, and there are a lot of health consequences to using it." Ben frowned. "Some wizards believe it shouldn't be wielded because it requires blood in the spellwork. Hunters believe it's evil for the same reason. I'm sure that made it all the more attractive to Sebastian."

"And Reginald approved this when you two were his apprentices?" I didn't see Reginald as a wizard who would buck the standards of using magic.

"He didn't know at first," Ben said. "I was the one to tell him. I convinced Reginald that, either way, Sebastian would use necromancy. Reginald wanted to make sure he was being responsible and staying safe."

"What do you think about it?" I asked. "Necromancy."

Ben shrugged. "Any magic can be dangerous. Even a wizard using mending magic, like Emma, could use it for the wrong reason. I feel it depends on the intent of the caster, not the type of magic." He reached over to set his hand on my thigh. "Sebastian views everything as a competition where he has to come out on top. A puzzle he wants to solve. He's always been that way. Please be careful around him tomorrow."

I smiled at Ben. He'd accepted the fact I'd be secretly poking around a Committee member's home without him, the access of which I'd get from his manipulative, necromancy-wielding ex-boyfriend. "I will."

14

THE NEXT DAY, my shift seemed to drag at the record shop. On my break, I sent my daily check-in to Trish. She and Nate had their hands full answering an endless stream of questions from the werewolf community about Stone's new laws. Though I appreciated them wanting to watch over me, I could carry on with my pursuit of Stone without them possibly deterring me.

When my shift ended, I drove east up the hill from downtown and into the wealthier part of the city. The Vissers were an established wizarding family in Hopewell, so that meant old money. I drove past Emma's more recently developed neighborhood and soon hit the area her parents called home. Sebastian's directions landed me a few blocks from Franklin Teuling's house in a parking lot shared by an organic grocer and a hot yoga studio.

I walked the remaining distance to a large home set back from the street. Unlike Emma's parents' place, it didn't look like a house that'd been misplaced from some southern plantation. The residence was still large, but I didn't think I'd get lost without a guide. I followed a footpath along the edge of the property that led to an unassuming side entrance.

After sending Sebastian a message that I'd arrived, I leaned back against the house to wait. He'd said the security cameras would be taken care of, but the tiny camera mounted on the stone wall above the door made me uneasy.

I began to worry he'd ghosted me when the side door opened. Sebastian held open the door with his hip and waved me in. I slipped by him into a tall hallway. He let the door close behind us and walked past me down the hall.

"Are we going right to the study?" I followed him, unsure if I should or not.

He gave me a bored, sideward glance. "Where else would we be going?" Sebastian paused at a steep, narrow stairwell. "This back entryway is for the household staff. The people working right now are in the kitchen. I'd suggest using this as your exit. The only other way back downstairs is the main stairway."

"You're not going to make sure I get out okay?"

"I can't stick around that long. They'll be expecting me at dinner." Sebastian smirked. "And you said you don't need me watching over you, right?"

True, but that'd been easier to believe when I wasn't sneaking through a stranger's house.

It was fine. I didn't need his help to check the study.

Sebastian climbed the stairs, and I followed. He stopped in front of a substantial set of double doors and tried the doorknob. It was locked. He rolled his eyes, as if served the largest inconvenience possible. "A house full of wizards, and you think a fucking lock is going to keep us out, Frank?"

As I waited, Sebastian withdrew the same small pen-like device he'd used at the warehouse. The fingers of his right hand were bandaged up to the first knuckle.

"What kind of tool is that?" I asked.

"A lancing device. I'm diabetic." With a click, it broke the skin of his left thumb and created a bead of blood. "I don't need it as much with the monitor I use now, but it's useful for getting blood for spells. It's more subtle than pocketing razor blades." He pressed his bloodied thumb against the door's lock plate and muttered words in that same eerie, surreal tone of voice. The metal momentarily glowed red until Sebastian's spoken incantation ended. He removed his thumb and gave the lock plate a thump with the side of his fist. Metallic, powder-like rust jostled loose from the door lock and sprinkled to the carpeted hall.

Smiling, he gave me a sideward glance. "Commoners can be so simple." He pushed open the double doors and entered the study.

I followed him into the large room. "Is that how you got into Rear Window Records?"

"Yes." He pressed a handkerchief against his bleeding thumb.

"But you didn't break into Ben's place?" I pulled a thin pair of gloves from my back pocket and slipped them on. One of Nate's hobbies was breaking and entering, so I'd picked up a few tips. "So it *is* possible for you to practice restraint."

Sebastian's gaze slid to me. "I told you multiple times, Ben is an old friend I want to reconnect with. Why would I break into his home?"

"Friend?" I wandered toward a bookcase. It held a plethora of books, mostly on finance, and a serving tray with glasses and a decanter filled with amber liquid. "Ben said you two dated." I uncorked the decanter and took a sniff. Bourbon.

When I didn't hear a reply from Sebastian, I looked back at the study's entrance. I wouldn't put it past him to walk out.

A small frown crossed his lips as he folded the spotless hand-kerchief. He looked up and tucked the handkerchief into his back pocket. "We did."

"And he's as uneasy around you as I am," I said. "Maybe you can understand why I'm not thrilled to have you in Hopewell, attempting to 'reconnect' with him." I shrugged. "You could come clean and tell me *why* you want time alone with him so badly. If it's as innocent as you insist, we could all relax."

Sebastian's frown deepened, but he didn't reply.

It'd been worth a try. I turned back to the bookcase. Some framed pictures of Teuling, a pretty woman with blonde curly hair, and a younger Julia sat on the shelves. I picked one up to take a closer look. "Why did you choose necromancy as your focus?"

"It's what I'm good at," he said. "I break things."

I returned the frame to the shelf. "And your mom doesn't care?"

He snorted. "Why would she?"

"Em says that necromancy is how wizards end up on a Hunter's hit list." Notably absent from the photos was any image of Sebastian. The dislike between Frank and his stepson must run both ways. "Your mom isn't worried a Hunter will be sent to track you down?"

"I'm a fucking Visser. Hunters know not to bother us."

I frowned and looked over at him. Nothing in his posture or expression communicated the instant terror the mention of a Hunter brought to the wolves. "Wow. Quite the entitled jackass, aren't you?"

A corner of his mouth curled up. "All day, every day."

"Reginald said your mom doesn't practice magic any—"

His features darkened and his reply was blunt. "She has nothing to do with why you're here."

I blinked. "I didn't think she did. I was curious if—"

"You're on your own now. You have until eight." He exited the conversation and the room, leaving me standing in the study.

"Huh." And just when he'd started to talk.

I stepped over to the double doors and carefully shut them. Hopefully I would find something to connect Teuling to Stone and Stone to Isaac's murder. Otherwise, I'd have to resort to the plan that even I thought was a bit harebrained. I'd have to somehow get a confession directly from Teuling.

I turned from the doors, took a large breath, and surveyed the room. It seemed to be the study of someone who liked the idea of having a study but didn't really work in it often. Either that or Teuling was extremely organized. The wooden hulk of a desk sat centered in front of the only windows. The ceiling, where large fan blades slowly spun, reached as high as the hall.

The heads of two deer and a collection of fish were tacked up on the wall. I shuddered and walked farther into the room to the desk.

I've never understood man's obsession with displaying carcasses like trophies. I also hadn't pegged Teuling as an outdoorsman.

I sat down in the high-backed leather chair. On the desk was another framed photo of a beaming Teuling hugging a smiling and gowned Julia with a diploma in her hand. I passed up the laptop in front of me for a browse through the desk drawers. There wasn't anything much of note, just the usual hanging files, paper and other office supplies, and a flask.

In one drawer, another framed photograph lay face down on a pile of papers. I pulled it out and my pulse skipped. The photo was more recent. Julia had pin-straight lavender hair, the same as when I first met her, and her arm rested around Isaac's waist. In the photo with them were Teuling and the curly-haired woman again, who must be Sebastian and Julia's mother. The small group stood smiling in a garden, holding small plates of food.

The stowed picture could have been a sign of Teuling's lingering guilt. He thought he was doing his daughter a favor by getting rid of Isaac. But having Isaac killed? I wondered if Teuling didn't care for Isaac because he didn't want Julia distracted from school or if it was simply because Isaac was a werewolf. I returned the picture to the drawer and reached for the slim laptop on the desk.

I checked the time and then booted up the computer. The login screen came up and required a password. My fingers drummed on the desk and I glanced around the room. If I were an old guy, where would I keep my password? I opened the desk's middle drawer, looked down at the neon sticky note stuck beside the pencil tray, and smiled. When you've worked a handful of temp office assistant jobs, you notice some common mannerisms among office staff.

I typed in *Tabbie94* and the computer finished booting to display a tidy desktop. I started to click around the different files, becoming more disappointed by the minute. What man uses his computer solely for work? All I could find were spreadsheets and comic strips about spreadsheets.

I finally turned to the mail program and thanked whichever gods were listening that Teuling preferred not to enter his password for every program he opened. I scrolled back in the history of sent mail to the dates when Anne and I had found Isaac's body. Chewing on my thumbnail, I frowned. There were a few emails to Stone, but most had to do with Stone's campaign.

I scrolled to emails sent even earlier, before Isaac was killed, and an email to Stone caught my eye. The subject line was blank. I clicked on the email to open it. There were only two words in the message window.

Isaac Laska

My pulse stuttered, followed swiftly by a wave of anger. One email, two words, and the wolves had a beloved community member taken from us. Meanwhile, a controlling father lounged in his plush study with dead animals, having an after-dinner bourbon.

I tightened my jaw against the rising buzzing in my head. It threatened to obscure my thoughts, something I did not need right now. Breathing heavily through my nose, I forwarded the email to myself and deleted the history of doing so. My phone chimed in my pocket.

I wasn't sure the single email alone would be enough, and I found it odd such an organized person would allow it to remain in his account. With my anger over Isaac's murder renewed, I continued to sort through the mail to find a more substantial piece of evidence.

That's how I lost track of time.

The jostling in the keyhole alerted me to the fact I'd stayed too long. I quickly exited the mail program and shut the laptop. I jumped up from the chair as Teuling pushed open the door, frowning down at the lock. I glanced all over the study, not seeing any places to hide. I finally dropped to a crouch behind the desk, my pulse pounding in my ears.

Incoherent grumbling came from near the study doors. Teuling's footsteps traveled toward the bookcase, and I saw his leather shoes from under the desk. The glass from the serving tray clinked. I tried to inch my way around the other side of the desk as Teuling poured himself a drink. The study doors were in sight, but unfortunately closed.

Teuling's steps moved toward the desk, and I knew time was up. Taking a deep breath, I dashed toward the doors.

"What the hell!"

The tumbler dropped with a muffled thunk to the floor behind me. I yanked open a door and dashed into the hallway with Teuling close behind. Without my amped-up speed and agility, I felt I was running through quicksand.

"Stop!" Teuling's voice sounded uncomfortably close. I hoped he didn't grab the handgun.

Reaching the end of the hall, I started down the stairs. My heel landed and slipped off the edge of a step due to the sharp incline. I reached for the railing, but not before I landed on my ass and slid down a few more steps. Wincing, I scrambled back to my feet.

Teuling's hand closed over my wrist at the banister. I tried to jerk it away and looked back at him.

"You." His eyes widened. "What are you doing here?"

For once my mouth remained closed. I twisted my wrist free from his grasp, turned, and rushed down the remaining stairs.

"Don't think I won't report this!" Teuling shouted after me.

The exterior door closed behind me, and I tried for a casual stroll as I moved away from the house. It probably looked more like some weird power walk. My pulse didn't begin to slow its hammering until I reached my car and sat behind the wheel.

"That could have gone better," I muttered. If I'd had my werewolf senses, I would've heard Teuling a lot sooner and had a better chance of a clean escape. Now he'd rat me out to the Committee for bad behavior while tethered.

Hopefully Trish could give me a better idea of what to expect. How serious should I take Teuling's threat? I drove toward Hell's Bells with a sick feeling in the pit of my stomach.

I didn't attack or harm Teuling in any way. Could Stone demand my head be put on the block simply for rummaging around in someone's office? It'd be a great way to get me out of his hair for good.

15

THE HELL'S BELLS park lot looked crowded when I arrived. From the road, the building appeared rundown, and I preferred not to think of what made the floors so sticky. But Trish and Nate's bar and music venue, a choice hangout for Hopewell's werewolves, served as our community hub. Most news concerning the wolves ran through the place.

I texted Emma and my parents to let them know I stopped to visit Trish and Nate. Ben and I hadn't planned on seeing each other tonight, and he hadn't messaged me for a status update. That meant I didn't have to tell him right now that I'd been caught snooping in Teuling's office.

I left my car and beelined to the club, trying not to make eye contact with anyone socializing in the parking lot. I'm sure the rest of the wolves already knew about my tethering sentence, so I wanted to dodge any of those questions as well.

I'd made it through the front door and past the doorman when someone caught my arm.

"Hey, Alex." A teenager, flanked by his friends, glanced past me toward the parking lot. "Is Emma with you?"

Gangly with a large scar at his throat . . . "Sorry, Roger, you only get me tonight."

"You haven't been by for days," he said. "We've been worried." There were nods from the others with him. They were trying to avoid looking at my throat, but they couldn't help themselves.

"Trish and Nate knew where I was," I said.

"Yeah, I finally asked," Roger said. "How're you doing?"

"Not that well, to be honest." The edges of my eyes prickled.

His fingertips wandered to the scar at his throat. "Does it hurt?"

"Yeah, it hurts. I feel like shit the majority of the time." I glanced at each in the group. "Where can I find Trish and Nate?"

Roger pointed through the crowded lounge toward the bar. "Trish is over there, and Nate is downstairs."

"Thanks." I slipped past Roger before he could ask anything else. Gaze lowered, I waded through the gauntlet of bodies toward the bar.

Trish perched on a barstool with a dwindling cigarette clamped between her red lips. She wrote hasty notes on a page already covered in her looped handwriting. When she saw me, she set the pen down and ground out the cigarette. "Before you say anything else, how are you?"

"My head hurts a lot. I'm not sure how anyone manages this," I said.

"Most struggle to."

I hugged her and sat on the next barstool. "Ben came to see me, so that was nice." I couldn't help smiling.

Trish raised an eyebrow. "And you let him stay?" She knew how not hearing from him affected my mood.

Heat rushed into my cheeks.

"I would have thrown him out on his ass." She lit another cigarette. "Just because we're wolves doesn't mean we have to settle. You deserve someone who contributes more than accepting who you are."

"He's a good guy," I said. "I like us together."

Trish's gaze flitted over me. She tapped the loose ash from her cigarette into an ashtray. "He's fortunate you're patient with him."

"About that being patient thing . . ." I fidgeted with the pen. "First, no one has *ever* said that about me. Second, I think I'm in trouble. A lot of trouble."

"You're in trouble?" Nate asked from my other side.

I startled, jerked away, and glared back over my shoulder at him. "Dammit, Nate."

"Right. Your nose and ears aren't working." He gave me a toothy grin and settled on the barstool beside me. "Sorry."

I slugged him in the side of the arm.

Nate looked at his arm and then at my clenched fist. He started laughing. "What the hell was that?"

"Nathan, please, let her focus." Trish turned her gaze from him to me. "Tell us what happened."

I came clean to them about my continued pursuit of Stone. I told them about what I overheard at the gallery and my confrontation there. Finally, I told them about meeting Sebastian, him helping me get into Teuling's house to find evidence, and me getting caught by Teuling.

"Your first mistake was not calling me," Nate said. "I'm a bit hurt you chose someone else, and a wizard no less, as your breaking-and-entering buddy."

"You've told me to get an inside guy if possible. Somehow I think you'll get over it," I said. "So, on a scale from one to ten, with ten being 'pack your bag and run now,' how bad do you think it'll be when Teuling tells the Committee what happened?"

Nate leaned forward to look past me at Trish. "What do you think, love?"

Trish set her smoldering cigarette down in the ashtray. Her jawline taut and twitching, she turned golden eyes on me.

"I didn't think I'd get caught! It seemed like an easy in-and-out." I motioned at the tether on my throat. "This thing has turned me into a bumbling idiot."

Trish frowned. "Don't blame your poor judgment and reckless behavior on the tether."

I dropped my gaze.

"Breaking and entering is considered a crime," Trish said, "whether it be in the Commoner law system or our own."

"But when Nate and I were caught at the Mind Center office this past winter, we walked out of the police station the next morning," I said.

"Yes, but you were with me." Nate pointed at Trish. "That means you had a direct line to her. Trish got us out of that one before it could reach the Committee."

"The Commoner law system is deeply flawed. I know how to navigate that," Trish said. "But I'm not able to clear every infraction every wolf incurs."

"My buddy, Floyd . . ." Nate swallowed and cleared his throat. "Floyd was nailed for carjacking in the Commoner system. When it was passed to the Committee by the Commoner law contact, they had him tethered."

And he took his life several months later because of the tether. I thought of Jakob. Floyd had been his older brother.

"When a gifted being like one of us is tethered, the Committee has us under a microscope," Trish said. "Any violation while serving a tethering sentence, no matter if it's a misdemeanor in the Commoner's system, is severely reprimanded."

"So being caught by Teuling, a Committee member, is all sorts of bad for me." My chest tightened.

"He won't bother reporting you to the Hopewell PD," Nate said. "He'll go straight to the Committee."

The Hopewell Police Department. Anne. But now she had a foot in both worlds. My mistake would be yet another reason for her to be disappointed in me.

The tether began its low buzz in my head. "Do you think Stone will use it to push for my execution again?"

Trish gave a curt nod. "Yes."

My stomach turned.

Nate looked past me to Trish. "Maybe it's time. We could finally tell the Committee to go fuck themselves. You leave your seat for good, and their rules wouldn't apply to us. When they come for us, we resist."

I'd heard Nate suggest the tactic before when I was still learning how the Committee operated in Hopewell. It seemed to be an ongoing tug-of-war between him and Trish. How much should the wolves bend to an organization that can cause them harm?

Trish shook her head. "I know you aren't fond of bending to their rules, love, but it prevents them from branding us as rebel monsters and using that as an excuse to round us up."

"They've already decided we're monsters." Nate snorted. "They have a single wolf on their side. We have our entire community. What could they possibly do if we decided we'd had enough?"

Trish frowned. "They have a wizard."

Reginald had created my tether, but I wasn't sure he could win out against all the wolves at once.

Nate spoke my thoughts aloud. "We stick together. One of us would take him down before he could harm us all."

Trish closed her eyes and pinched the bridge of her nose. "Living under the new laws Stone put into place isn't sustainable for us." She looked back at Nate and me. "Alex is on the right path. We find a way to dispose of Stone."

"Trish!" Roger rushed up beside the bar. He trembled, his nostrils flaring. "Jakob DeBoer is here looking for you. He has his Commoner partner with him, the woman cop, and there's something . . . off . . . about her."

Anne told me they were looking deeper into Isaac's case, but Roger's words still caused dread to pool in my stomach. I didn't need my heightened sense of smell to notice the fear that gripped him. Why would Anne, a Commoner, elicit such a reaction from a werewolf?

Nate stood, snarling. "I'll tell them to get lost."

Trish grasped his arm. "Be careful. We have to step lightly with Jakob, now more than ever."

Jakob and Anne were here for Trish. It was possible Teuling hadn't reported me yet. I stood and jogged ahead of Nate to the front door.

The police cruiser parked as close to the club entrance as possible. Jakob kept his gaze forward, and Anne scanned around them as they walked to the door. The gathered werewolves shrank away from Jakob and Anne like a sea made of glowing eyes and rumbling growls.

"Anne." I passed through the doorway. "Is there a break in Isaac's case?"

Jakob saw me and immediately frowned. His face carried a sheen of sweat that made him appear ill.

Anne's eyes momentarily widened. "I should have realized you'd be here." She glanced around at the agitated werewolves. "Leave, Alex."

"What?" My dread grew. "Why?"

"Please step aside, Miss Steward." Jakob's gaze jerked upward and past me. He tensed. His eye color immediately changed from brown to gold.

"Evening, DeBoer." Nate leaned in the doorway behind me, greeting the two officers. His eyes were copper, and his grin included sharp teeth. "What can we do for you tonight? Stop by to check out some music?"

"We're here to speak to Patricia Drake," Jakob said.

"Sorry. Trish is busy." Nate scratched behind his ear. "Anything I can do for you?"

"Cut the shit, Osterberg," Anne said.

Growls rippled through the werewolves. Nate's eyebrows raised, and his attention refocused on Anne.

Her eyes narrowed. "You and your sweetheart are no longer immune to the law."

My pulse sped up, and I looked around at the other wolves. All eyes were trained on the two officers. "Anne," I said, voice lowered. "Careful."

She ignored me and spoke to Nate again. "Go fetch her. Now."

Nate's lips pulled back from his pointed teeth in a sneer. "What did you say to me, Commoner?" He pushed away from the doorframe. With the sound of popping joints, his fingers elongated and his fingernails grew to curved points. A fresh chorus of growls rumbled from the crowd in the parking lot.

Jakob glanced around, swallowed, and stepped closer to Anne's side. His facial muscles and fingers twitched. He quickly wiped away the sweat on his upper lip.

Anne, jawline tight, glared at Nate. I stood close enough to notice the slight tremble in her hands.

Trish appeared at Nate's side, her golden eyes fixing on the officers. "What is it you need from me, Jakob?"

"I'm sorry." Face red, Jakob addressed the threshold at Trish's feet. "Patricia Drake, we have a warrant for your arrest in violation of Committee Safety Guideline 11: Protecting Citizen Safety and Wellbeing. I ask that you come with us. If you resist arrest, we have permission to use whatever force is necessary."

My heart lurched and my eyes widened. Nate let loose another snarl, and murmurs wove through the crowd.

No humor shone in Trish's smile. "Protecting citizen safety and wellbeing by following laws made for Commoners whose lives look nothing like ours. I've never broken a Commoner law that caused a Hopewell Commoner citizen physical harm."

Anne jabbed her forefinger at Trish. "I could wallpaper this dump twice over with the paperwork logged on you at the Hopewell PD. None, not a single one, of those visits ended in charges that were passed on to the Committee. How in the *hell* is that possible?" Anne's cheeks were hot with anger. "But no more. Every last one of your infractions from the past twenty years is now with the Committee."

"Anne, please." My own body shook from adrenaline. I didn't like how anxious the other wolves were acting, how they seemed laser-focused on Anne. "This is a really bad idea. You don't know what you—"

The heat of Anne's glare fell on me. "Don't you dare say I don't know what I'm doing."

"Alex is right, Jakob," Trish said. "You're putting your partner at risk by confronting me here with Stone's orders. He's wielding your moral code against you." Trish glanced at Anne. "Both of you."

"We're here to enforce the new laws," Jakob said. "You and I were both there for the vote."

"I'm not going with you," Trish said. "People are confused and scared by the Committee's actions. I'm needed here."

"Trish, please." Jakob's voice almost cracked.

Anne gave Jakob a sideward glance and frowned. She shook her head, set her jaw, and marched toward the door as she reached for the handcuffs at her belt. "Patricia Drake, you are under—"

In a burst of motion, Nate pinned Anne against the doorframe, her arm twisted and her hand raised behind her back. It happened before Anne's surprised cry passed her lips.

"Nate, no!" I lunged toward Anne, but Jakob caught me by the shoulder. He shoved me backward as he dashed past. I stumbled, lost my balance, and fell onto my ass in the parking lot.

Nate's nostrils flared and his eyes widened to the point of showing white. Snarling, he recoiled from Anne. He drew his clawed hand back to strike, but Jakob tackled him off his feet into the club.

Quick to recover, Anne spun and attempted to restrain Trish. She ducked away from Anne's grasp. Trish's nostrils flared as well. I followed her wide-eyed gaze to Anne's hand where a thin surgical scar disrupted the skin. Anne moved nearly as fast as a werewolf and captured Trish's wrist in her cuffs. Trish bared her teeth, seized the cuffs, and yanked Anne through the doorway and into the front lounge.

The crowd collapsed toward the door. I scrambled to my feet among the other wolves. "Stop! Everyone stop." I slipped out of the pack, put my back to the club, and waved my hands over my head. "I know you want to help, but don't give them a reason to take you, too! Please, step back. Trish would want you to go and stay safe."

Uneasy glances were exchanged within the crowd. Their beloved leader faced danger, and I asked them to pack it up and head home.

The sounds of smashing glass, shouts, and snarling came from behind me. I took one last glance at the crowd, turned, and dashed inside.

The lounge area was a mess of overturned furniture and broken glass. The patrons were either pressed up against the walls, attempting to stay clear of the fights, or pushing past me to get out of the building.

Jakob and Nate crashed around the room like a growling wrecking ball. Every bit of me wanted to leap in and help, but I was useless without my inner wolf's strength and agility. Instead, I hurried through the lounge, encouraging other werewolves to evacuate the building. Surprisingly, most listened.

When I returned to the ongoing fights, Anne held her own. She'd introduced me to boxing, her favorite form of hand-to-hand combat, before we had our falling out. Anne ducked, wove, and threw punches with sharper and quicker movements than I'd ever witnessed in our practices. Trish struggled to defend herself, even with her heightened reflexes.

How was that even possible?

"I've told everyone to back down, Trish," I shouted over the noise. Only Jakob, Nate, Trish, Anne, and I remained in the empty lounge

Trish raised her hands, the cuffs dangling from her wrist, and stepped back from Anne. "Nathan, stop!"

Anne held a defensive stance, her chest rapidly rising and falling.

Nate leapt back from where he'd been fighting with Jakob. Panting, bloodied, and his shirt soaked through with sweat, he retreated to Trish's side. "Did you feel it?"

Trish watched Anne. "Yes."

I looked between the two. "What's going on? Feel what?"

"The Commoner," Nate said. "She has a Hunter's key."

The words caused fear to flood my body. A Hunter's key blessed a Hunter with special abilities, like heightened strength and stamina. It also gave Hunters the ability to agitate and disorient werewolves. I hadn't sensed it like everyone else because I didn't have access to my wolf. My heart clenched, and my gaze jerked to Anne. "Is that true?"

Anne's brow furrowed. She didn't lower her raised fists as she watched Trish and Nate.

"Is it?" It couldn't be. Anne wouldn't embrace a weapon created to dispose of people like me. "Anne, talk to me!"

"You can't go with them, Trish," Nate said. "People are going to lose their shit."

"Everyone is at risk with her here. You and Alex can help people remain calm. I'll sort this out and be home soon." Trish lifted her chin. "I'm ready when you are, Officer Reid."

If Anne had a key . . . I looked at Jakob.

His whole body trembled, and his eyes were a vibrant gold. Nate's blood stained Jakob's claws. As he spoke, his sharp teeth appeared. "Nathan Osterberg, we also have a warrant for *your* arrest in relation to violating Committee Safety Guideline 11: Protecting Citizen Safety and Wellbeing. I ask that you come with us. If you resist arrest, we have permission to use whatever force is necessary."

"What!" The anger hit me hard. The fact Jakob, who knew what it was like to be a werewolf in Hopewell, would do this to us made me furious. With both Trish and Nate gone, our community would spiral into frightened confusion. And why in the hell would he subject himself to the disorienting irritation of a Hunter's key?

The painful buzz of the tether's feedback vibrated in my head. "Who's going to keep this place open and care for everyone while they're gone? I can't do it on my own."

Anne lowered her fists. "Under Safety Law 45: Ensuring Safe Spaces in Hopewell, this club is considered an illegal gathering space and will be closed."

It felt as if the floor dropped out from beneath me. The buzzing in my mind pitched to an unbearable high whine. I winced and grabbed my head. My eyes watered.

"Coward." Nate spat at Jakob's feet, his voice a low growl. "You're a traitor, DeBoer."

Jakob leapt forward, snarling, and cracked Nate across the jaw. Nate stumbled backward, his eyes wide.

My insides were on fire, and my mind raged. The tether screamed in my head, threatening to black out my vision. With an angry scream, I charged at Jakob.

Trish easily swept me off my feet. She dropped to a crouch beside me, pinning me down.

"No!" I twisted and kicked, trying to wrestle free of her. "They can't do this to us!"

Trish drew back her fist. "Be careful, Alex." She struck me. Everything went dark.

16

ROGER SHOOK ME awake, and I found myself lying beside my car in the empty Hell's Bells parking lot. The metallic taste of blood lingered on my tongue. I sat up quickly, and the side of my jaw throbbed with dull pain.

"They took Trish and Nate," Roger said, his features pinched. "There's a chain and lock on the doors." He pulled me to my feet.

"She hit me." I touched my fingertips to my split lip and winced.

He nodded, as if I wasted time stating the obvious. "What do we do?"

I looked at Roger, my eyes wide. "Why are you asking me?"

"Everyone knows Trish wants you to be her second," he said. "She's been working with you for half a year now."

My face grew warm. Everyone believed that but me. My honeymoon with self-denial was at an end. "I mean, I have an idea of how to take down Stone, but I can't direct everyone."

He frowned. "What do you mean? You did earlier when the cops showed up."

I chewed at my thumbnail. He wasn't going to let the idea go. "Okay. But can you help me?"

Roger grinned and straightened his posture. "Yeah, of course. Whatever I can do to get Trish and Nate back home."

Roger's response supported what I already believed about Trish, Nate, and Hell's Bells. This place was our home. I couldn't let Stone take that from everyone.

"I need you to tell the rest of the wolves how important it is that everyone keep a low profile. No lurking around here," I said. "We can't give the Committee any excuses, no matter how far-fetched, to come after any more of us."

Roger nodded. "I can do that."

"While you're doing that, I'm going to try to delay Trish and Nate's trials," I said. "Then it's time to go after Stone."

I managed to stay under the speed limit on the way to St. Anthony's Cathedral. Even though Father Aiden and I didn't see eye to eye on most things, he had a past with Trish. They'd been close friends at one time. A few months previous, Aiden made an exception to his neutral role on the Committee by providing me info on Hunters. Hopefully, he would bend the rules again, this time for Trish's sake.

I parked my car and hurried through the fading daylight across Cathedral Square to St. Anthony's. When I pulled on the large handle of the front door, it refused to open. "No." I read the hours posted on a plaque near the door. The cathedral closed at 6:00, before I'd snuck into Teuling's study. "No, no, no."

Jakob had brought me through a metal door in the back when he arrested me. I rushed around the cathedral. Also locked. Had Trish and Nate already been dropped off? My thoughts raced. The awful sound of the tether's feedback whined inside my head. I pressed my eyes closed and pounded on the metal door with my fist. "Aiden! Aiden, open the door!"

"Miss Steward!"

My eyes flew open, and I spun toward the voice.

A dark-haired man with graying temples stood scowling in the open doorway of a small single-story residence to my right. "What are you trying to accomplish by standing out in the dark and yelling?"

A priest's collar, sharp features, and hooked nose. Click. Aiden.

"They took Trish and Nate." I rushed over to him. "Are they here yet?"

"They? 'They' who?" His forehead wrinkled. "What happened to you? You're bleeding."

"Jakob and Anne." I wiped the blood from my split lip, wincing.

Aiden frowned. "One of the officers struck you?"

"No," I said. "They showed up at Hell's Bells and arrested Trish and Nate under the new laws."

Aiden's gaze darted around the dim alley. "Come inside so we can talk." He stepped back from the doorway.

I entered the house. "You're acting shifty. What's going on?"

"I have this disturbing feeling I'm being monitored. But that is nothing to concern yourself with." He closed the wooden door. "These arrests . . . This is the first I heard of them."

"But you're the Committee Chair," I said. "Don't Jakob and Anne have to tell you when they make an arrest for the Committee? Or aren't you involved in approving it?"

"The safety laws have removed many approvals needed from the Chair, citing them as a hindrance." He glanced toward the window and the cathedral next door. "Perhaps officers DeBoer and Reid were going to inform me in the morning."

"Well, you've been informed now," I said. "What are you going to do about it?"

The corners of his mouth dipped down, and he looked back at me. "As I've told you many, many times before concerning Committee business, there is nothing—"

"No!" The angry noise in my head pitched upward. "No more excuses for standing by and allowing awful things to happen! You're in a position to help."

Aiden's shoulders sagged. "Miss Steward, I am not able—"

"What about the trial?" I asked. "Is there anything you can do to get it delayed?"

He studied me. "To what end?"

"Find something to slow the process," I said. "I'll do the rest."

"And as a neutral party, I'll choose not to hear that." Aiden frowned. "I suppose if I review the Committee's bylaws closely enough, there may be a way to delay the trial. It would of course be pursued in the interest of maintaining proper procedures and order."

Inklings of hope flickered in my chest. "Whatever you have to tell yourself, Father."

He gave me a flat look.

"Can you please tell Trish and Nate what you're doing?" I asked. "If they're here, their phones have been taken. Let them know everyone at Hell's Bells is okay, too."

Aiden took down a key with a fob from a row of hooks by the door. "I'll follow you out and check if they've arrived."

We exited the residence, he locked up, and we walked the short distance toward the cathedral. The large floodlight outside the back door had switched on.

"Did Trish bring you the Hunter's key that belonged to David Eastman?" I asked.

"Yes," he said.

I tipped my head toward the cathedral. "Was it stowed in the basement with the silver daggers?"

Aiden turned to me with a frown. "Why do you ask?"

"Because I think Anne . . . Officer Reid has it." Just saying it aloud made me nauseous.

"That can't be," he said. "It was given to Reginald Sharpe to protect since it's a powerful magic object. You must be—"

"She has a key," I said. "Trish and Nate felt it at Hell's Bells. All the wolves did." And if Reginald gave such a potent object to Anne, why didn't Aiden know?

He shook his head and turned to the back door. "I'll speak to Patricia about it, and then Reginald if necessary."

"Hey, Aiden," I said, "thanks for doing this."

He ran the fob over a sensor. The lock clicked, and he pulled the door open. "Miss Steward, whatever it is you're planning to do, please be fast and discreet about it." Aiden walked through the back entryway, and the door closed and locked behind him.

I checked "talking to Aiden" off my mental to-do list and walked back around to the front of the cathedral. I needed help to expose Stone's role in Isaac's murder before Trish and Nate's trial. Someone who harbored the same frustrations about the Committee but who wouldn't shy away from opposing them. Luckily, I knew such a person.

An occasional park light lit the main pathway from the cathedral to the street. From the corner of my eye, I noticed a large man approaching from across the shadows of the square to my right. I turned my car keys in my hand to position a key between my fingers like a spike. My grip tightened when another person, a woman, approached from my left. Both had the threadbare and stained clothing of people who didn't live with the creature comforts most others were used to.

Heart thudding against my ribs, I stopped to wait for the two strangers, eyeing both. When the larger man grew closer, he looked vaguely familiar. But while others' identities slowly resolved themselves in my mind, this one eluded me.

"Alexandria Steward?" he asked.

I swallowed and nodded, still grasping the key.

The woman stopped several paces away and remained silent. She wasn't familiar at all.

"Fillip wants to see you," the man said.

I remembered where I'd seen the guy before. One of Fillip's flock, he worked as a bodyguard of sorts for the vampire. My stomach turned. "Now?"

There were currently too many fires I needed to put out. I didn't have time to verbally spar with Fillip, especially while tethered. Without my inner wolf's abilities, there would be no way to protect myself against him if our conversation got heated.

"Yeah, now," the man said.

"We'll take you to him," the woman said.

I was in the red with the vampire, so he was more than likely calling in some of my debt. The last time I'd tracked down Fillip without requesting an appointment first, he'd sent out an immediate order to kill the young man who'd given away his location. In other words, he took his business dealings very seriously. I couldn't simply ignore his request.

Fillip's two stooges were less than chatty as they guided me west from the cathedral further into downtown. The large guy remained a few steps behind me, I'm sure to nab me if I decided to run.

Nate said only a few vampires lived in Hopewell because of the city's small size. Fillip referred to a large section of the unhoused population he protected as his "flock." In turn, they provided him not only with the blood needed to sustain him but also with an impressive spy network. Fillip then sold or traded the information to people like Trish.

"Where's he hanging out tonight?" I waited, but neither of my guides answered. Fillip moved around a lot, taking up temporary residence in different locations each evening, but always downtown. Since members of his flock congregated near the city's shelters, he'd established his territory there. We turned onto a street that took us south, past a large market.

"Crazy I'm hearing from him now." My chuckle sounded forced. "I wondered if he'd forgotten about me." I'd *hoped* he'd forgotten about me.

"He doesn't forget anybody," the man said.

We crossed the street and approached a redbrick building stamped with a story-tall name of a defunct furniture company. The current use of the historic building seemed to be lofts. I couldn't imagine the cost of rent.

The woman leading us didn't head for the main entrance, but to a maintenance door tucked around the corner in an alleyway. A sputtering fluorescent bulb lit the doorway, which set off my internal *This May Not Be Your Best Idea* alarm. The woman pulled a key from her pocket, unlocked the metal door, and stepped inside.

I paused at the doorway. More flickering fluorescents created patches of animated light on the landing of a utilitarian stairwell.

The guy behind me gave me a rough shove. "Keep moving."

He easily pushed my weight forward, forcing me to step through the doorway and follow the woman down the stairs. She unlocked another door and held it open to a rank tunnel even my dulled sense of smell found offensive.

The woman remained outside, but the guy entered after me and closed the door. A safety light above an EXIT sign provided a sphere of illumination that melted into the dark reaches of the tunnel. The guy waited, placing his body as a barrier between me and the exit.

"Are you staying here to keep me safe?" I asked him.

He frowned down at me and crossed his thick arms over his wide chest.

"Alexandria." The raspy voice leaked from the shadows shrouding the tunnel, connecting the name in my head to the creature speaking. "Thank you for meeting me on such short notice."

My skin tried to crawl away from the sound. "Your people didn't really give me a choice, so . . ." I squinted my eyes but only saw a vague shifting of shapes in the dark.

A stooped figure crept like some sort of awful insect into the halo of light. The vampire was shorter than me, and a heavy, patched peacoat wrapped his huddled form. It made me sweat just looking at him.

"Please, forgive them. It was by my instruction." Fillip's pale skin, marred by liver spots, was wrinkled in some areas and pulled taut over a bony frame in others. His head was bald and everything about his face appeared long: ears, nose, chin . . . and teeth. "Step closer, child, so I can see what they've done to you." His beady red eyes twitched as he looked me over.

"I'm good here." I suppressed a shudder.

His shape blurred, and Fillip suddenly stood inches from my face. I gasped and tried to pull back, but he seized my chin in his bony hand. He gently lifted it up and to the side. His dagger-like nails pressed into my skin.

I reached for his wrist to free myself but couldn't move his hand. For such a frail-looking creature, his grip was powerful. The angry buzzing ignited in my head.

Fillip studied my throat, and a sneer bent his lips. "So barbaric." He released my chin. "I'm sure Patricia is not pleased."

I backed away, struggling to keep my mouth under control. No one was allowed to manhandle me like that.

"I can sense you aren't in the mood for conversation tonight." He smiled, flashing yellowed, rodent-like teeth. "I'll get on with our business. You are familiar with the Commoner politician Joseph Stone, correct?"

The noise in my mind intensified. "Yes."

"I want you to bring him to me."

My heart skipped, and my eyes widened. "What? Why?"

"The man is an idiot, but as many men like him, he's stepped upon others' backs to elevate himself to a prominent position. Through bribes, blackmail, and blatant lies, he has gained a powerful hold on the feeble-minded members of the Committee. He will more than likely win Hopewell's mayoral election."

I swallowed. Maybe I'd lucked out and Fillip would take out Stone for me. "What will you do with him?"

Fillip's eyes glinted. "Come now, you know information carries a price."

Being so far in debt to Fillip, the warning didn't mean much to me. "Add it to my tab."

"I will place him under my command," he said. "A puppet like him would be a valuable asset."

"So you plan to mess with his head? Brainwash him?" I had enough dislike for Stone to go around, but I despised the idea of someone's mind being controlled even more.

"He has managed to ensnare many representatives on the Committee and even the city council into less-than-moral deals," Fillip said. "I'm not the only one who sees the opportunity to influence many through one public figure. Others may attempt to claim him first. That is why it is important you bring him to me as soon as possible."

"Because you being in charge of Hopewell and the Committee would be better?" I wondered what a vampire would prioritize if in charge.

"The health of my flock members would no longer rely on city officials who would rather have them disappear than feed or house them." He watched me over arched fingertips a moment longer before he added, "And if I control Joseph Stone, the werewolves will no longer live in fear of wearing a collar forged by a wizard."

It was tempting. Fillip's info was always rock solid, so I believed the information about the Committee members' integrity being compromised, but I didn't know if the vampire's campaign promises were as reliable. Plus, he despised wizards, and I didn't want rules he set through Stone to harm Emma or Ben. "What if I take a pass on this request?"

"That is not an option," Fillip said.

"It'd be faster if you or one of your people pick Stone up." I pointed to my tether. "I'm working with limited resources."

"I prefer people to be brought to me, and I will not endanger any member of my flock to apprehend such a prominent target."

My mind raced, trying to find a way to wiggle out of the task.

He didn't smile this time. "If you do not do this, I will kill you."

My stomach cratered, and the buzzing in my head intensified. *Defy him. He'll end you. Your family and friends will no longer have to deal with you.* "It might take longer than usual since I'm still adjusting to the tether," I said. Maybe I could at least delay.

"True." Fillip nodded. "I will give you three days."

I managed through clenched teeth. "Great. Super generous of you. Thanks."

"You're a delight to do business with, Alexandria." He gave a slight bow of his head. "I wish you a good evening." Fillip turned his back to me and waded into the shadows.

Behind me, the door unlocked and opened. I turned to see the larger guy.

He jerked a thumb at the door. "Get out."

I jogged back to Cathedral Square and my car, eliciting catcalls along the way. Night emboldened those who would otherwise be satisfied just leering. Like any woman, I was cautious when walking to my car at night. But it'd been nearly a decade since I'd felt so unsafe. I readied my car keys like a weapon again in case anyone decided to get too friendly.

In my car, I brought up the message thread with Joan. I read the last message in the thread to Joan, sent from my phone. I hadn't typed it. The timestamp matched the night Emma and I attended the gallery event.

Joan, it's Sebastian. Tell Ben I'm in Hopewell and want to see him. xoxoxo

"That jackass." Not only had he added his contact details to my phone without asking, he also messaged Joan. A flare of irritation and a bit of jealousy burned in me.

I edited my message a few times before I sent it to Joan.

I know who gave Isaac's name to Stone. Trish and Nate arrested and awaiting trial. I'm done playing Committee's games. I want to take down the whole thing, but I need your help.

The group Joan created with Isaac's help wanted to replace the Hopewell Committee but went into hiding after their tethering protest went south. As Ben said, Stone was trying to sniff them out. I wasn't sure Joan or the group she helped lead would put their safety on the line for my plan.

Not only did I have to find evidence against Stone before Trish and Nate went to trial, but now I raced against Fillip wanting to make Stone his hand puppet. Joan and her group were currently my best option for accomplishing that . . . if she agreed to work with me.

I hoped she could make quick decisions, because I was running out of time.

17

I DROVE BACK to Emma's place to find my family watching a film on the enormous screen mounted to the living room wall. Seeing them together, laughing and eating popcorn, I wondered if I'd made the right decision to stay in Hopewell. We could be back in New York, enjoying a movie night in our family home.

But Trish and Nate would still be facing trial. Ben would still be in limbo, hoping Joan could come to some agreement with the Committee. It's not that they couldn't make it without me, it's that I couldn't rest knowing I'd left them while they were in trouble. And having experienced the tether's feedback, there's no way I'd survive without them.

I joined my grandmother on the couch, put my arms around her, and snuggled close.

"They have you working such long shifts at the store," she said.

I snagged a piece of popcorn. "I don't mind." I chewed, imagining Styrofoam had a similar taste. "Where's Em?"

"She left with a man a little bit ago," Grandma said, "but not before she made us a snack and taught us how to work the television. She's so thoughtful."

I sat up. Emma *always* told me if she had a guy on her hook. "Did she introduce you?"

My grandmother tapped at her chin, her gaze lifted to the ceiling. "Yes, but I can't remember his name. He had lovely curly hair like yours and wore more makeup than you do, dear."

"Sebastian." My dad glanced over at us. "We're trying to watch a movie, ladies."

I frowned. Emma had ignored my warning about him.

"When will Ben be visiting again?" Smiling, my grandmother patted my wrist. "He seems like a nice young man, and he's very easy on the eyes."

"Mother," my dad said, "please."

She lowered her voice, leaned toward me, and gave me a knowing wink. "You were practically glowing beside him."

My face burned. I'd hoped we could all forget the whole *my-grandmother-catching-me-in-bed-with-my-guy* thing. With my family, apparently not.

I glanced at my mother, confirming the glare I'd felt. "What?"

"Nothing." My mother shook her head, the punctuation to her unspoken disapproval, and turned her attention back to the film.

I'm a grown woman! She is not going to make me feel guilty about Ben. A bit of guilt soured my stomach. "Why don't you like him, Mom?"

"I never said that. He seems nice enough."

"Mom."

My parents looked at each other before my dad answered. "Alex, we noticed Ben has the same mark on his throat as you do. We're ... concerned. Did you ask him what he'd done to deserve that?"

"Deserve?" My throat went dry. "Because, like me, everyone who gets tethered *deserves* it?"

Dad's eyes widened.

Mom shook her head. "You know we don't mean it that way, Alex. We want to make sure Ben is a safe person for our daughter to be spending time with."

"I wouldn't be with him otherwise." A faint whine spun up in my head. Having my family here complicated everything. I took a moment to breathe deep and slowly exhale. "I know you're worried about how I'm feeling. But as you've seen, I have good friends here for emotional support. I really think you could go home, and then

I'll visit when I have some time off?" If they left, they wouldn't be in harm's way if things turned nasty with Stone or Fillip.

"You don't want us here?" My mother frowned. "Why?"

I shook my head. "No, I just thought—"

"Your mother and I don't feel comfortable leaving yet, Alex," my dad said.

I didn't know how to tell them they could be in danger because I was involved in something that would worry them even more. They'd never leave then.

I gave my grandmother a kiss on the cheek. "Enjoy the movie." I stood and walked to the back patio, passing through the screen door and sitting down in a chair next to the pool. I pulled out my phone and sent a message to Emma.

Make good choices.

It was an ongoing joke between us, but I was concerned for her. After my conversations with Sebastian, and given Ben's opinion of the guy, I didn't quite trust Sebastian had my best friend's happiness in mind. But then again, Emma viewed most men as an accessory. Maybe they would balance each other out and have a good time.

My phone chimed, and a reply came up in my message thread with Joan.

Tomorrow morning I'll send an address. Someone will meet you there.

So at least she'd listen. Tonight would be better because of the short timeline. I'd have to sneak out so my family wouldn't be alarmed. I sent a message back.

Tonight instead?

Joan swiftly replied.

Tomorrow.

I also had to work the next morning. Rear Window was closed for the night, so I left Sarah a message. "It's Alex. My family is visiting from out of town, and something came up tonight. I won't be able to make it into work tomorrow. Sorry."

Hopefully I wouldn't get fired for such late notice. If I lost the job, my parents would be packing my few belongings for me.

THE NIGHT BROUGHT little sleep, so I got up early for a run. Usually my favorite form of exercise helped clear my head, but this time it didn't quell my anxiety about meeting Joan. With Trish and Nate locked away, I'd lost valuable allies. I needed Joan's help to nail Stone and begin breaking apart the Committee.

When I returned to Emma's house, I noticed a box of pastries and the prepped coffee maker. I hadn't heard her come in the night before. She must not have planned to join us for breakfast. After a quick shower and change, I debated slipping into her bedroom and asking if she was okay. Instead, I cracked the door just enough to confirm she'd made it home.

I didn't smell the freshly brewed coffee until I went downstairs and into the dining room and kitchen. The patio screen door was cracked open. I walked out onto the patio, and Sebastian turned in one of the chairs to look over his shoulder at me. Deep shadows lurked beneath his eyes like bruises. He wore lounge pants and a shimmery tank top. The shirt may have been Emma's.

"Good morning." He sipped at the steaming mug of coffee he held. His fingers were no longer wrapped in bandages. A bottle of whiskey sat on the patio table beside him. "Early riser? Pull up a seat."

I remained standing. "What are you doing here?"

"The fuck if I know." He looked away from me. "Emma must have brought me here at some point." Sebastian raised a finger. A lacework of scars covered the inside of his forearm. "When going out for an off-the-rails night with a wizard, choose one that practices mending magic. You'll wake up in a bed instead of a gutter."

"Em takes care of people," I said. "I bet she offered to heal your fingers before even thinking to ask what you'd done to them."

"You're correct." Sebastian set aside the coffee mug. "Healers are always taking in strays." He looked back at me again and smirked. "But you already knew that."

I gave him the finger.

"Alex, I feel everything started off wrong between us, and I still don't understand how it happened. It can't be that some harmless charm with a Commoner clerk made you despise me like this." He pushed the whiskey bottle toward me. "Get some coffee. Join me. Let's talk."

I hesitated. I hadn't felt any magnetic effects of charms. Maybe whatever he and Emma had gotten up to the night before had exhausted him. I pulled out a chair and sat down. "You have five minutes."

Sebastian shifted to sit more upright. A grinning skull with smoke rolling from its empty eye sockets leered at me from the skin on his shoulder. Beneath the tattoo and near the back of his arm, a small pod-like device was attached. He noticed me staring. "It's a glucose monitor. It's nice not to have to stab myself whenever I want to eat."

"Sorry," I said. "I noticed your tattoo. Did Sandra do it?"

"Yeah." His grin looked eerily similar to the skull's. "Sandra does great work, doesn't she?"

"She seems to. My Shield has warded everything thrown at me so far." I paused. "Everything except Reginald's spells."

"That old bastard is a master of the craft, though," Sebastian said. "Has Sandra repaired your Shield yet?"

I shook my head.

"You should do that," he said. "And take Emma to get one."

"Why?" I wasn't convinced my safety was top of his mind. "Are you planning to spam us with your shitty charms again?"

He watched me from behind his hooded eyelids. "You're right. I suppose a Shield isn't going to stop the bullet the Committee puts into your head after they get wind of your fantastic fuckup last night."

My stomach tightened. I immediately thought of Ben. "They *shoot* people?"

Sebastian chuckled. "What did you think they did? Behead people with an ancient sword?" He closed an eye and aimed his pointer finger at my face, his thumb cocked. "It's quick, clean, and not even a lupine can survive one right between the eyes."

I licked my lips. The whine of the tether started. "I'll get Stone before that happens."

"And if you don't?" he said. "Have you thought that far ahead?"

"I'll feed him to Fillip." The words escaped before I could stop them. My hate for Stone was eroding my moral boundaries. I couldn't let him take that from me, too. "But it won't come to that."

Sebastian arched an eyebrow, showing interest for the first time since he learned his stepfather was involved in Isaac's death. "And who is Fillip? Another lupine?"

I frowned. I assumed he knew Fillip since Ben did, but maybe Ben's encounter with the vampire happened after he and Sebastian had parted ways.

"Alex, you can tell me." He hit me with his smooth smile. "I'm curious about him now, so I'll find out eventually."

"Fillip is a vampire," I said.

"Vampire? There are only like two in Hopewell." Sebastian smirked. "I'm having a hard time believing *you* would know one."

"He's an informant of Trish's." I swallowed. "I owe him debts. He ordered me to bring him Stone so he could work some kind of mind magic and use Stone like a puppet to influence the Committee."

Sebastian's other brow rose. "You've suddenly become more intriguing."

I snorted. "I'm glad my unfortunate business dealings with a blood-sucking creature of the night entertain you."

"Can you introduce me to Fillip?"

I blinked. "Why?"

"Vampires have powerful abilities fueled by blood magic adjacent to the type that I wield," he said. "I'd be interested in discussing it with him and possibly learning from him."

"Fillip hates wizards," I said.

"He hasn't met me." Sebastian cocked his head to the side and smiled. "He'll love me."

"I'm not sure why anyone would like you," I said.

Sebastian rested his elbow on the table and his chin in his hand. "Why do you despise me so much?"

"Are you serious? I don't trust you," I said. And maybe I disliked him a bit because Ben remained upset years after they split. I echoed Ben's words, trying to find some reassurance in them. "You're arrogant and selfish."

"Not confident and driven?"

I snorted again.

A corner of his mouth turned upward. "Those were words Emma used to describe you."

I blinked and my face warmed. "What?" It wasn't how I'd describe myself. I defaulted to *barely-keeping-it-together*.

Sebastian sighed and fell back in his chair. "She wouldn't stop talking about you. 'Alex risked her life for this,' and 'Alex is an amazing friend because of that.'" He stifled a yawn with the back of his hand and reached for his coffee mug. "It sounded more like you being impulsive and, frankly, asinine, but now I have a better idea of why Ben would even bother with you."

My fingers curled into a fist on the tabletop. "And I'm getting a better idea why he doesn't want anything to do with you."

"I've helped you twice now. I don't know what else you need from me before I can gain your trust." A frown twitched Sebastian's lips. He turned the coffee mug in his hands a few times. "I'm trying to make long overdue amends with Ben while I'm here. But I won't get anywhere with him without your approval."

"Ben is his own person," I said. "You don't need approval from me."

Sebastian disregarded my response with a wave of his hand. "But he cares for you and what you think."

"Why in the *world* would I help my guy's ex, who I don't trust, weasel back into his life?" The idea alone brought an ugly wave of jealousy.

"You have nothing to worry about." Sebastian dropped his gaze to his coffee mug. "He's enamored with you . . . disgustingly so. Nothing I do is going to change that."

Romance hadn't been on my radar when I met Ben. It was a frivolous thing meant for other people, not someone whose focus should be not wolfing out. But with Ben, I didn't have to hide any part of me. Yet our relationship still felt fragile. Intimidating. What if I messed up? And now his smooth-talking, necromancy-practicing ex-boyfriend shows up, wanting my blessing for alone time with Ben?

Hell. No.

"I'm not here to harm him or steal him away." Sebastian's lazy smile and half-lowered eyelids slipped back into place like a mask. "But if you ever need insider advice on how to please him, don't hesitate to ask."

Jealousy clawed its way up out of my chest as a low growl, followed by an eruption of pain from my tether. I choked and lifted my hand to my throat. My mind exploded with feedback noise, but my pulse quickened from the unanticipated reaction of my inner wolf.

Sebastian's eyes widened. He lowered his mug. "How often has *that* been happening?"

I bit back my first reply. He'd put himself at risk to help me, though I wondered if only for his own benefit. He also served as my keycard to Teuling's home, so I still had to play somewhat nice with him. "This is the first time since you tried to remove the tether."

He sat up again, set his coffee cup aside, and turned his chair to face me. "Let me try again."

I leaned back. "What?"

"Breaking the tether." He stared at the area of my throat hidden from his sharp gaze by my fingers. "I haven't stopped thinking about it. I know how to improve Ben's spell, and the necromantic translation is fairly simple. Let me have another go at it."

My initial thought was to agree, but Ben's warning lingered in my mind. The spell symbolized a puzzle for Sebastian to solve. He didn't care if the attempt harmed me. I shook my head. "No. I don't think that's a good idea."

"Alex," Sebastian's chin dipped and the edges of his mouth slowly curled. "I can give you what you want." His velvety voice was full of promise. "I'll make you whole again. Let me help you."

Anticipation and longing rushed through me. I wanted nothing more at that moment than to be reunited with my wolf, and Sebastian could make it happen. My body leaned toward him like a plant toward sunlight.

The tingling heat of desire was doused by another bout of rumbling growls in my chest and corresponding noise in my brain.

I shook my head, the dreamlike effect of his spell falling away. He'd exploited my broken Shield, and the flickering presence of my wolf had sensed it.

"You asshole!" The chair legs screeched as I stood. I snatched up his half-full coffee cup from the table and tossed the contents into his face.

Sebastian flinched back, raising an arm too late. He leapt to his feet, his chair tipping over with a clatter. "What the actual fuck!"

"I said no more charms!" A snarl edged my voice, and pain stabbed inside my throat.

Frantic, he wiped at the coffee on his face and front of his shirt. "What is wrong with you? Are you trying to burn my face off?"

"*This* is why I don't trust you!" I shouted. "The *second* someone lets down their guard, you take advantage of them!"

"Alex?" My mother stood at the slider, her eyes wide. "What's happening out here? Are you okay?"

Sebastian glared at my mother, turned away, and pulled off his shirt. He used it to sponge away the coffee dripping from his face and hair.

"Nothing important." Scowling, I slipped past her into the house. "I'm okay."

"Are you sure?" She turned and followed me. "Why is that man here? Should I ask him to leave?"

"Mom, ignore him. Grab some breakfast and coffee." I sat at the dining room table, trying to eat a pastry and calm myself. The angry noise in my head faded to a low murmur. Getting the info I needed from Teuling to entrap Stone couldn't happen fast enough. I wanted to rid Ben and myself of Sebastian Visser.

"Emma is such a nice person." My mother sat down beside me and lowered her voice. "Her friend seems . . . weird. Maybe we should talk to her about him."

"Emma is going to do what she wants." I pushed the nibbled pastry aside and tried the coffee instead. My phone chimed. The address I needed to meet Joan. My dad entered the dining room right before I stood and pocketed my phone. I gave each of my parents a hug and a peck on the cheek. "I'm off."

My mother frowned. "Already?"

"Good morning?" my father said.

"I have to get to work," I said. "Sara has me opening today."

"Maybe you could ask for some vacation time," Mom said.

"It's a minimum-wage job and I just started," I said. "There is no vacation time. Plus, it helps me to stay busy. When I'm busy, I'm not thinking of this." I pointed to the tether.

My dad joined us at the table with a steaming cup of coffee. "Alex, have you given any thought to going back to college? Finishing your last semester?"

I blinked. "What? Where is *this* coming from?"

"Since you don't have to hide anymore, maybe you can start thinking about your future," he said. "You could get your degree and earn a decent income."

"It breaks our hearts to see you struggling," my mom said. "What if you want to have a house? Start a family?"

The walls of the room pressed in on me. I swallowed back growing nausea. "Have we all forgotten what I am? I don't get to have those things. I *still* have to hide from the Commoners."

"Your grandfather was able—"

"I'm not him!" The static whirred inside my skull. I pressed my fingers to my temples. "I don't *want* those things. A family?" I frowned at my parents. "Why would I ever put someone else at risk to become what I am?"

My mother's features crumpled, and I realized my mistake. She raised her hands to cover her face.

"Alexandria." My dad spoke my name as a reprimand.

"Mom, I'm sorry. I didn't mean—"

"We knew there was a chance, but we wanted a child," she said. "And your grandfather made it look so easy."

My mother's crying tore at my heart. Why couldn't my mouth *ever* check in before opening? "Mom, it's okay. I understand."

My father shook his head and looked down at his coffee.

"I'm sorry, but I can't talk about this right now." I backed away. "I'm going to be late."

I escaped the house to my car and sat in the driver's seat for a few minutes to regain control of my breathing. Deep inhales and slow exhales caused the painful noise in my head to fade. I'd never told anyone but Emma that I didn't plan on having kids, which is what my parents meant when they said "family." She'd only asked after bemoaning the fact it was taking too long to find the right partner to help raise kids of her own.

House? Family? Other werewolves had them, and they'd be in danger if Stone and the Committee were allowed to continue business as usual. And beneath that urge to protect the wolves, I recognized my own, darker reason for wanting to put an end to Stone and the Committee.

To hurt those who hurt me.

18

SWEATY PALMS CLAMPED to the steering wheel, I drove to the location Joan sent. The address landed me at a five-story brick building downtown. A man several years older than me, closer to Joan's age, waited on a public bench in front of the building.

"Alex?" His eyes wandered to my throat and his nostrils flared.

"Yes." I recognized him as another werewolf I'd met before. "You're Joan's friend, right?"

He nodded.

"I remember you from Ben's place after the protest went south earlier this summer," I said. "You'd bogarted the shower."

Recognition flickered behind his eyes. "Yeah, that was me." He stood and extended his hand. "I'm Lars."

I shook it. "Like the drummer?"

He grinned. "Yeah, like the drummer."

"Are you from Hopewell?" I hadn't seen him around Hell's Bells. Though it was a popular gathering space for wolves, I'm sure not everyone frequented the club.

"Yeah, I'm local. I knew Joan before she moved away." Lars motioned me to follow him. "They're waiting for us. We don't like to give out our exact location. The Committee has been trying to find us ever since that protest you mentioned."

I followed him a few blocks to a stairway beside another brick building. We descended the stairs to a door beneath street level. A faded metal sign beside the door, stamped with a pyramid of three upside-down triangles, read *FALLOUT SHELTER*.

He pushed a button at the door, and the small speaker above it crackled to life. "It's Lars with our guest." The door unlocked with a mechanical click, and he pulled it open. When the door shut behind us, we were left in darkness.

I stopped, reminded again of what was taken from me. "I'm sorry. I can't see anything."

"Let me have your hand." He led me across the room and opened another door.

I squinted against the sudden artificial light in the low-ceilinged room. Two additional doors led off the windowless area. A dozen or so people were gathered around a salvaged table. Lars and I entered, and their conversation halted. Everyone's attention turned to me.

I recognized Joan and another person I didn't expect to be there. "Ben?"

He crossed the room in several strides and embraced me. "Are you okay? Joan told me about Trish and Nate."

I savored the comforting pressure of his body against mine. "I'm okay. Pissed, but otherwise okay." We parted, and I frowned up at him. "But what are you doing here?"

"Someone put it into his head that the time to negotiate with the Committee is over." Joan approached with a slight smile. It brightened her eyes, the same beautiful blue-grey color as her brother's. She had identical dark hair, too. Joan's fell just past her shoulders. "And I can keep a better eye on him if he's with me." She held out a hand and clasped mine. "I know I've made myself scarce, but it's good to see you again."

The small twinge of happiness her words brought surprised me. We hadn't talked since we worked with Trish to shut down Stone's Hunter. Joan and I had a tense relationship since she didn't completely trust my intentions with her brother. "Thanks for getting back to me so fast. I'm in a bit of a time crunch," I said.

She nodded, but like so many others I'd seen since my trial, her gaze settled on my throat. Her smile faded. "I'm sorry for what they did to you."

"Thank you for bringing Ben to see me." I gave him a sidelong glance. "I know you're worried about keeping him safe, but having him visit helped."

"You're welcome," she said. "He hasn't smiled so much in months, so thank you."

Ben rubbed at the back of his neck and blushed.

I couldn't help my own smile. "Will there be an agreement with the Committee on his sentence?"

"It felt like we were almost there," she said. "They were close to settling for an additional year added, but then all negotiations were suddenly halted."

"We're assuming it's the new safety laws," Lars said, both startling me and reminding me a group of people waited on us. "If the Committee plans to retroactively punish supernatural citizens, they don't want to be seen as weak by negotiating with someone who is tethered.

Joan faced the table and raised her voice. "Everyone, this is Alex Steward. She wants to pitch us her idea to topple the Hopewell Committee." Joan gestured around the room. "Alex, this is everyone. The majority of them are from Hopewell. Only three of us are from Chicago."

"Are you here representing the Chicago Delegation?" I asked.

Joan shook her head. "No. I've worked with the Delegation there, but I've never been a member. This group is independent. I helped Isaac create it since I'm native to Hopewell and had personal experience with how the Committee here harms instead of protects supernatural citizens." She gave a fleeting glance at Ben. "Isaac didn't have to search long before finding others who had the same experience and were ready to help create change." She motioned to an empty chair at the table. "Have a seat and tell us more about your idea, Alex."

I told the group about Stone's influence on the Committee and how he'd used it to push through the new rules and regulations. I told them about Trish and Nate's arrest, the closing of Hell's Bells, and my request the wolves lay low. Then I told them about Teuling's role in Isaac's death and how I wanted him and Stone off the Committee.

"Teuling is already battling a heavy conscience. I think we can get him to confess." I shifted in my seat. "If I can get him to listen after he caught me snooping in his study."

"How do you plan on getting a private one-on-one with him?" Joan asked.

"His stepson is in town and helped me get inside the house the first time," I said. "He *really* doesn't like his stepfather, so he'll be willing to get us in there again."

"So that's how you know Sebastian," Joan said. She looked at Ben, her brows drawn together. "Are you going to be okay with this, or should I be worried?"

Ben shrugged and avoided Joan's gaze.

"I hoped to have your help taking Teuling somewhere private, without distractions or interruptions," I said to Joan. "We convince him he needs to confess, ratting out Stone in the process."

Joan looked around the group of people. "What do we think?"

Lars shook his head. "I don't see how removing Stone and Teuling is going to cause the Committee to collapse. Trish Drake had Reverend Jansen kicked out and that's how we got Stone. What if the next guy is even worse?"

"I have it on good authority that Stone's shady dealings among Committee members goes beyond Teuling," I said. "We could intimidate the others into resigning."

"We're going to need more than 'on good authority' if you want us to put ourselves in the Committee's crosshairs to help you," Lars said. "Consequences are more severe since those new laws went into effect. Agreeing to help you is agreeing to be tethered if caught."

Several people exchanged nervous glances. I wondered how many of them were wolves like Lars and me.

I looked at Joan. "Fillip is the one who told me about how far Stone's reach extends into the Committee." I turned back to the rest of the group. "He brokers information. The reputation of his business relies on the authenticity of his word."

"She's right," Joan said. "As much as I find Fillip unpleasant, I don't believe he'd give out false information." She turned her gaze on me. "Or free information. What did you pay for it, Alex?"

I shifted my weight. "I have a running debt with Fillip. He wants me to bring him Stone," I said. "Something about controlling Stone to do his bidding."

Joan leaned back in her chair, her eyebrow arched. "Fillip wants Stone to be his thrall? So if we go with your approach, we'd be removing Stone but pissing off a vampire." She chewed at her lip and glanced around the group again.

"Wizards and vamps in Hopewell have never had a good relationship," a young woman said. "If we help her, we'll rid ourselves of Stone and prevent a vampire from influencing Committee rules and making trouble for us."

Joan looked at me. "Would Fillip be happy with the consolation prize of a Commoner mayor if we get Stone removed from the Committee but he still wins the election?"

"I'm not sure that's an option," I said. "There's a lot of crossover between the Committee and the City Council. Stone's support for mayor will more than likely plummet when the Committee members desert him."

Lars watched me. "How do we know you're not working undercover for Stone?"

I scowled. "Are you kidding? Why the *hell* would I *ever* work for that bastard?"

He shrugged. "Struck a deal with him? Turn in our group and get your sentence reduced? He's been trying to use Committee resources to nail us since he had Isaac murdered."

Joan looked back at me, speaking to the group. "I know Alex enough to know her dislike of Stone. She isn't a spy for him." She grinned. "And outright lying isn't in her skillset."

Lars frowned at her. "But as a wizard, you don't know what she'd do as a wolf to rid herself of a tether."

The young woman looked at Joan. "I think we need time to discuss this and make a decision together as a group." She glanced at me. "In private."

"I don't have much time," I said. "Fillip told me he wanted Stone in three days."

"The Committee has to go away, and Stone can't win the election." The corners of Joan's mouth turned upward. "I'm in." She looked around the group. "I'll respect your choice if you don't want to take this chance. Let's have a decision to her within the hour." Joan stood, a signal the meeting had ended. The group dispersed into several clusters, their conversation filling the room.

She reached out to place a hand on the side of my arm. "I'll be in touch with an answer from everyone else. Then we can put together the details of a plan."

Even though I had successfully recruited her, I had mixed feelings about having Joan on board. She was a talented wizard to have in my corner, but she could be unpredictable. Hopefully the rest of the group would pitch in as well.

I thanked everyone, exchanged a kiss with Ben, and followed Lars back through the dark room toward the front door. He released my hand and pushed the door open into the sunlight. His body tensed, and he yanked at the door to shut it again. The door stayed open. Someone seized Lars and pulled him outside. There were sounds of a scuffle, and I stepped back.

Anne, holding a large mag light, braced her body against the door to prop it open. She swung the beam of light toward me. "Alex?"

I raised my hand to shield my eyes.

Jakob stepped past her into the building, scanning the area.

My throat went dry and my pulse raced. Had they followed me here? I took a deep breath and turned in the direction of the back room. "Police!" I shouted.

Growling, Jakob dashed across the room.

"Dammit, Alex!" Anne tried to shove past me to follow Jakob.

I grabbed her left wrist. "Anne, please, you're going after the wrong people!"

Anne turned on me, her face a mix of anger and frustration. "These *people* were behind the riots. Let go of me and get out of our way."

"No." I tightened my grip. "The Committee is pointing you and Jakob in the wrong direction. How many times do I have to say it? You should be looking into Stone!"

Jakob made it through the door into the adjoining room. The sounds of shouting and crashes of overturned chairs echoed across the space.

Anne glanced toward the noise and then back to me. She clasped the fingers of her immobile hand over my wrist, rotated her hand, and turned her hips away from me.

The swift move tweaked my wrist and forced me to stumble past Anne. I released her to keep my balance. But not before I saw the long scar across the top of her left hand and the grotesque bulge beneath the skin. My chest tightened.

The Hunter's key.

Anne scowled. "If you're still here when we're done, I'll arrest you, too."

"Why did you agree to it? Why are you carrying his key?" I asked. "He killed Isaac!"

She stopped short, and her features went still. Anne's gaze twitched down at her hand and back at me. "I need a way—"

"He was a monster," I said. "He had a box of trophies from the people he murdered!"

The color drained from her face, and she swallowed. The flashlight beam wavered.

"That key sets you at odds with every supernatural citizen in Hopewell. Why do you hate us so much that you'd endanger yourself before letting us live in peace?" The awful feedback from the tether buzzed in my mind. "Tell me!"

There were more shouts from the adjoining room. Anne backed away from me, shaking her head. "No. I don't have to tell *you* anything." She turned away to run across the room.

A sudden anger seared my gut. Anne had chosen the Committee and its rules over me. I remained useless, this time in helping Joan's group escape . . . in helping Ben escape. My throat spasmed, and a growl slipped past my lips.

Heart hammering, I reached out for my inner wolf.

Nothing.

I clenched my teeth against the escalating tension in my head and dove for Anne. With a grunt and a stream of curses, we tumbled to the paved floor. "Please, stop!" I begged. "Ben is in there. They'll kill him."

Anne's struggles paused briefly before she tossed me off her. She pinned an arm behind my back and hauled me to my feet. My thrashing did nothing against the iron-clad grip the Hunter's key granted Anne. She dragged me, kicking and yelling, back to the front door of the building.

With a final shove from Anne, I found myself outside in the blinding sunlight. I stumbled over Lars's leg, and the door swung closed. I spun, seized the door handle, and tried to yank it open.

Locked.

The tether's whine in my head became deafening. Heat erupted in my chest. I screamed and punched the metal door. The surface crumpled like tin foil beneath my fist, but the jarring collision vibrated up to my elbow. My fist stung, along with my throat, and brought instant tears. The door's lock stubbornly held.

Panting, I held my injured hand against my chest. That glorious feeling, the flush of heat warming my body again. The release. I wouldn't survive without it. I couldn't live with her locked away.

I crouched down beside Lars. A check of his pulse confirmed he was just unconscious. I wondered if, when Lars awoke, he'd be convinced I worked for Stone after all. Jakob had bound him with a pair of handcuffs.

When my fingers came into contact with the metal, my skin tingled. I jerked back my hand. Narrowing my eyes, I leaned closer. The cuffs had an odd plastic rim where the person's wrists would be. I hesitated before touching a fingertip to the metal. The same tingling sensation traveled up my skin, and my finger started to itch.

The cuffs were silver, but the tether muted its effects on my body to a mild irritation. I snorted, wondering if I'd discovered the one and only benefit of being a tethered werewolf. The moment of humor was short-lived. Silver handcuffs were yet another Hunter's weapon the Committee now seemed to be using.

I located the shim that I kept on my keychain, a gift from Nate. Wiggling it down between the lock house and the teeth, I opened the cuff. The same technique opened the other, and the handcuffs clattered to the ground. I stood and moved the cuffs away from us with the toe of my sneaker.

With my hands under his armpits, I dragged Lars away from the door and toward the stairs leading up to street level. I didn't have the strength to haul him up the stairway and to my car. I blew out an exhale and sought my inner wolf.

No answer.

I rested his body against the building wall and chewed at my thumbnail. Sticking around wasn't a great idea. I had to leave him behind and hope he'd wake up before Anne and Jakob came back for him. "I'm sorry." I rushed up the stairs to the street.

When Anne had said that following up on Isaac's case had nothing to do with me, I'd hoped a fragment of our friendship still survived. That a small part of her still cared for me like I did for her. She could have cuffed and hauled me into the Committee twice now, but she didn't. Had she somehow instead used me to find Joan's group? I wasn't sure I could trust her anymore.

As I hurried down the sidewalk to my car, I worried about the possible fallout my visit would cause Ben, Joan, and her friends. Pausing beside my car, I pulled out my phone to message Joan. A white stationery envelope, tucked under the driver's side windshield wiper, caught my attention.

I yanked the blank envelope from beneath the wiper and almost tore it in half in my rush to open it. Familiar handwriting with elegant loops inscribed the card inside. It'd been on every note from Fillip. The single sentence filled me with dread.

No wizards.

The pressure inside of my head made my eyes water. I tried to swallow down my anger, but my throat spasmed and a small burst of heat opened in my chest. Another snarl left my lips, and my hand flew to my mouth to stifle the sound.

I turned in place, looking around for the person who must have followed Lars and me, then called Jakob and Anne. Fillip's flock consisted of people society often overlooked, allowing them to be the perfect spies, collecting intel for him in plain sight.

None of the passing people caught my attention. I got into my car, leaving the door open to vent the heat, and sent a text to Joan.

Fillip had me followed. I'm sorry. Please let me know if Ben and you are okay.

My phone rang from an unknown number. "Hello?"

"Benjamin Sharpe," said the familiar voice. My stomach turned. It was Stone.

I waited a moment too long to reply. "Who's that?"

"Don't play an idiot with me, bitch," he said.

My mind raced.

"An anonymous call giving us the address we've been trying to locate for months." Stone chuckled. "I'm not sure who to thank, but someone must dislike you or Reginald Sharpe as much as I do. We've been after Sharpe's grandson as long as we've been dealing with his granddaughter. I already have the case prepared to argue for his execution."

I swallowed back a wave of nausea and crumpled the note still clutched in my hand. "No, wait. You don't want anything to do with the person who gave you that information." I couldn't believe I was warning Stone about Fillip, but I would try almost anything to protect Ben and delay his trial. "It'll be dangerous for you."

"Suddenly you're worried about me? Too late. You've had your chance to back off." Stone's tone darkened. "This will be our last conversation, Alexis."

"Wait! Do you have Ben or not?"

"I cannot say it's been a pleasure knowing you," he said. "I'll be sure to pass on my regrets to your family."

The line went dead.

19

I LOWERED THE phone from my ear, the adrenaline coursing through me causing it to shake. After having Isaac murdered, I didn't doubt Stone would attempt getting rid of me, permanently, without the Committee's help.

"Alex?"

I screeched, flinched back, and did some sort of kick in the general direction of the voice, all the more ridiculous because I was seated in my car. Eyes wide and gasping, I lowered my raised arm from in front of my body.

An older man stood outside my car, turning a tattered and stained Lions ball cap in his hands. It was John, one of Emma's clients and an acquaintance of Ben's. A member of Fillip's flock.

"You startled me." I got back out of the car and shut the door. "Don't tell me you were the one to call the cops on us. It put Ben and his sister in danger."

John's bushy eyebrows bunched together, and he drew a cross over the left side of his chest with a finger. "Wasn't me. I'm here to take you to Fillip."

John led me toward the riverfront. As we walked together, he said, "I wish I could do something for you and Ben, but Fillip takes care of us."

"It's okay." I didn't like it, but I understood. Fillip offered John protection when most other people would rather people like him disappear.

We descended a set of stairs to a little pocket park, tucked away from the main sidewalk and facing the water. Fillip waited on the single bench.

John stopped and nodded to me. "Good luck." He turned, walked back up the stairs, and away down the sidewalk.

My anger with Fillip threatened to be a problem. I inhaled slowly, then exhaled just as slowly before I approached him. Diplomacy would be needed. I'd spent months watching Trish, trying to learn from her repeated examples of restraint.

I stopped at the bench and scowled. "That was a dick move."

Well, I'd tried.

Fillip watched the river. "In my business relations, I expect anyone I work with to remain true to their word. Instead of retrieving the politician for me, you attempted to scheme with Joanna Sharpe." He spat on the ground upon mentioning the wizard's name. "I don't take unprofessional behavior from my partners lightly."

"How can I concentrate on getting Stone when you've put Ben in danger? I don't know if he got away or if Stone has him." I frowned. "You know Ben is important to me."

"If you remain on task and bring me Joseph Stone, I will have the time needed to take control and spare Benjamin," he said.

My face flushed and the goddamn buzzing started in my head again. I pinched the bridge of my nose and squeezed my eyes shut. "The tether is slowing me down too much. I need allies. You must know Trish and Nate are locked up at the cathedral. Please, let me work with Joan."

Fillip looked from the river to me. "Wizards cannot be trusted."

"Let me worry about that," I said. "She'll want Ben safe, too. All that matters in the end is that I get you Stone, right?"

He watched me in silence, his red eyes seeming to peer into me. I shifted my weight. The noise in my mind intensified. Fillip finally spoke. "Only Joanna Sharpe," he said. "Is that understood?"

"Yes."

"Good. Let's be done with this so you can spend time with your grandmother and parents while they are in Hopewell," he said.

The static in my head pitched sharply upward.

"Goodbye, Alexandria."

I walked back to my car, trying to regain control. Not only did Ben face danger, but my family as well. My hands flexed at my side, but the emotion to power shifting lodged like a shard of glass between my eyes. The pain added fuel to the bonfire of my discouragement and self-doubt. *Give up. You make everything worse. You're hurting everyone around you.*

Everything was falling apart.

Let the Committee execute you instead. This will all stop.

I tried to start my car, but the engine sputtered and stalled. I turned the key again and it didn't turn over. "No!" I slammed my hand against the steering wheel and startled myself with a blare of the horn. I fell back in my seat, massaging my temples, and tried to have a coherent thought.

I pulled out my phone again and dialed my lifeline. "Hey, Em. I need your help."

"WHEN ARE YOU going to trade in that piece of junk?" Emma asked. She glanced over at me from the driver's seat of her Prius.

"It's not a piece of junk. It hasn't fully recovered from being smashed by an angry werewolf. *Most* of the time it works." The car had been towed to a repair shop, and Emma picked me up to give me a ride back to her place. The ruckus in my brain dulled to a low hum.

Emma gave me another glance, her bottom lip caught between her teeth.

"What is it, Em?"

"I'm only saying this because I love you, but you look like shit. Are you not sleeping? Is retail work really that hard?"

I snorted. "Have you ever worked retail?"

Emma's cheeks turned rosy. "You know I haven't." She paused. "Sebastian told me that you were caught snooping in his stepfather's study. Is that true?"

I closed my eyes.

"Alex?"

"Yes," I said. "I tried to find something to link Stone and Teuling to Isaac's death."

"Will he report you to the Committee?" Emma said.

"I wouldn't be surprised if he already has." I shook my head. "And after this raid by Anne and Jakob, I'm not sure how many of Joan's group have been taken in. Stone called to say he knew Ben was there. Then he threatened to kill me." The tether's feedback whined in my head.

"Tell me what I can do to help."

I looked over at Emma.

Scowling, she tightened her hold on the steering wheel. Emma scowling was about as intimidating as an angry kitten.

My heart warmed. "Give me a ride to Teuling's house tonight?"

"Of course," she said. "I wanted to see Sebastian later anyway."

"Yeah, about that, I'm not sure it's a good idea to hang out with Sebastian," I said.

Emma gave an award-worthy eye roll. "We're just playing."

"He wants time alone with Ben, and I suspect getting close to you is another way he's trying to get that." I frowned and shifted in my seat. "They were together for a while."

Emma's eyebrows shot up. "Oh. Are you sure *that* isn't why you don't trust him?"

Maybe.

"Ben told me Sebastian is unreliable," I said. "I don't want Sebastian hurting you or getting you in trouble. These new laws the Committee voted in aren't a joke."

"Alex, stop fretting." Her response didn't surprise me. Wizards weren't affected as strongly by the Committee's rules.

"I don't like those charms he uses," I said. "It's like he dissolves people's inhibitions. It really pisses me off thinking he'd pull something like that with you."

Emma forced a smile. "I know what I'm doing."

"How much do you really know about him?" I asked. "Ben said that Sebastian practices necromancy."

She cringed. "How mad would you be if I said I knew that?"

"What the hell, Em?" I threw up my hands. "You're the one who told me necromancy is bad news! Dark magic. It's the number-one way for a wizard to be nailed by a Hunter. But now it's okay to have a casual fling with someone who practices it?"

"I know, I know!" Emma pouted. "He's really fun, though. And it's not like he's going around raising the dead."

"What! They can do that?"

"Of course not," Emma said. "At least I don't think so. The only wizards I've ever heard about who could do that were villains in kids' stories."

My arms crossed, I shook my head and looked out the window.

She reached over and patted my arm. "Stop worrying. I promise to be careful. Plus, if Ben was . . . friends with him, he can't be *that* bad, right?"

Emma had always had shitty taste in guys, but Sebastian worried me. I'd feel better if he stayed away from both Emma and Ben. In my desperation to get to Stone, I seemed to be putting the people dearest to me in danger.

When we got back to Emma's, she went upstairs to preen and cycle through several clothing options for the evening. My parents were on the back patio together.

"Where's Grandma?" I closed the screen door and sat down at the table.

"She's taking a nap," Dad said. "We have dinner reservations at a restaurant Emma recommended. Can you come with us?"

"What's wrong?" My mother studied me. "Something is wrong."

Dad looked between the two of us, frowning.

I took a deep breath. "I need you guys to leave Hopewell. Tonight. Within the next hour would be preferable."

"Are you in trouble?" Mom said.

"Someone I'm indebted to knows you're visiting and threatened to hurt you," I said. "I'll call when this is all over."

"Indebted? Threatened?" Mom's voice rose. "When *what* is all over?"

"Dad, please," I said.

My father looked between us again. "There's nothing we can do to help with this debt? We can give you any money you need."

I shook my head. "You three leaving is the best way you can help me. Trust me."

"Kim—" my father began.

My mother's eyes widened. "No. We can't leave our daughter when she's in trouble."

"There's a lot she deals with that we don't understand," he said. "Dad was the same way when I was a kid. Let's trust Alex."

The screen door slid open, and Emma stepped out. "Ready to go?"

I stood and hugged my parents a bit tighter and longer than usual. "Please say goodbye to Grandma for me. I'll call you as soon as I can."

My mother started crying. "Please be careful."

"Love you," Dad said.

"Love you guys, too," I said. "And thank you."

"Are you leaving?" Emma frowned. "But your reservations."

Dad smiled. "Our daughter thinks it's best we head out. Thank you for hosting us on such short notice, Emma."

Emma's smile shone bright. "Of course! Anytime." She hugged them both as well.

My chest ached as I left my family on the patio, but part of me exhaled in relief. They would soon be outside of Fillip's reach.

Emma glanced over as we got in her car. "Is everything okay with your family?"

"Things are getting messy, and I'll feel better if they're out of harm's way," I said. I took out my phone and texted Sebastian. *Emma and I have a stop to make and we'll be on our way.*

My phone chimed with his response. *Is Ben coming with you?*

I clenched my teeth and debated reading Emma the message as evidence that Sebastian didn't have any interest in her. But I'd already voiced my concerns, and Emma had me doubting why Sebastian irked me so much. Was I just being the jealous girlfriend or was he really a threat?

Emma caught me frowning at my phone. "Everything okay?"

I put it away. "I'm anxious to be done with this. I want Ben safe and Stone taken down."

Emma reached for my hand and gave it a squeeze.

We stopped at a wine shop on the way to Teuling's place. Emma insisted nothing she had at home would be something Sebastian liked and she would be as fast as possible. I went into the shop to make sure she didn't lose track of time. As I followed her down the aisles, I couldn't stop thinking about the upcoming confrontation with Teuling—or about Ben being in danger.

And why hadn't Joan returned my message? If Jakob and Anne had caught and arrested Joan and Ben, surely Stone would have gloated.

On our way back through the parking lot, Emma and I passed an idling red truck. A campaign sticker that read *Joe Stone: Putting Your City First* adorned the back bumper.

I scowled and motioned back at the bumper sticker. "How can people even like Stone? Are they really willing to put a complete asshole in a seat of power and endanger everyone else just to feel safe? It's ridiculous how easily he's fooled everyone."

Emma shifted her wine tote and placed an arm around me. "I'm sorry you're frustrated and everything is so awful right now."

I slipped my arm around Emma to return the hug. Her comment didn't rid us of Stone, but it made me feel the tiniest bit better. The validation alone felt nice.

We got into her car and started toward the Teuling residence. When we turned onto the expressway, I noticed the red truck from the parking lot did the same.

"Are you sure you want to do this?" Emma asked.

"I don't have any other choice, Em." I watched the truck in the side mirror. "I'm running out of time, my allies are dropping left and right, and now Stone might have Ben."

I frowned at the side mirror as the truck passed a car and pulled up behind us. I took note of the dealer's plates and the make and model of the vehicle. The truck increased its speed to close the space between it and Emma's car.

Emma glanced at the rearview mirror. "Is that necessary? Just pass me already." She slowed down so the truck could pass.

It didn't.

"That's the same truck from the shop's parking lot," I said.

"What? It is?" Emma accelerated, creating more space between the vehicles.

I turned in my seat to look out the back window. Two young men I didn't recognize were in the truck. "Maybe we should get off the highway."

Emma nodded and signaled to merge into the far-right lane to exit. The truck jerked around to our right. It sped up to pace beside her car. She couldn't change lanes. Her eyes widened. "What are they doing?"

I looked out the passenger-side window at the driver. He was laughing at us. Did they think this was a joke? My mouth went dry and my face flushed with heat. "Jackass!" I gave the guy the finger. "Get out of the way!"

The driver responded by edging the truck to the left, closer to Emma's car. My stomach twisted. The space between the truck and my side mirror rapidly closed.

Her body rigid and tilted forward in the driver's seat, Emma twitched her eyes between the road and her rearview mirror. She signaled again and merged to the far-left lane. A ditch served as the median to our left. Emma gave a frantic glance past me out the passenger-side window.

The truck merged across the middle lane to follow us. The driver's friend leaned toward us and made lewd gestures. Both men were still laughing as the driver wove in his lane. Each swing to the left edged Emma's car closer to the shoulder of the road.

Emma was near tears, her knuckles pale. "Why are they doing this?"

I felt helpless, stuck in the passenger seat, only able to watch everything unfold. "It's okay, Em. You can do this. Let's stop. Pull over to the side of the road." At least we wouldn't be moving at such a high speed in a metal box.

Emma sniffled and nodded. Her car's speed dropped as she signaled her intent to pull off onto the road's left shoulder.

The truck swung left and careened into the car's side mirror.

The Prius shuddered.

Emma cried out. She slammed her foot on the brake.

Tires screeching, her car fishtailed.

I grabbed the dash, catching one last glimpse of the laughing men before Emma's car slid off the shoulder into the median and rolled.

My world shrunk to a cacophony of shattering glass and crunching metal. I didn't know which way was up. Something struck me in the chest. My head snapped backward, and my vision went dark.

20

I DRIFTED IN and out of consciousness. At first, I found myself suspended upside-down, my seatbelt cutting into my shoulder and my head pounding. There were blurs of faces and conversation in the back of an ambulance. The whirring of machines, and cold on my exposed legs and arms.

Finally, my eyelids raised and remained open. I rested in a dimly lit hospital room. A machine beeped next to my bed, and some tubing ran from me to an IV. I looked to the side, the movement causing pain in my neck and head.

My grandmother sat in a chair at my bedside. She lowered the magazine she held. "Are you awake, dear?"

"Yes," I croaked. My throat was void of any moisture. As I regained my bearings, I remembered the accident. My heart lurched, and I risked my aching neck to look on the other side of my bed. A privacy curtain separated me from the rest of the room. "Where's Emma?"

"She was a little more banged up than you," Grandma said. "They took her into surgery."

"What!" I started to cough.

My grandmother handed me a Styrofoam cup with a straw. She gave me a reassuring smile. "Emma will be okay. They have to do something for her arm or wrist. I'm sorry, dear, I can't quite remember." She patted my arm. "Did you know Emma's father is a doctor? He's caring for you. Such a talented man."

The supernatural community relied on Charles Artzin, a wizard who excelled at healing, for both his talent and discretion. Emma adored him, but often referred to her parents as "Charles and Susan" when they frustrated her. I wondered how Charles felt about uninsured patients. "Yeah, Em's talent for taking care of people comes from him."

"You already look so much better than when we saw you last night." My grandmother nodded sagely. "Dr. Arztin said you should still rest, though, so your body can heal."

"Wait." I frowned. "What are you doing here?"

"Well, your parents were exhausted from sitting up with you last night," she said. "I came to switch places with them this morning."

"No, I mean, you shouldn't be here. Mom and Dad shouldn't be here." I struggled up to my elbows, clasped the hospital bed railing, and carefully sat up. My body bemoaned the movement.

"Emma had the hospital contact us since she woke up first," Grandma said. "We weren't too far on our way yet, so we simply drove back."

Anger burned the last dregs of sleep away. How much time had I lost stranded in this bed while Ben could be in danger? And now my family returned and remained within Fillip's reach. The dull throbbing in my head forced me to recline back on my elbows again.

It pissed me off.

The feedback from the tether started. *Close your eyes. There's no use in getting out of bed.* That pissed me off further. I gritted my teeth and shoved my body to sit upright in bed. My eyes watered from both the pain and the frustration of the task.

My grandmother leaned forward. "What do you need, dear? Are you in pain? Should I call a nurse?"

What did I need? I thought of the loss of Isaac, and the family and community he left behind. I thought of Joan and her group's efforts to bring about change for the supernatural citizens in Hopewell. I thought of Trish, Nate, Ben, and my family in danger.

I thought of Emma, the person who loved me for who I was, nearly losing her life while helping me.

And finally, I thought of Stone and the tether he'd so easily hobbled me with. I'd been fighting tooth and claw to put him away since Isaac's death. He simply bent a few words, greased a few palms, and now I was no longer whole.

"Alex?" My grandmother stood beside the hospital bed. Her small hand rested on my back. Her touch is all it took for me to burst into tears. My grandmother lowered the bed railing and sat on the bed so she could put her arms around me.

I leaned into her, sobbing. "He keeps hurting people I care about. There's no way to stop him. I'm broken and useless." The pain in my head sharpened, a bright slash from my hairline to the bridge of my nose. *There's no more use in trying. You've lost.*

"Shh, shh . . ." My grandmother rocked a bit, just like she had when I was a little girl. "Who is that? Who is hurting people?"

"Joe Stone. He's the reason this happened." I gestured to the mark on my throat. "I hate him. I hate him *so* much."

"Don't let that fester, dear." My grandmother rubbed my arm. "It will eat you from the inside."

"But I can't do anything about it!" Crying, I rubbed at the spot between my eyebrows. "Everything I learned to be is shut away and out of my reach."

Grandma's tone remained soft. Soothing. "Do you remember when you were in grade school and couldn't go to Amy Schwartz's birthday party because you got in trouble?"

I sniffled and leaned back to look at her. What was she talking about? "No."

"I'm surprised you don't." She smiled. "You were absolutely devastated. You'd gotten in trouble because of a fight at school."

Memories flickered in the depths of my mind. Kids laughing and shouting. The taste of blood for the first time.

My grandmother handed me a tissue. "A boy twice your size tried to lift up Amy's skirt on the playground. You told him to stop. When he didn't, you latched onto his arm with your little nails. You sunk them deep and didn't let go, even after he struck you. The principal said you only released him after the playground monitor hauled the two of you off to the office."

I remembered now. My friend had been screaming and crying. I recalled how the bully's face looked as he tugged at her skirt, his grin an ugly slash of bravado. The playground monitor excused the behavior with "boys will be boys."

I'd met that bully over and over again throughout life. He had different names and wore different faces, but it was the same guy. "I guess I had a low tolerance for jackasses even back then."

My grandmother chuckled. "I guess so. Or you recognized the boy used his size to harm someone smaller than him. And even though you yourself were tiny back then, and he gave you one heck of a split lip, you weren't going to allow him to hurt your friend."

"How old was I?"

"Eight years old."

Third grade and the boy already believed it was acceptable for him to hold down a crying girl and paw at her clothes. "If I stood up for Amy, why wasn't I able to go to her party?"

"Your parents thought you should stay at home and think about the rules you'd broken." My grandmother shrugged. "You're my granddaughter, but you're their child. Even if I disagreed, I didn't interfere. Remember, we all lived under the same roof." She winked. "Though your grandfather did sneak you a slice of pie."

I smiled, my heart warming with love for my grandparents.

"Alex, dear, I had a suspicion, even before your gifts awoke, that your instinct for protecting others would continue to grow. And you have too much of your stubborn grandfather in you to give up." She smiled. "Heaven help the man who steps in between you and what you want."

The room door opened, and someone spoke from the other side of the privacy curtain. "Miss Steward, it's Dr. Arztin. May I speak with you?"

I wiped the last lingering tears from my cheeks and cleared my throat. "Sure."

My grandmother left the bed and took a seat in the chair.

The curtain slid back on its rings and Charles—Dr. Arztin— walked to my bedside, reviewing a clipboard he held. "Do you prefer Miss Steward or Alexandria?" He looked up from the paperwork, took a pen out of his jacket's breast pocket, and studied me with the same clear blue eyes his daughter had.

"Alex." I gave him a break since over the three years I'd been friends with his daughter, I'd only talked to him once. "How's Em?"

"She's out of surgery and in recovery. Her doctor said the breaks in her wrist were clean. They'll heal without issue." He scribbled a few things on the clipboard and set it and the pen aside.

"You can't be her doctor?" I asked.

"It's against the Medical Association's Code of Medical Ethics to treat my family or myself except in case of emergencies." He reached toward my head.

I scowled and leaned away.

He paused, hands held inches from my face. "I'd like to check your neck."

I hesitated.

"Your CT scans were clean, but this is a standard neuro check," he said.

"Okay." I flinched when his hands, this man I didn't know well, came into contact with my skin.

Dr. Arztin turned my head and prodded my neck. "You ladies were lucky. Emma's car almost rolled into the southbound lanes." He reached for the clipboard and scribbled more notes. "Can you stick out your tongue and wiggle it for me?"

I did so. "Did anyone find the bastards who ran us off the road?"

"No. Detective Grey will be here later to speak to you and Emma. He's on his way back from Chicago." Dr. Arztin set aside the clipboard again and held out his hands to me. "Can you please take hold and squeeze my hands?"

I did as he asked. "I have the make, model, and plate number of the truck."

"Be sure to let Detective Grey know. We'll find those men, and I'll personally ensure they're dealt with." He made more notes on the clipboard. "And finally, could you please point and wiggle your toes."

I resituated the hospital gown under the sheets before I flipped the sheet aside. Point. Wiggle.

Dr. Arztin nodded. "Thank you." More writing.

"I think those guys are connected to Joe Stone," I said.

His pen stopped, and he looked over the clipboard at me. His wife, Susan Arztin, was a huge financial supporter of Stone's campaign. "That's a very serious accusation, Alex."

"The guys driving the truck had one of Stone's campaign stickers," I said, "and Stone had already personally threatened my life."

He cleared his throat. "Please pass this all on to Detective Grey."

I didn't want to wait.

"I'm still concerned about possible whiplash or concussion," he said, "but overall you made it through the accident with minimal cuts and bruises."

"How long before I can get out of here?" I asked.

"I'd like to watch you for twenty-four hours, so the earliest will be this evening." Dr. Arztin returned his pen to his pocket. "Any other questions?"

"Can I go outside and get some fresh air?" I asked.

"If, and only if, someone is with you. I don't want you to have a fainting spell and hurt yourself. Ring for a nurse when you're ready, and they'll rearrange your monitors." He glanced at the clock. "Anything else?"

"No." Nothing he could give me answers for. I frowned as I watched him pull the curtain back around and leave.

My grandmother leaned toward my bed, her eyes twinkling. "Your friend Emma has a very attractive father."

"Grandma." My face reddened.

"It's only an observation, dear."

"Where are Mom and Dad? Back at Em's place?"

"Yes. She gave us a house key." My grandmother smiled. "They'll be here when visiting hours start."

I chewed at my thumbnail, checking the clock on the wall.

"Alex," My grandmother reached down beside her to lift her flowered purse onto her lap. She extracted my phone from its depths and handed it to me. "This buzzed while you were trying to rest. Now that you're awake, you might want to check it in case any of your friends are looking for you."

"Thanks." The screen had a starburst-like crack spreading across it from the top right corner, where the case lost a chunk of plastic. I quickly checked my messages. One was from Sebastian a few hours after our accident.

Tired of waiting. Going out.

There were also not one, but two missed calls from Joan. She must have escaped Jakob's and Anne's surprise visit. Like Trish, Joan preferred texting. I switched back to the messages and saw an overlooked text from her.

They have him.

21

MY HEART STUTTERED, and the blood drained from my face.

"Alex, what's wrong?"

I looked at my grandmother. My voice hoarse, I said, "I need to go. I can't stay here."

"You're not able to leave yet. Didn't you hear the doctor?"

I tried to figure out how to get disconnected from all the hospital monitors. My voice threatened to crack. "The man who tried to have me killed has taken Ben, and I don't know what he'll do to him." I wasn't sure if Stone still planned on putting Ben through a Committee trial, or if he would deal with Ben like he did me.

My grandmother frowned. "Oh no."

I grew more frantic and started to get tangled in the wires and tubing.

"Shh, wait a moment." My grandmother picked up a small, box-like device from beside the hospital bed. She pushed a big button with a nurse icon. "Let's go about this in a more discreet way, instead of setting off alarms."

Within a minute, a nurse entered the room and appeared at my bedside. "Can I help you with something?"

"Hello, dear. My granddaughter and I would like to go for a walk together." My grandmother's smile appeared as sweet as they get. "Can you help us?"

The nurse returned the smile. "Let me check what the doctor said." She flipped through my chart and nodded. "As long as you accompany her, you're allowed to walk the campus. There's a pretty garden on the tenth floor or an open-air courtyard on the ground level." An efficient flurry of activity, the nurse hit buttons, flipped switches, and helped me out of bed.

"Thank you," I said.

"You're welcome. Anything else?" she asked.

My grandmother smiled. "No, thank you."

The nurse nodded and left the room.

I sat back down on the bed and messaged Joan.

Sorry I missed your call. Available now.

My phone rang and I answered it.

"Where the *hell* have you been?" Joan's breathing was labored. "I called hours ago."

"Em and I were run off the highway and her car rolled. I'm at the hospital."

A brief pause. "Can you walk?"

I blinked. "I believe so. I'm just really sore and my head hurts a bit."

"I have something for that," she said. "How soon can you be ready?"

I glanced at my grandmother. "I'm ready now. I need a few minutes to get outside."

"Meet me at the northwest corner of the hospital just beyond the entrance to the guest parking ramp. And call Sebastian to let him know we're on our way."

The line clicked and the call ended. I looked at my grandmother again. "I need to get outside. Someone is coming to pick me up."

I pulled the curtain shut and changed out of the hospital gown into my clothes. The nurse had unhooked me from all the machines, so when I pulled the IV, no alarms signaled my intentions to the staff. I tossed the tubing and the medical tape into the trash.

Grandma handed me a Band-Aid. "Are you sure you're doing the right thing, dear?"

"I think so." I frowned, not without a bit of doubt. "Do you have a piece of paper and pen?"

She nodded and offered me both from her purse.

"Here are the truck details of the guys who forced us off the road." I scribbled the info on the scrap paper. "Can you give this to Em so she can pass it to Detective Grey when he gets here?"

"Of course, dear." She tucked the pen and the note back in her purse, then offered me her arm.

I wanted to check-in with Emma, but I'd have to take her father's word that she was okay. There wasn't time for me to stop in her room, and I didn't want her trying to come with me.

My grandmother and I found the location outside the hospital that Joan had described. I pulled out my phone and dialed Sebastian's number. It rang through to voicemail. I hung up and called again several times.

Finally Sebastian, his voice tense, answered. "What the *fuck* do you need that can't wait for me to call you back?"

"Em and I were run off the road last night. The car rolled and we ended up at the hospital," I said. "That's why we never showed up to see you."

The sharp edge left his voice. "Are you both okay?"

"I'm just banged up a bit, but Em needed surgery," I said.

"Which hospital?" he asked. "What's her room number?"

"Sebastian, Em will be okay, but I still need your help. Like, right now. Ben's sister is on her way to pick me up."

"Joan?" he asked. "Why is she coming here with you? Is Ben in trouble?"

"Yes." I cut off his question before he could ask it. "We'll tell you everything when we see you. Is Teuling at the house right now?"

"I don't know," he said. "I'll find out."

"Thanks. We'll be there soon." I hung up the phone.

Joan's car pulled up to the sidewalk where my grandmother and I waited. The passenger window lowered. Joan leaned toward us, eyeing my grandmother. "Who's this?"

"This is my grandmother, Lunella. Grandma, this is Joan Sharpe. She's Ben's sister."

My grandmother smiled and wiggled her fingers. "Hello, dear."

Joan gave a pained smile. "Hello, ma'am." She motioned for me to get into the car.

I turned to my grandmother and gave her a tight hug. "Thanks for helping me . . . and for letting me do what I need to do."

"I was married to your grandfather long enough to understand the support he needed." She kissed my cheek. "Please be careful. I love you."

"Alex! Let's go!" Joan shouted.

"I love you, too, Grandma." I ducked into Joan's car and barely closed the door before she pulled away from the curb. "Sebastian is expecting us." Buckling my seatbelt, I glanced over at her. "Is Ben at Saint Anthony's?"

Joan shook her head. "No. The cops arrested him with a few others during the raid, but they took Ben away in a different car. We've been watching St. Anthony's. Everyone but him turned up there." She gripped the steering wheel, her features pinched and eyes stormy. "Someone will notify me if by any chance he's dropped off."

"Stone has Ben, doesn't he?" The dreaded thought caused the buzzing to begin in my mind.

"I think he does, and that worries me." Joan rolled through a stop sign. "I want to offer Stone Teuling's confession in exchange for Ben."

The noise in my head increased. "We need that confession to prove Stone's involvement with Isaac's murder!"

"We need to get Ben back!" Joan shouted, her cheeks flushed.

I flinched. Of course. We had to save Ben, but Stone would get away. Again. And would he really be happy with only the confession? Wouldn't he want Teuling as well?

"We grab this Teuling guy," Joan said, "take him somewhere we won't get interrupted so we can get the confession, then call Stone."

The tether's awful noise made my eyes water. I nodded and rubbed at my temples, my voice hoarse. "Okay."

Joan glanced at the glove compartment. "There are painkillers in there if you need them."

I opened the glove compartment and several bottles threatened to roll out and fall to the floor near my feet. "On-the-go pharmacy?"

"It's Ben," she said. "He's been clean for almost ten years, but he doesn't want any kind of pills in the house where we're staying, so I'm stashing them there."

"Oh." I turned the bottle over in my hand, thinking of the medicine cabinet in his apartment. Guilt soured my stomach. I'd *teased* him about how empty it was, only containing deodorant and toothpaste.

She spared me a glance and a frown. "I take it he didn't mention anything to you?"

"No." The letters on the medication bottle blurred. "He didn't."

"Yeah, that's my baby brother." Joan shook her head. "It's not just you. He doesn't tell anyone anything. It's infuriating."

I nodded and wiped my eyes with the back of my hand.

She reached over and gave my shoulder a brief squeeze. "You said you and Emma were in an accident. What happened?"

I cleared my throat. "Stone had some lackeys from his fan club run us off the highway last night." I popped a few pills and shut the bottle back into the glove compartment. "I finally pushed Mr. Friendly Neighborhood Politician to his breaking point."

"Yeah, I'm done playing nice with that asshole. He has to go." She glared ahead at the road. "They all have to go."

WE MADE IT to our destination in record time and parked on the street a few doors away from Teuling's house. Joan opened the trunk, took out a roll of duct tape, and handed it to me. "Here, take this."

I looked at the grab bag of items scattered in the car's trunk. "Do you keep an actual kidnapping kit back here?"

She gave me a sideward glance. "I'm not able to simply punch someone in the face to keep them from squirming." She pulled out a few rags, stuffed them into her pocket, and shut the trunk.

Sebastian met us at the same entrance he'd let me in before. He wore his lazy smile. "Joan, it's—"

"Don't talk to me." Scowling, she pushed past him into the house. "Where's Teuling?"

"He's in his study." Sebastian looked at me. "What's happened to Ben?"

Joan started up the stairs. "Where's the study?"

I frowned at Sebastian and rushed after Joan. I grabbed her elbow. "Joan, wait."

She turned on me from the step above and yanked her arm away, eyes blazing. "We don't have time for waiting. Let's grab this guy and go."

"We didn't discuss details," I said. "Should we ask him for the confession first before we tie him up and haul him out of here? It'd save us a lot of trouble." It may also remove Teuling himself from the equation during an exchange with Stone. We could warn Teuling to seek protection.

"He's not going to voluntarily tell us anything. We need to take him somewhere else in case it gets messy." She turned and continued up the stairs.

I frowned and looked at Sebastian. He shrugged in response to my unspoken question. "How the hell should I know what he's going to do? There is a lot of staff in the house right now, though."

I climbed the stairs after Joan and lowered my voice to a whisper. "First double doors on the right."

Joan lowered her voice as well and looked back at Sebastian. "If you want to help Ben, do what I tell you to do." She held out her hand for mine. "You don't have your strength. We need to take him by surprise."

I glanced at her hand and up at her.

She snapped her fingers. "Give me your hand, Alex."

I extended my hand. Her fingers clasped mine, and she began to recite a spell in a poetic cadence. Beginning at the top of her head, her body became translucent, the effect flowing down to her feet. I knew from seeing her cast the spell before that the same would happen to me. We'd be able to see each other as semi-transparent, but neither of us would be visible to anyone else.

"Joan Sharpe: the reason invisibility is the most annoying spell in existence," Sebastian said. "Alex, do you know how many times Big Sister put an end to my fun with Ben with that fucking spell? I'd be aware of that if I were you."

My cheeks warmed. It hadn't even crossed my mind she would use it to spy on us. But she *did* err on the side of overprotective.

Joan ignored him and finished the incantation. "Sebastian, let us into the room and then distract him."

Sebastian leaned against the wall and crossed his arms. "Not until you tell me what's happened with Ben."

"Are you kidding?" She glared at him even though he couldn't see her. "Open. The. Door."

He shrugged, pushed his body from the wall, and started to walk away. "Good luck."

I lost my patience. "Stone raided Joan's hideout and caught Ben. We're planning to hand over Teuling's confession to Stone if he'll give us Ben."

"But first you need Frank to get his confession," Sebastian said.

"Yes," I said.

"If I were Stone and knew Frank gave the confession," Sebastian said. "I wouldn't stop with destroying the recording. I'd want to deal with the source of the confession, too."

I frowned and looked to Joan. Had the thought crossed her mind as well?

"He's right," Joan said. "It's possible Stone won't be happy with a simple recording."

Not only would Stone get away with Isaac's murder again, he may attempt to have Teuling killed. Would it be better to turn Stone over to Fillip? No one else would have to die.

Sebastian drummed his fingers on his arm. "If I help now," he glanced at the study door, "I also want to come along with you to wherever you're taking Frank."

I thought of my conversation with Fillip. *Only Joanna Sharpe.* But Sebastian didn't live in Hopewell anymore. He was visiting. Did Fillip even know Sebastian was a wizard?

"Fine! Quit wasting time and open the damn door," Joan said.

We needed Sebastian's help right now, so I didn't object. Sebastian turned from us and pushed his way through the study doors. "Hello, Frank."

I shadowed Joan as she crept deep into the room toward where Teuling sat at his desk. The invisibility spell made me uneasy. I felt exposed, and yet Teuling didn't react to our presence.

Teuling tucked something away in his desk drawer. A glass of bourbon and a rumpled handkerchief sat on the desk in front of him. "What is it, Sebastian? Does your mother need something?"

"No. She and Julia are out." Sebastian closed the door and strolled toward the bookcase. He poured himself a glass of bourbon, turning to Teuling as he did so. "You don't mind, do you?"

As we drew closer, I noticed Teuling's eyes were watery and his nose and cheeks flushed. He waved a hand at Sebastian. "Of course not."

Sebastian sipped his drink. "You aren't looking well, Frank." He sat on the front edge of Teuling's desk and tipped the top of the picture frame back to peek at it. "Something weighing on your mind?"

Teuling looked at the photo of Julia and himself as well. He shifted in his leather chair and turned his gaze up at Sebastian with a frown. "Feeling a bit under the weather, I guess."

Joan and I had reached Teuling's side of the desk. I covered my nose and mouth, as if my breathing would give us away. Joan's eyes scanned the area where Teuling sat. I pointed at the wheels on his office chair. Joan nodded and mouthed a word.

Ready?

I tightened my hold on the roll of duct tape and nodded. Joan took a step back and launched into an incantation.

Teuling's frown deepened, and he looked to his side, straight through Joan.

"Something wrong, Frank?" Sebastian asked.

"You don't hear that?" Teuling asked.

The corners of Sebastian's mouth curled upward. "Hear what?"

Joan extended a closed fist in front of her body, and then with another spoken word, rotated her wrist with a jerk, as if she were going to give someone a "thumbs-up" sign. The office chair jerked and flipped backward to dump Teuling onto the floor.

He gasped and rolled to his side, trying to free himself from the frame of the chair. I lunged forward and seized his free hand, but his body pinned his other hand beneath it. As soon as my skin made contact with his, the effect of Joan's spell melted away.

"You!" Teuling shouted. "Sebastian, help!"

Sebastian crossed one leg over the other, watching from beneath hooded eyelids our circus of an attempted kidnapping. He took another sip of bourbon.

Joan pulled the rags from her pocket and crouched beside Teuling's head. She blindfolded and gagged the man, dampening his next cry for help.

Meanwhile, I heaved at his body to roll him to his stomach. Kneeling on his back, I tried to grasp his other hand. Joan pinned her weight atop him too. Teuling wasn't a large guy, so our combined weight held him stationary. I pulled his other hand behind his back and wrapped the duct tape around his wrists, securing them.

"His legs, too," Joan said.

Despite being blindfolded, gagged, and his wrists bound, Teuling still flopped about, reminding me of all the fish on his wall. I tried to secure his ankles with the duct tape, but he kicked his legs and nearly cracked me in the chin with the heel of his shoe.

"He's making too much noise." I glanced at the study doors, waiting for someone to burst through them at any moment . . . someone from the house staff or Sebastian's mom, having returned home.

Joan attempted to help and cursed as his foot struck her in the side.

The eerie, echoing murmur of Sebastian's incantation caused a chill to race down my spine. Teuling heard it too and redoubled his efforts to free himself.

Sebastian lowered himself next to Teuling's head. Rubbing his bloody index fingertip and thumb together, he leered down at the bound man. He pressed his thumb to Teuling's forehead. Teuling's body went rigid, shivered, and fell limp.

Sebastian patted Teuling's cheek. "Goodnight, Frank."

I turned wide eyes on Sebastian as he stood. "What did you do to him?"

"Shut him off for now." He smiled down at us, smug. "Brilliant plan, by the way." He pulled a small handkerchief out of his pocket and wiped the blood from his thumb and fingertip. The blood started to disappear from the fabric even before he returned it to his pocket. "I really enjoyed the part where you two seemed surprised he'd fight back."

Fuming, Joan snatched the duct tape from me and bound Teuling's ankles. She glared up at Sebastian. "Why don't you make yourself useful and see if we have a clear path out of here?"

"Ah, how I've missed your warmth and kindness, Joan." Sebastian's hands slipped into his pockets, and he strolled from the study into the hall.

I helped Joan lift Teuling free from the office chair. "You seem to like Sebastian as much as I do."

Joan scowled. "He was Benjamin's best friend and a constant nuisance. They were inseparable." She lowered Teuling's shoulders to the ground in front of the desk, and I did the same with his legs. Joan straightened, flushed from the physical strain of the task. "I've never liked him."

I looked after Sebastian with a frown, hoping I hadn't made a mistake working with him. Even if he lied about his reason for wanting a solo meeting with Ben, Sebastian seemed to want to help him.

Joan startled me when her hand settled on my shoulder. "It's okay. I know you don't have many choices for allies right now."

I nodded and looked down at the unconscious man at our feet. "Ready to haul this guy down those stairs and out to the car without attracting anyone's attention?"

"Yeah." Joan actually smiled. "Let's go rescue my brother."

I'D NEVER GIVEN much thought to how a human body would fit into a vehicle's trunk. A hatchback would have been easier, but we managed to wedge Teuling into the sedan without drawing attention to ourselves.

Until we were driving away with a Committee member stuffed in the trunk, I also hadn't thought of what would happen if we were caught. The realization of those consequences sat like a dead weight on my chest. I'd moved well beyond years added to my tethering sentence. If we were caught and tried by the Committee, I wouldn't be walking away from it.

I gnawed at my thumbnail, lost in thought, when Joan asked, "Does Stone know his plan to kill you failed?"

"I would think so," I said. "I'm not sure, though. Seems like a task you'd follow up on."

Joan grinned and I smiled.

"Do you know what you're going to say to Stone?" she asked.

"Our first priority is getting Teuling to come clean to us," I said. "Then we'll actually have a recording to threaten Stone."

Sebastian snorted from the backseat. "It'd mean Frank would have to admit he made a mistake." Sarcasm thickened his voice. "Frank's never wrong about any choices he's made."

I turned in the passenger seat to look at him. "You do realize by helping us you're a criminal in the eyes of the Committee, right? Aren't you worried about getting tethered?"

"No." Sebastian lounged with his arms resting across the top of the seat. His head leaned back so he could look up through the back window.

Joan frowned at the rearview. "Vissers don't get tethered."

Sebastian lifted his head and pointed at Joan. "Correct." His gaze slid to me, a corner of his mouth quirking upward. "We're not a pack of wild animals."

I clenched my jaw. "Joan is wanted and Ben faces a possible death sentence. Their grandfather is a member of the Committee, and that doesn't protect them. Why are you so confident you'll be safe?"

"Reginald is an exception. He chooses to follow the rules instead of enjoying the system that benefits families like his and mine," he said. "He probably believes it makes him a better person than the rest of us."

The awful buzzing descended on my mind. "That imbalance doesn't bother you?" I wondered how Anne and the Hunter's key fell within the rules, but I wasn't sure Reginald gave the item to her.

"What does it matter if it does or doesn't?" He chuckled. "I can't do anything about it."

Joan looked in the rearview at Sebastian. "He's comfortable. Why would he want it to change?"

Even though I had to call Emma out every now and then for overlooking the advantages she had as a wizard, she at least tried to learn and help. I exhaled aloud, turned to face forward, and scraped at the chipped polish on my nails. "After we take down the Committee, something new can be built, and it won't matter what your family's name is."

"Yes," Joan said. "Change will finally take hold."

"I've heard that since I was a kid." Sebastian sighed and rested his head back again. "I'll believe it when I see it."

Within ten minutes, we'd crossed the river to the west side and arrived at the three-story warehouse Joan had selected as our interrogation site. We drove through the small gravel lot and parked in front of the blond brick building.

"They used to manufacture flypaper here," she said, "but now it's only used as studio space for artists."

"You couldn't find a place that wasn't being used?" I waited by the car's trunk as Joan unlocked it.

"We already know the layout here," Joan said, "and we arranged for it to be empty."

"We?" I glanced around the vacant lot and building exterior.

"Several people at the meeting wanted to help put an end to the Committee, but they didn't want to be around you when we dealt with this guy." She grasped Teuling's armpits and looked at me. "Others believe you led the Committee's cops straight to us."

My face flushed. "I told you, Fillip gave away your location! His network of spies is enormous." I grabbed Teuling's ankles and helped to lift him out of the trunk. We lugged the unconscious man toward the building. "I had no idea someone followed me."

Did Fillip know about the car accident? Had he sent any of his people to keep an eye on the hospital? My stomach lurched. Did he know my family was still in town?

"That's what I told them." Joan struggled with the door a few moments before glaring over at Sebastian. "Hey, some help here?"

He strolled to the warehouse, pulled open the door with a dramatic flourish, and held it for us.

Joan glared at him as we passed. We carried Teuling to a metal stairway. "Third floor and then to the left," she said.

We schlepped Teuling up a stifling hot stairwell and turned through a doorway. It opened into a sunlit, vacant space with high exposed-beam ceilings. A wall of high windows faced the parking lot.

Joan and I propped up the still blindfolded and gagged Teuling in a chair in the middle of the room. We stood panting and sweating to catch our breath. The air in the room felt only slightly less warm than the enclosed stairwell.

I pulled up another chair to face Teuling. "Any idea how long it'll be before he's awake?"

Joan shook her head. "Sebastian would know, but I can't look at him right now without wanting to strangle him."

"Would that be a bad thing?" I asked.

She laughed, the sound expelling the tension from around us.

Smiling, I said, "I'll go talk to him." I left Joan with Teuling and went back outside. Sebastian, sitting atop the sedan's hood, didn't look up from his phone as I walked up to him. "How long before your stepdad is back with us?"

His shoulders briefly lifted. "Don't know."

I snatched the phone from him. "Are you here to help get Ben back or not?"

Sebastian rested back on his hands. "I wouldn't be spending time with you otherwise."

My eyes narrowed. "So I'll ask again . . . When is Teuling going to be conscious?"

His chin dipped, his gaze settled on me, and a smile curled his lips. "Ten minutes, give or take a few."

Goddammit if I didn't blush. "Drop the charm bullshit and pay attention, Sebastian."

His eyebrows rose. "No charms here. That only gets me a hot drink in the face."

What the hell? My face blazed. I tossed his phone back at him and blurted. "You're so damn annoying. I don't know how anyone can stand being around you."

"Me?" He chuckled. "People love being around me."

"Ben doesn't seem to," I said.

Sebastian's smile vanished, and his fingers tightened around his phone.

I shrugged. "In fact, I'd never heard your name until you and I met. He and I have been together for over six months."

Something shifted in Sebastian, and his unyielding gaze held the same unnerving intensity I'd noticed when he'd tried to break my tether. He spoke slowly, as if considering each word before he said it. "Now you're being cruel."

I turned and walked toward the warehouse. An awful sense of satisfaction warmed my chest.

The next ten minutes dragged by while we waited for Teuling to regain consciousness. When he did, he whipped his head to the left and right, like it would help him sense where he was. Joan removed the cloth secured around his mouth.

I sat down in the chair opposite him and got out my phone. "Teuling, we need something from you."

His face swung toward me. Sweat beaded on his upper lip and dampened the blindfold at his temples. Teuling's features were tight, and his words rushed. "What is it? Money? Property? Just let me go and we can work something out."

Arms crossed, Joan scowled at him.

"Tell us about Isaac Laska," I said.

Teuling paled. "Who?"

"Isaac. Laska."

"I can talk to the Committee," he said. "Explain to them that it was all a big misunderstanding. You were a guest of my stepson's. That's why you were in our home."

"Isaac. Laska," I repeated.

Teuling licked his lips. "I don't know anyone by that name."

"You're wasting time. Stone turned you in." I lied, but I took the chance. The two men seemed cut from the same cloth when it came to saving themselves at the expense of others. "He knew the investigation by officers DeBoer and Reid would lead to him, so he threw you under the bus."

Teuling shifted in the chair. His feet tested the ankle restraints.

"You're the reason Isaac's dead," I said.

He frowned. Sweat trickled down his temples and along his jawline. "Look, what happened to the kid is unfortunate."

"Unfortunate?" The buzzing in my head grew louder. My patience dwindled. "Your actions got a young man murdered!"

Teuling flinched away from my raised voice. "I didn't kill him! Please, I have a wife and daughter. My wife is sick. They'll be worried about me. Let me go."

"You didn't trust Isaac with your daughter and didn't like the changes he wanted for the Committee, so you had him marked as a target for the Hunter."

"No, I didn't know Stone intended to order the Hunter to *kill* Isaac! Julia refused to end her relationship with Isaac, so I went to Stone." Teuling's voice cracked. "I wanted Isaac tethered so he couldn't turn into a monster around Julia." His body sagged in the chair, and he began to cry. "I didn't know. I wanted my daughter to be safe. That's all. I didn't know."

I looked over the blindfolded and weeping man, remembering how he'd already been bleary-eyed when we found him in the study. "Isaac had a family, too," I said. "He had parents and a little sister."

Teuling shook his head. "Please, stop. Let me go."

I managed to keep my voice conversational. "It must be awful knowing you played a part in taking him away from his friends and family."

Joan frowned and mouthed, *What are you doing?*

Sobbing, Teuling nodded.

"Mr. Teuling, you're being given a second chance. You can help Isaac's family find a bit of peace. You're in the unique position to make sure Stone doesn't take away someone else's son or daughter." I swallowed. "If I remove the blindfold and untie you, will you allow us to record your account of what happened to Isaac?"

Joan's eyes widened. "He's going to run."

"No." Teuling's crying subsided. "I won't run."

"So, you agree to letting us record you?" I asked.

"Yes," he said.

I stood and looked at Joan. Cursing, Joan walked away to stand near the room's door. I untied the soggy blindfold and crouched behind the chair to peel away the duct tape binding his wrists and ankles.

Teuling rubbed the raw skin at his wrists and looked around the room. He watched me as I returned to my seat in front of him. Gone from his red and watery eyes was any of the previous anger or fear. In their place was . . . relief?

"Thank you for doing this," I said.

"If I give you this confession, who'll protect me from Joe Stone?" he asked.

My jaw tightened. Of course he'd make sure to save his own neck. But he believed, like we did, Stone would come after him. "We won't let him hurt you. Are you ready to start?"

He took a large inhale and blew out an exhale. "Yes."

I raised my phone and started recording. Teuling gave his confession, a complete and detailed recount of the plan to rid himself of what he viewed as a threat to his daughter. Memories of Isaac, finding his discarded body, and the sense of loss among the wolves left in his passing overwhelmed my mind. So did the screeching noise of the tether.

When Teuling finished, I stopped my phone and rose from my seat. I trembled as I walked from the room. Once outside, I took gulps of fresh air to clear my head and settle my stomach, but it was no use. I covered my ears against the painful uproar the tether directed into my head, doubled over, and dry heaved.

I wanted all of this to be done. For people to stop getting hurt. For my mind to be quiet. I wanted to close my eyes and not have to open them again.

Do it. Give up.

"What happened?" Sebastian's voice came from the direction of the car.

Footsteps crunched on the dirt and gravel. I expected Sebastian, but Joan crouched beside me. "I bound Teuling's wrists and ankles again. I still don't trust he won't run otherwise."

I nodded. "Okay."

She rested her hand on my back. "I'm sorry you had to relive that. Take a few minutes, and then we'll call Stone."

I chanced looking at her. "Thank you."

Her expression, dark brows pinched together over blue-grey eyes, reminded me of Ben. I bit my lip, and her image blurred. She leaned toward me and encircled me with her arms.

JOAN PLACED HER phone on speaker and called Stone.

"Hello, this is Joe Stone."

Joan spoke before I could. "I want my brother back."

"Can't do, Miss Sharpe. We need him as insurance for something we have in the works. Then he'll be delivered to St. Anthony's for violating his sentence."

"Hello, Joe," I said.

The line remained silent for a moment. "Miss Sharpe, I'm willing to strike a deal with you. You hand that creature over to me, and I'll give you back your brother."

Joan glanced at me as if considering the offer. She may be able to overpower me since I couldn't fully tap into my werewolf abilities. And my broken Shield gave her the option to use her magic, not requiring her to exert any physical effort.

"No," I said. "We have the better offer." I played part of the audio recording of Teuling's confession. Dead silence on the other end of the phone line. "Bring Ben to us, and we'll hand over this recording."

Stone's tone darkened. "We've been here before, Alexis."

"We'll give you the recording and Teuling himself," Joan said. She stared at the phone, avoiding looking at me. We knew it was something he might want.

"Now I feel we're approaching more of a win-win," Stone said. "Where should I meet you?"

Joan gave him our location. "If you bring either of the cops, or anyone else for that matter, we're done. We'll disappear, and that recording will be sent to everyone on the Committee."

"I'll be there." The call disconnected.

I frowned at Joan. "I told Teuling we'd protect him from Stone if he gave us his confession."

"I don't care." Joan glared at me. "Stone wouldn't have come otherwise. I want Benjamin back and safe. Don't you?"

"Of course I do! But what if Stone kills Teuling?" A low static spun up inside my head. Was it too late to bring Stone to Fillip?

"I'm sure he's planning on it." Joan frowned. "And I *still* don't care. Why would you? We have what we need from him." Joan motioned to Sebastian. He lay on the hood of her car, possibly asleep. "Even his stepkid hates him."

"I've told you before. I don't kill people, and that includes setting them up to be killed." I felt a small twinge of guilt, remembering my fleeting hope Fillip would dispose of Stone.

"You're seriously hung up on honoring your promise to Franklin Teuling? The man who gave Stone Isaac's name!" Joan shouted. "I thought you asked everyone to be all in, Alex. You wanted our help to take down the Committee. I need you to be all in, too, because I'm going to do anything to get Benjamin back from Stone."

Wincing, I rubbed at my temples. I hoped I could be of any use at all with the faulty tether. "You know I'll do what I can."

Joan studied me, weighing my words as if she didn't quite trust them. "I hope so." She strode back into the building.

"Isn't she pleasant?" Sebastian sat up and slid off the car's hood. "Was always a bit intense."

"Please don't bother me." I paced beside the car and shot agitated glances toward the street.

"When are we expecting Joe Stone to roll in?" Sebastian asked.

"Soon," I said. "You should make yourself scarce so he doesn't see you."

He shrugged. "So he sees me."

I stalked over to the car, my head already a shitshow from the tether's feedback. "He won't be expecting anyone other than Joan, your stepdad, and me. You'll be better use to us if you stay out of sight, and then help if we need it."

"Ah, I see," he said. "Good point. Just try to do better than your less-than-stellar performance in Frank's study."

"If you goof off, and Ben gets hurt—" I couldn't find the words to describe the misery I'd bring down on Sebastian. "Now go."

He held up his hands. "Calm down. I thought you'd want this first." He passed me an envelope with the elegant handwriting I'd come to dread.

I snatched the envelope from him, my eyes wide. "What's this?"

"An old bag lady brought it for you," Sebastian said.

The open envelope ripped in my haste to extract the note inside. "Why would she give it to you instead of me?"

"I told her to," he said. "Is it from the vampire you mentioned?"

I numbly nodded. On the folded piece of paper was a single sentence, followed by a location and time. *Bring Stone to me or Lunella will not return.*

Ringing began in my ears, and my knees weakened.

"By the look on your face, this Lunella person is important to you," Sebastian said.

My voice sounded distant. "She's my grandmother."

"I'll go with you. I wanted to meet this Fillip anyway," he said. "I'll help you take Stone to him."

I looked from the shaking note in my hand to Sebastian. "Joan thinks we're going to swap Teuling and the recording for Ben."

"All Joan cares about is Ben," he said. "We make sure Ben is safe, then you and I can take Stone to your vampire. Otherwise your grand—"

"Please go." I shook my head and looked back toward the street so he couldn't see the tears filling my eyes. "Stone will be here any minute."

"Give it some thought," he said. "I'm a persuasive guy. I could broker some sort of deal with Fillip to get your debt reduced." Gravel crunched as he left around the corner of the building.

My mind spun with thoughts of my grandmother being held against her will. White-hot anger unfurled inside me. I pressed on my temples, clenching my teeth against the shrieking of the tether. Through measured breathing, the awful sound in my head dulled to a faint whine.

Like Sebastian said, I'd make sure Ben is safe and then disable Stone and take him to Fillip . . . alone. I'd have one last chance to convince Fillip to let me turn Stone over to the Committee for the murder of Isaac.

Not a few minutes later, Stone's car pulled into the lot. I waited at the front door of the building and watched the sleek car crawl toward Joan's dusty rental. When the vehicle parked, the back driver's side door opened, and Stone stepped out. He'd employed a driver.

Stone walked behind the car to the passenger side. He opened the back door. His lips moved as he spoke to someone in the vehicle. Ben stepped out of the car. His mouth was gagged, and his hands must have been bound because he held them behind his body. Ben saw me and his eyes widened.

Rage erupted inside of me, and the backlash in my head stung behind my eyes. I'd have to keep control, otherwise the tether's feedback would turn my brain into mush and render me useless. There'd be no way I could help Ben, grab Stone, and face Fillip.

Stone closed the car door and urged Ben forward with a prod at his lower back. He halted a good distance from me and grabbed Ben's shoulder.

Ben flinched, and his steps faltered to a stop. His chest rose and fell in short bursts.

Stone's tone remained dark. "Where's Teuling?"

I jerked my thumb over my shoulder, focused on keeping my voice steady. "We're upstairs on the third floor."

Stone frowned. "I'm not leaving my back open to you."

I backstepped. "I'll see you up there, then." Once I'd passed into the building, I jogged up the stairs and walked across the large room to where Joan stood beside Teuling. "He's here and on his way up."

Joan frowned when she saw me. "What's wrong? Is Ben with him? You look like—"

"Miss Sharpe." The shadows of Ben and Stone fell across the doorway. Stone saw Teuling and his features twisted into a scowl. Stone transferred the anger to a nasty jab in Ben's back, and they both entered the room to cross toward us.

Joan's hands clenched, and she vibrated with fury beside me. Teuling shrank back into his chair and averted his gaze.

Joan cut the binding at Teuling's ankles, grasped his arm, and pulled him from the chair. "Let him go, Stone," Joan said. "Then we'll send Teuling over to you."

Teuling's eyes widened, and he looked at me. "What!"

Stone smirked, his tone flat. "Frank, I thought we'd worked past your concerns."

"No! Whatever these women said about me, they're lying." He struggled against Joan's hold. "They kidnapped me from my home and were holding me hostage."

I took his arm from Joan. "I'll walk him over." She might attack Stone, no matter how awful the idea was. And then Ben might be hurt.

Joan hesitated, studying me before releasing Teuling and letting me guide him forward.

I was less than ten feet from Stone when he said, "Stop there." He flashed his artificially whitened grin. "I've lost some trust in you. You have this awful tendency to attack me. I suppose it speaks to the true nature of your kind."

I frowned. "Let Ben go and I'll release Teuling."

Stone's grin didn't falter. He locked eyes with me as he said, "Kneel down, Sharpe."

Ben lowered himself into a kneeling position, revealing the handgun Stone had hidden behind Ben's body. Stone aimed it at the back of Ben's head.

Joan cried out. My mind exploded into panicked chaos. Tears leaked from my eyes from the pressure. My body started to shake.

"Alexis, be a sweetheart, and send Mr. Teuling over to me," Stone said.

I couldn't believe he was going to win. Again.

I squeezed my eyes closed against the pain and frantically sought out my inner wolf. My throat spasmed, and I choked.

"Now!" Stone shouted.

I wiped at my leaking eyes and shoved Teuling toward him.

Teuling stumbled forward. His voice trembled. "Joe, I can ex—"

Stone raised his arm, and the gun popped.

An awful grunting noise came from Teuling, and he crumpled to the dusty floor. Stone swung his arm to point his weapon at me.

With a shouted word from Joan, the gun twisted in his hold before he could fire it again.

Ben dropped to his side and looked back. He nailed Stone in the ankle bone with the heel of his boot.

Stone swore, buckling from the pain, and lowered the gun to point at Ben.

I leapt forward past Ben, throwing my weight into Stone.

He stumbled away from Ben, holding the gun out of my reach.

Another shout and an abrupt gesture from Joan, and the gun spun out of Stone's grasp. The weapon zipped like a bullet toward the tall windows. With shattering glass, it exited the building for the parking lot below.

I didn't have my normal strength, but I tapped my boxing drills with Anne and the hours of training with Trish and Nate. Stone saved his nose from my first punch, but that allowed me to swing a hook around to collide with the side of his mouth. He raised his hands to shield his face again. I jabbed him in the side. Stone staggered backward.

"You messed up." My knuckles and wrists throbbed, but the adrenaline curbed the pain. "There's no way you're getting away with shooting a Committee member in front of an audience."

Cruelty colored his laugh. "You stupid bitch. What don't you understand?" He wiped blood from the corner of his mouth and thumped himself on the chest. "I *am* the Committee. I can shoot whoever I want and *still* be elected mayor!"

Movement by the door caught my attention, and Stone's driver appeared behind him. The man leveled his gaze and a handgun on a target over my shoulder. I glanced back. Joan had released Ben from the gag and untied the rope that secured his wrists.

"Joan, the doorway!" I shouted.

She jerked her gaze toward the driver, the rope still clutched in her hand. Ben seized her wrist and yanked her back behind him. His lips moved. He swung his hand in an upward arc. Ben's tether blazed to life with a hot glow.

The driver's gun fired.

Ben grasped at his throat, and his knees buckled. The bullet struck a type of invisible barrier in front of him and Joan. Electric blue light sparked at the point of impact. The collision drove Ben backward into Joan.

The raging in my mind verged on unbearable. Large dots began to obscure my vision.

I turned on Stone, who screamed at the driver. A leg swipe Nate taught me brought Stone crashing to the ground onto his back. I dropped my knee to his breastbone and pulled back my fist. My instinctive reflex to reach out to my inner wolf was awarded with a small blossom of warmth in my chest.

Another gunshot sounded, and something punched my shoulder. I looked down to see a hole in my shirt. Blood seeped up out of the wound and bloomed around the wrecked fabric.

I'd been shot. My attention snapped to the man in the doorway. His gun was pointed at me.

A pale skull materialized behind Stone's driver. Sebastian emerged from the dark doorway. His lips barely moved as he cast his incantation.

The driver's eyes widened. He spun around.

Sebastian closed blood-marred fingers around the barrel of the gun. The weapon immediately crumbled apart. It fell from his fist as rust-colored dust.

Stone took advantage of the distraction. He shoved me off him and delivered a punch of his own. The strike to my midsection left me curled up and gasping for air.

Stone stood unsteadily, his chest heaving. He reached down to seize the front of my shirt collar. With a grunt, he pulled me to my feet. Stone twisted the fabric in his fist and dragged me toward the tall windows.

Choking and growling, I kicked and threw my weight around to jostle loose from Stone's grasp. My senses started to blend together, adding to the ongoing riot in my brain. I let my knees buckle so my body became dead weight.

Stone expended more effort and lifted me up toward the sharp edges of the broken window's ledge.

A tingling sensation raced over my skin. At another shout from Joan, the remaining glass still clinging to the frame were blown out. I squeezed my eyes shut to keep them safe from the shards that showered down.

Stone glanced back over his shoulder, cursed, and turned his attention to me. His eyes were wild, the whites visible, as he pushed me back over the window's edge. "If the Committee isn't going to do its job and get rid of you, I'll do it myself."

I redoubled my efforts to free myself, but I only had my legs available to kick at him. My hands were busy preventing him from strangling me with my own shirt. As a werewolf, I had a good chance surviving the nosedive to the parking lot Stone intended to send me on. As a tethered werewolf, I wasn't as confident.

Stone's hand caught my pant leg. He heaved me upward.

My feet left the floor, and my balance tipped back out the window. Panting, tears running down my cheeks, I locked gazes with Stone.

His cruel grin was triumphant.

Deep within my core, she thrashed. I cried out from the sudden searing agony at my throat, but it didn't stop the warm flood of strength through my body. Sebastian's attempt at breaking the tether had weakened it enough. She heard me. The tether could hobble us, but it could no longer separate us.

The look of victory in Stone's eyes shifted to one of doubt. Then to one of horror.

It must have been my eyes that gave us away, that made him realize he hadn't been able to keep us apart. I grinned, and my canine teeth lengthened.

I've always struggled to hide my eyes.

The tether fought back, and my throat spasmed. Choking, I directed my fury and strength into shifting my hands. I welcomed the hollow sound of popping cartilage and the dull ache in my knuckles. I released the collar of my shirt and sunk every single one of my claws deep into the flesh of Stone's upper arms.

The scream of pain barely left his lips before I pitched my body backward out the window. We plummeted toward the parking lot.

23

I DIDN'T HAVE as much control over my body as I'd expected while falling from a third-story window. The pain from the tether surged. My hands began to slip back into human form.

Since my claws were no longer hooked into him, I attempted to grab a hold of Stone's arms while he struggled against me. I didn't care if Stone broke a few things, but death offered a Dodge the Consequences Card I didn't want him to have. I reached out to my wolf, hoping we'd be able to absorb some of the impact for Stone as well.

A prickling sensation raced over my skin. Side by side, Stone and I slowed before striking the gravel of the parking lot. An electric-blue web of crackling light radiated across the ground from our point of impact. My shoulder crunched, and my organs felt like they jostled against the wall of my body. The warm, coppery taste of blood flooded my mouth.

Stone moaned beside me. I tried to sit up, but a wave of nausea stopped me. My vision danced with black spots. A shadow fell over us, and a pair of dark shoes entered my line of vision.

"Ben?" My voice was thick from the blood in my mouth.

"No." Sebastian crouched beside me and glanced up at the building. He had the driver's hat cocked atop his head.

"Are Ben and Joan okay?"

"Yes, though I'm sure that spell he used to break your fall didn't feel good." Sebastian smirked down at me. "They'll be down here any minute, and the door won't hold them long. We need to go." He brushed some curls from my forehead with cold fingertips and pressed his wet thumb to my skin. "I'll wake you when we're there."

A soothing calm spread through my body, and I drifted away.

"GOOD NAP?" SEBASTIAN'S sharp features swam into focus.

I sat in the passenger seat of Stone's car, parked someplace I didn't recognize. My injured shoulder, bound in rags, burned as if aflame. A strange haziness fogged my mind. I wiggled my toes, relieved I could do so. Next were my fingers.

Sebastian leaned on the open passenger door, looking down at me. "Before you ask, Joan and Ben aren't here. We don't need them fucking up what we have to do, and that's something Joan does better than anyone else I know."

The scents of metal, blood, and earth filled my nose. "Where are we?"

"At the address Fillip sent you," he said.

"What? Goddammit!" Instantly, the terrible noise inside my head sprang to life. Unlike before, its volume pitched erratically up and down.

"The suspense killed me at first," Sebastian said. "Would she hand over the politician to the vampire? Would she bring me along and introduce me? It's not every day I get a chance to discuss blood magic with a vampire." The edge of his mouth quirked up. "But then I grew bored with waiting, so I made the decision for you."

I pushed him aside, earning me a painful flare in the shoulder, and got out of the car. "It wasn't your decision to make." Stone's car seemed to be the sole vehicle in a short row of parking spaces near the entrance of a wooded city park.

"You're welcome," Sebastian said. "How're you feeling?"

"Surprised to be standing." The pain in my body was bearable, not anywhere near the level I'd expected after being shot and falling out of a building. "Why am I still standing?"

"My guess is a combination of your werewolf stamina, Ben's janky magic, a hangover from my spell, and a hell of a lot of luck." Sebastian's narrow shoulders lifted. "It doesn't matter as long as you're well enough to help carry this guy to our meeting." He pointed past me.

A bloody, bruised, and incoherent Stone sat on the ground. The erratic hitching of Stone's chest expelled wet and ragged breaths. I wished Emma could be with us to stabilize him.

Indecision threatened to paralyze me. I still wanted Stone to stand trial for Isaac's death but knew I couldn't show up to meet with Fillip without Stone. I'd at least haul Stone along with me. With my injuries, I needed help carrying him.

If Sebastian came with me, I took the chance of pissing off Fillip. The vampire had threatened to harm my family if I worked with any wizard other than Joan. But Sebastian no longer lived in Hopewell, so it was possible Fillip didn't know him.

Then the breeze shifted, and my nose picked up the faintest traces of lavender. I snarled, and my attention snapped to the sporadically lit pathway leading back into the woods.

"Grab his feet," I said.

We lifted Stone and started slowly down the path. The instant I reached out to my wolf, the park lights burned brighter and the various aromas of the woods magnified. The tether blazed in response, causing pulse-like bursts of pain in my throat. I covered my mouth to quiet my choking and almost lost my hold on Stone.

Sebastian eyed me. "Do you want me to be the one to talk?"

"Absolutely not." The rich, coppery odor of Stone's fresh blood lured my wolf further to the surface, and the tether lashed out again. My eyes started to leak tears.

"Let me at least introduce myself," he said.

"What part of *hating-wizards-with-every-bit-of-his-undead-soul* don't you understand?" I glared at him. "Don't say anything. I'm hoping we can pass you off as a Commoner."

Sebastian scoffed. "I'm not some—"

"Don't mess this up for me," I said.

Movement and light off the path, deeper in the woods, caught my attention. Twigs snapped under our shoes as we waded through the underbrush into a small clearing. Fillip's huge henchman stood scowling with a flashlight. He had a black eye and a bandaged chin. Beside him, bound, gagged, and looking more pissed than a cat in a bath, was my disheveled grandmother.

"Alexandria, you received my letter." Fillip seeped from the shadows. His eyes shone with reflected light.

I looked between him and my grandmother, my stomach tying itself in knots. The awful noise created by the tether spun up in my head.

"What happened? I smell blood everywhere." Fillip motioned me toward him with a skeletal hand. "Come closer, child."

Sebastian and I lowered Stone to the ground. I did as Fillip asked, wondering if he would be able to hear my thundering pulse. "I'm here for my grandmother, but I can't give you Stone," I said.

"Yet you brought him to me." His piercing gaze switched to Sebastian. "Who is this one, and why is he here with you?"

"Sebastian Visser, sir." He gave a respectful nod. "It's an honor to meet you."

My stomach cratered.

Fillip's eyes widened, and his liver-spotted face twisted. "Viss—"

I quickly interrupted. "We've decided to hand Stone over to the Committee because of his involvement with the murder of Isaac Laska."

"We?" The question came as a sneer. In quick succession, Fillip appeared next to Sebastian, seized him by the nape of the neck, and drove him to his knees. The driver's hat tipped off Sebastian's head onto the leaf-strewn ground. Fillip's eyes gleamed a vibrant red. "You would conspire against me with a Visser, a wizard, even after my warning?"

Like a rabbit spotted by a predator, Sebastian froze with the whites of his eyes visible. Amazingly, he remained silent.

"Wait!" I held up a hand. "He's just an errand boy. I'm injured and needed help carrying Stone. I'm sorry."

In a jolt of movement, Fillip released Sebastian and stood in front of me. I flinched back. He scrutinized me with his unblinking stare. "Tell me why you brought this wizard to help deliver the politician, but now you wish to renege on our arrangement." His gaze darted to Sebastian and back to me.

I glanced at Sebastian as well and swallowed. "I've had a change of heart. I'll have to find another way to repay my debts." My mind spun through the static noise from the tether to keep ahead of the vampire. "Please, let the errand boy take my grandmother back to the car. You and I can finish this conversation in private."

Fillip stared at me a moment longer before his pallid face split into a grin. "Your naivety never ceases to amuse me. Why do you believe our business deal is so easily rewritten?"

"He won't be any use to you." I gestured to Stone. "We have a confession from one of the Committee members who worked with Stone to have Isaac Laska killed. After that's given to Aiden, any allies Stone has on the Committee will desert him."

Fillip's grin dissipated. His gaze refocused on Stone.

If I could convince Fillip that Stone was a waste of his time, maybe we'd all leave the park alive. "He'll have lost all those positions of power you were hoping to exploit."

"That is a valid point." Fillip's gaze slid back to me. "Unless you were to destroy the recordings."

My throat spasmed, and the words left me as a snarl. "No! He doesn't kill a wolf and get away with it."

Fillip's intense gaze twitched to my tether and back to my face. "Though unfortunate for us both, the loyalty to your pack is admirable." He gave a slight nod. "Then a compromise it will be. Both Stone and Lunella will die."

Fillip's body flickered. He no longer stood near me.

"No!" I rushed to my grandmother, knocked her down, and stood over her.

The henchman lunged. He swung his flashlight like a club.

I ducked, the flashlight whooshing over my head. Warmth and adrenaline charged my muscles. Snarling, I nailed him in the kidney with a punch. He grunted and turned back to swing at me again. I caught him in the temple with a second punch, and he crumpled to the forest floor.

The feedback pitched upward in my head as the tether seared my throat. Choking, I lowered myself beside my grandmother.

An awful, moist choking noise sounded near Sebastian and Stone. Still on the ground, Sebastian had fallen back onto his hands to put distance between himself and Stone. Blood rushed in a dark stream from a large, ragged gash across Stone's throat.

The scent of the newly spilt blood hit me hard. I clenched my teeth. The pressure in my head increased, and my eyes stung with tears. "Sebastian, help him!"

A light breeze brushed over my face. Fillip stared down at me. His lips and chin were dark and glistening. "You wasted my time and damaged my confidence in you, Alexandria. It disheartens me to do so, but I must terminate our business relationship."

I dodged Fillip's long fingers. His knife-like nails severed strands of my hair rather than cleaved open the side of my head. I reached for my inner wolf to shift form. Only sharp pain from the tether answered.

Fillip caught me by the upper arm and dragged me onto my feet. He tossed me like a ragdoll into a stand of saplings. The young trees bowed and snapped as my body crashed through them. I lay on the ground, gasping for air.

The hem of the vampire's long coat rustled plants and leaf litter as he walked toward me. At least he preoccupied himself with me instead of harming my grandmother. "You've had multiple chances to follow the orders given to you," he said.

I tried to roll away to my side, but his shabby boot caught my injured shoulder and pinned it back to the ground. Fillip drove a broken branch through my upper arm like a spike. The tether choked out the sound of my scream.

His smile appeared as red as a circus clown's. "Patricia will be angry with me at first, but she will eventually replace you. I hope her next selection will know how to keep one's word in business."

Sobbing, I tried to jerk the chunk of wood from where it nailed my upper body to the ground. The distortion in my mind raged, but renewed strength charged my limbs.

Fillip lowered himself to a knee beside me. He gently brushed back my hair to expose my throat. "Goodbye, Alexandria."

A rippling sensation rushed along my skin.

Fillip's features contorted. He spun around, hissing, to catch Sebastian's wrist. In a flicker of movement, he had Sebastian by the front of his shirt, lifting him so his boots didn't touch the ground.

It allowed me the time needed to jostle loose the branch sunken into the soil. I focused the agony from both the gruesome wound and the burning tether into shifting form. All my senses were boosted. My ears and canines lengthened, along with my fingers, which now ended in nasty claws.

Fillip glared up at Sebastian. He twisted the shirt's fabric. "You arrogant and conniving creature."

Sebastian choked, his face reddening. He hooked his legs around Fillip's waist. A single word, gasped in his warped voice, left Sebastian's lips. He drove his thumb down into Fillip's eye.

Fillip's inhuman wail echoed around us. He released Sebastian to paw at his smoking and damaged eye. The stink of burning, decayed flesh filled the air.

Sebastian fell onto his back with a thud, gulping for air.

I sprang toward Sebastian, seized his upper arm, and pulled him back along the ground with me to my grandmother. He lay in the dirt beside her as I spun to face the vampire. Flexing my fingers, my heart hammering and every muscle taut, I waited in a crouch for Fillip to move.

Fillip hesitated, his ruined eye squeezed closed as its remains oozed down the papery skin of his cheek. His hunched figure, glowing eye, and blood-stained chin destroyed any illusion he'd fabricated to look human. He glowered at me and, with a blur of movement, vanished.

But not his scent.

My grandmother's muffled cries cluttered the night's sounds around us.

"Hold still," Sebastian croaked at her. "I can untie you."

"Shh . . . quiet." I waited, standing in front of them, scouring the area with all senses.

No snapping twigs. No rustle of leaves. No shifting forms within the shadows.

Nothing.

I exhaled and turned toward the two. "Grandma, are you okay?"

Sebastian had freed her of the gag and bindings at her wrists.

A force slammed into me from behind, and a white-hot pain spread from my back to my abdomen. Fillip's long-fingered hand clasped around my already-injured upper arm.

I coughed.

Blood dripped off my bottom lip onto my shirt.

"I will never understand why you chose to align yourselves with the wizards." Fillip's voice, behind me, whispered. "Be thankful I am merciful and, unlike them, offer you a swift end." He yanked free his nails, like so many blades buried deep in my body, and released me.

I stumbled, collapsed down onto my hands and knees, and fell forward onto my stomach. Sebastian and my grandmother lay motionless beside me. My nose filled with the scent of damp earth, decaying leaves, and my own blood. The edges of my vision melted, and I receded into my body. Fell backward and far below.

DARKNESS AND COLD, like a deep well. Somewhere quiet where I could be alone and finally sleep.

Or so I'd thought.

Hesitant footsteps startle me awake. No one is meant to find me here. I was locked away so long ago. They believed me to be too large. Too loud. Filthy in my unapologetic nakedness.

Dangerous.

I'm frightened. And furious.

A young woman approaches. I growl and snap my jaws at her, straining against the bindings keeping me in my place. Mud and the scents of spring cover her running shoes. Terror is frozen in her hazel eyes.

Recognition breaks through my deep-seeded heartbreak.

My rage.

She was younger when I saw her last. Smaller. Still fresh with promise and full of brazen curiosity. We ran as one, howling and leaping. Our hair snarled with wind, and our knees bloodied by adventure. Every shared cell vibrated with life. Freedom.

Until I was stripped away. Severed. Buried in the depths of this darkness.

Had she forgotten?

I am her, and she is me.

The young woman inhales. She reaches out to pull one of the straps impeding me. Her voice trembles as much as her fingers.

"I've found you," she says. "You'll be okay."

I exhale. As the bindings fall away, I swear I'll never allow myself to be torn from her again.

"I'll protect you," I say. "You'll be safe."

They tried to separate us with magic symbols and restraints woven of words. They'll continue to try. But they will fail.

We will always find each other again.

Woman and wolf. One body. One mind. One heart.

I STOOD, A hulking figure in the dark forest.

The adrenaline from shifting form dulled the pain from my injuries. It quieted the torment of my bones and muscles breaking and tearing . . . stretching and realigning. My balance shifted. Tattered clothing lay scattered over the ground, and a sleek coat of gray fur covered my body. Both my hands and feet were larger. Taloned. My jaws were elongated, distorted, and full of sharp teeth.

Unlike the previous two times I shifted this far from woman to werewolf, I knew this body. I remembered it. Strong, alert, and agile. Capable of so much. Deadly.

It was my own.

It had always been my own.

My nostrils quivered, decoding the night air until it gave the location of my target. A deep growl rumbled like thunder in my massive chest.

Fillip spun from where he hunched over Sebastian. He raised a hand to protect his face.

My serrated teeth snapped down upon his forearm. I yanked him off his feet and shook my head, an abrupt and contained movement that whiplashed Fillip's body. Broke bones.

He hissed and sliced at my muzzle with the razor-sharp nails of his free hand.

I tightened my jaws and, with a damp crunch, separated his forearm from his body.

Fillip fell to the ground, keening like an injured animal. Bitterness filled my mouth. I opened my jaws to let the vampire's limb drop from my tongue onto the forest floor.

He rolled to his stomach and made it up to his knees, only to be driven to the dirt again by a swipe of my huge, clawed hand. I stepped on his back to hold him against the ground and sunk my teeth to the canines into his shoulder. With a swift jerk of my chin, I tore fabric and flesh away from his body.

The vampire flailed beneath my foot, screaming. A part of me wanted to end him, to release him . . . to let it be known by all what happens when you fuck with my family. Nate had assured me vampires don't heal when they're missing their heads.

But who would step into the void Fillip left? Would it be someone more dangerous? Someone without Fillip's predictable code of conduct?

I stepped back. The hunk of cloth and meat drop from my jaws. When he struggled to stand again, Fillip shrank away from me. He hissed and bared his fangs. I snapped at him, but my jaws closed around empty air. His figure blurred and was gone.

Lifting my shaggy head, I tested the air with my nose. Fillip's scent had vanished as well.

I returned to my grandmother and crouched beside her. She lay pale and still. Her eyes were open, and blood smeared her bottom lip. No breath visibly moved her chest.

A giant fissure seemed to split inside me, and a long whine left my body.

Sebastian sat up, blinking and gasping. Getting onto his knees, he grabbed his handkerchief from his pocket. He reached toward my grandmother's face.

My hackles rose, and I growled. I drew forward to block her tiny body from him.

He waited, watching me. "The spell suspended her pulse to hide her from Fillip." He motioned toward her with the handkerchief. "If you want her to live, I need to wake her."

I backed away and stood. Sebastian whispered a word that made my skin twitch. He wiped the blood from my grandmother's lip. Instantly, color bloomed in her cheeks. She wheezed and sputtered. He helped her sit upright.

Frowning, her bun and glasses askew, she squinted at Sebastian and immediately demanded. "What happened! Where's my granddaughter?"

Sebastian chuckled. He pointed past her at me.

"Oh, Alex!" Her hand flew to her heart, and her eyes filled with tears. "You look *just* like your grandfather, dear."

A crashing through the understory caused me to spin and face the woodline. I crouched, growling, waiting for Fillip's form to emerge. If he wasn't going to leave us alone, I'd have to separate him from his head after all.

Instead, familiar, nonthreatening scents wafted to my nose.

Joan and Ben ran out into the small clearing. They both drew up short when they saw me, eyes wide. Joan seized Ben's arm and pulled him back toward her.

I wasn't ready for Ben to witness this part of me, the part so many saw as a monster. The shift back to human form would be unpleasant, too. I turned to escape deeper into the woods.

"No, wait! Alex." Ben rushed forward but halted a few steps away. "Are you okay? We heard screaming."

"She drove off Fillip." Sebastian stood and helped my grandmother to her feet.

Ben looked from them back to me. He swallowed and took those last few steps to stand in front of me. With one snap, I could crush him between my jaws. He lifted his hand, reached out, but then paused as if he wasn't sure he was allowed to touch me. "Your face is bleeding."

I didn't know how to communicate in this form. I lowered my shaggy head and pushed my forehead against his chest, keeping my claws clear of him.

Ben chuckled. His hand brushed up the length of my nose, between my eyes, and back behind my ear.

His light touch eased the flight response in me. I focused on my breathing, assuring myself the immediate danger had passed. My body relaxed . . . and then began to shift.

I made another attempt to slip out of sight. My shaking limbs allowed me a single step before I lowered myself to the ground. Nausea hit me first. The fine coat of fur withdrew.

Then came the pain as my joints popped, slid, and shifted under my skin. I cried out as each leg felt broken before the bones realigned. The claws receded on my feet and then my hands.

The overwhelming feedback of the tether hit me like a bus. I wailed and pounded at my ears with the sides of my fists, trying to vent the pressure.

"Stop!" Ben knelt beside me and caught my wrists. He brought them toward his chest. "Shh . . . Alex, it's okay."

I shook my head and screamed. "It's not!"

He'd already taken his shirt off and held it ready to cover me. Ben let go of my wrists, helped me into the shirt, and pulled me close. I collapsed against his chest, closed my eyes, and tried to curb my tears. Deep inhales of his scent and slow exhales brought the cursed noise in my mind to a tolerable level.

I'm okay. I'm safe.

When my eyelids rose, I looked into the glassy and blank stare of Joe Stone. His corpse lay only several feet away. The sight of Stone's broken body, the lingering taste of Fillip's bitter blood, and the aftereffects of shifting back into human form turned my stomach. Bile rose in my throat, and I urgently tapped at Ben's arm. "I'm going to get sick."

He released me. I crawled a few paces away on my hands and knees and proceeded to get violently ill.

24

I SAT ON the park bench, my teeth chattering, in the toasty summer evening. My skin was clammy, and I couldn't get warm. I huddled closer to Ben's side.

A police cruiser and an unmarked squad car were parked near the other vehicles. Jakob, Anne, and Detective Grey had all been sent to the scene after we'd called Aiden to let him know what happened. Fillip's disgruntled henchman waited in the cruiser.

When I asked Aiden again about the Hunter's key, he confirmed it had belonged to David Eastman. Detective Grey convinced Reginald that Anne needed a magic item for protection in her new line of work. Grey cited Anne's pristine performance record as proof she had the moral stamina needed to carry the key. I still didn't like the idea of a Hunter's key back in the mix.

Ben shifted to tighten his hold and kissed the top of my head. His shirt fell to mid-thigh on me, so Joan found a blanket in her car's trunk to offer a bit more coverage.

Sebastian lounged on Ben's other side, reclined back with his ankle resting on his knee. "How long do we have to stay here?" He watched the medical examiner and his assistant gather their tools before walking deeper into the park for Stone's body.

"They want to question us." Ben rubbed my upper arm. "We wouldn't be in this situation if it weren't for you, Bash."

"I saw an opportunity and took it. Everything worked out in the end." Sebastian groaned. "Can you imagine what I could have learned from that vampire? Fillip seemed older than, well, dirt. I missed out on so much knowledge."

"You're lucky you aren't missing the majority of your throat," I said. "Not much of a mighty necromancer when you're dead."

"Well, that's debatable," Sebastian said. "But thank you for preserving my throat."

"Thanks for keeping Grandma safe with your creepy-ass death magic," I said.

He smiled. "You're welcome."

I pulled the blanket tighter around me. Footsteps sounded at the park's trailhead. Moments later, Anne, Jakob, and Joan emerged from the woodline. Detective Grey had already left to take my grandmother back to Emma's and question her there.

"I'll wait in the car," Joan said as she passed by our bench.

"Mr. Visser, you're with me." Jakob motioned Sebastian to follow him to a bench further away.

Anne waited until the two were gone before she turned her attention to Ben and me. She sat down on the bench. "How're you holding up, Alex?"

I looked at her and sunk my teeth into my bottom lip. The tears came anyway. My emotions were *all-of-them*, and I was exhausted. "Not well."

"Joan Sharpe gave her account of what went on tonight at the warehouse. We got a statement from the thug in the car, too. I'm sorry you had to witness something so gruesome," she said. "I need to question you, but we can go as fast or slow as you want. Let me know if you need a break."

I nodded and wiped my eyes. With Anne so close beside me, an awful pain for our broken friendship stung my heart. "I'm sorry I didn't tell you . . . about me. I miss you."

Her lips pressed into a thin line, and she opened her notepad. The Hunter's key created an ugly bulge on her hand, but Anne didn't need to call on its powers for her conversation with me. "Three years of lying, Alex."

"I never lied to you!"

"Withholding information is still deception." Anne shook her head as she flipped to a new page. "It hurt. It still hurts. I lost a friend, too."

I reached for her, but stopped when I noticed Fillip's still-sticky blood marring the creases of my hand. My stomach heaved, and I withdrew my hand back beneath the blanket.

"But now that I'm part of this," She gave a vague gesture around us, "this other world you live in, I understand why you couldn't say anything to me. Without these laws of secrecy, it could get chaotic fast."

"I'm sorry you were pulled into it," I said.

"I'm not. I feel this is where I'm meant to be right now." She cleared her throat and looked at me. "Miss Steward, can you please tell me your account of what happened here tonight?"

Finally, I could tell Anne everything. I no longer had to hide anything from her. It felt good.

THE FOLLOWING MORNING Ben and I sent my parents and grandmother on their way home to New York. Since Fillip was MIA, I didn't want my family anywhere within Hopewell city limits.

We all exchanged hugs several times over. Mom smiled at Ben beside me. "We would love for you to come along with Alex for a visit."

I internally cringed. My mother didn't know it would be two more years before Ben could leave the Midwest because of his tether. If the Committee collapsed like we hoped it would, maybe that would change soon.

Ben returned her smile anyway. "Thanks, Mrs. Steward. I'd like that, too."

A week passed while Ben and I hunkered down at Emma's place. We were anxiously waiting for the fallout of Stone's death.

Dr. Arztin healed the deceased Stone's throat before the corpse transferred to the city morgue.

His widow ID'd the body, and his death was ruled a suicide. She tearfully admitted to the media how the campaign had been hard on him . . . how he tossed and turned in his sleep, muttering about monsters in Hopewell.

Dr. Arztin's willingness to help gave me the chills. Healing to aid deception? Even when I asked Emma, she seemed eerily comfortable with it. I wouldn't miss Stone and was relieved we wouldn't be prosecuted, but it felt wrong to hide the cause of someone's death.

As hostess, Emma made sure Ben and I rested and relaxed. That meant eating delicious food and sitting poolside in the summer heat . . . after hauling Ben's vinyl collection up to my room, of course. I'd already grown restless with our state of limbo, but Ben contently worked his way through a stack of library books.

The patio door slid open, and Joan stepped outside. "I can't believe you got my brother out into this gorgeous sunlight, Alex." Grinning, she pulled a chair up beside the long lounge chair where I'd been napping.

I smiled over my shoulder at Ben. "Sort of."

He smirked at Joan from his chair beneath a large patio umbrella. Joan stuck her tongue out at him.

"Here you go." Emma handed her a sweating glass filled with iced tea.

Joan squinted up at her and accepted the glass. "Thank you."

"You're welcome," Emma said. "You should stay for lunch."

"No thanks," Joan said. "Too much to do. I'm only here to share Committee news."

I sat up and scooted over on the lounge chair. Emma sat down beside me.

Joan's eyes were bright. "Apparently Teuling's confession was only the beginning of unburdening his conscience. He gave Aiden a list of Committee members who were working on the sidelines with Stone. Representatives resigned like crazy. Rats from a sinking ship! There's no way the Committee can continue. With seven seats gone, they can't even meet quorum."

"They won't assign new representatives?" Emma asked.

Joan shook her head. "No. The members who remained agreed the Committee as it appears now no longer fits the needs of the city Hopewell has become."

"Trish texted me mid-week when she and Nate were released from St. Anthony's," I said. "At that time, she didn't know how much longer the Committee would last. It's gone, then. We're finished." No more fighting. We'd finally be allowed to live our lives in peace like the Commoners.

"Well, we're not finished yet," Joan said. "Now comes the hard part. We have to create a new system that will work for all supernatural citizens in Hopewell."

The task sounded overwhelming to me, but if it kept the werewolves safe . . . "I want to help," I said.

"We'll need all the help we can get," Joan said.

"What does Reginald think of all this?" Emma asked.

Joan winced. "Well, things are a bit tense at the Sharpe household right now. Granddad is struggling a bit. But I think he's relieved that Ben isn't in immediate danger anymore."

I glanced back at Ben. He frowned.

"You're welcome to stay with him, too, Benjamin," Joan said. "You both could."

Ben's body had drawn in on itself, and he fidgeted with the cover of the paperback he'd been reading.

"I think we're good here, thank you," I said.

"The thing with Granddad is he's part of the old guard," Joan said. "He genuinely wants everyone to thrive in Hopewell. He's willing to learn and adapt, and for that reason I'll continue to be patient with him."

Her words made me think again of the Hunter's key Anne carried. Was Reginald, like Detective Grey, only concerned with

Anne's safety? Or did something deeper in him, even at a subconscious level, want the relic in circulation.

I hesitated. "What about everyone who's been tethered?"

"Tethering will more than likely go the way of the Committee, as it should," Joan said. "Everyone's cases will be reviewed."

"Did Reginald say anything about removing mine?" I asked. She smiled.

"They will?" My pulse pounded in my ears. Sebastian's casting of Ben's spell had weakened my tether, but it wasn't enough for me. I wanted to be whole again.

Joan nodded. "Without Stone here to blackmail anyone, the Committee had the few votes needed to repeal the safety laws before the organization dissolved. That means Reginald will remove your tether."

Emma's eyes widened, and she threw her arms around me. I hugged her back, my eyes prickling with tears.

"They're even going to reward my baby brother for fifteen years of good behavior." Joan looked past me at Ben, her eyes shining. "They agreed to remove your tether, too."

"What!" I shrieked, leapt from my seat, and tackled a startled Ben. His chair flipped back and dumped us on the patio. I tried not to squeeze him too tight as we hugged each other, laughing.

BEN SAT OUTSIDE a door in the large hall of St. Anthony's, watching me pace.

"I don't know how you can be so calm," I said, shaking my hands by my sides. "I feel like I want to crawl out of my skin."

He chuckled. "You're excited enough for both of us."

"I barely made it twenty-four hours before I wanted to shake Reginald until he removed the thing." I frowned. "You'd told me once that being tethered felt like you weren't a whole person. I understand now." I wrapped my arms around myself. "I woke up after my tethering and they had taken part of me." I shook my head. "How did you manage being incomplete for so long?"

"I almost didn't, but like you, I had help," he said.

I stopped and hesitated, but I had to know. "Sebastian?"

Ben dropped his gaze. "Sebastian tried, but his type of help turned destructive. Then he left. I slid into a dark place. Joan is the one who pulled me out of the downward spiral."

"I'm glad she did."

Ben looked up and smiled, his blue eyes bright. "Thanks."

My stomach flipped and my face warmed. "Great album, by the way. Did you help write it?"

Ben chuckled again and shook his head. "Felt like it at the time."

I glanced at the door and started to pace. "Do you think it'll be as awful as when they put it on us?"

"I don't know," he said.

I groaned. "What's taking them so long?"

"Alex."

I paused.

"Sit down and relax," Ben said. "I'm sure they'll call us when they're ready."

I walked back over to him, considered the chair beside him for all of a second, and instead settled onto his lap to face him. His hands rested on my hips. I put my arms around his neck and grinned. "I'm excited for this." I kissed the tip of his nose. "And I'm excited for you."

He smiled. "It's going to be strange. It's been such a long time. I hope I can manage it."

The stairwell door opened, and someone cleared their throat. When we looked over, Aiden stood in the doorway. The corners of his mouth dipped downward. "Miss Steward. Mr. Sharpe. If you're not too busy, please follow me."

I wiggled off of Ben's lap, and we stood and walked over to the door. "Why do we have to go to a dungeon for this?" I asked Aiden. "Wouldn't your office work?"

Aiden didn't find my remark as funny as I did. "There is still a need for discretion, Miss Steward. I'd prefer my office administrator's largest concern to be her grandson's standing in the children's choir."

I blinked. Did Aiden attempt something adjacent to humor?

Aiden and I jockeyed for position. He finally released the door to me and descended the stairs. I went next, and Ben followed. The air cooled. Soon we walked along an underground hallway with stone walls.

"Will Ben and I be together?" Not sure of what would happen when they removed my tether, I'd been fretting over it. I knew my body more than ever, understood part of me would always be wolf, but didn't completely trust myself yet.

Aiden didn't bother to turn around. "That is completely up to Mr. Sharpe and you."

"There's no chance I'll . . ." I searched for a different way to say *lose my shit*. "I'll be able to stay in control, won't I?"

"That has been what I've witnessed," Aiden said. "But as Patricia has told you, not many werewolves live to see this day. I'm unsure if what I've seen is the norm or the exception."

I glanced over my shoulder at Ben. "What do you think?"

Frowning, he looked up from the floor as I spoke to him. "I'm sorry?"

"Should we go in there together?" I asked Ben.

Aiden stopped by the door and turned to us.

Ben's eyes widened slightly, glancing to Aiden and back at me. "I, uh, I'm . . ." Suddenly *Mr. Sit Down and Relax* seemed a bit nervous.

Aiden's features softened. "Each of you are bringing your own experiences to this room. It'd be wise to share what you carry with the other. Being vulnerable can be frightening, but it's the best path forward if you plan to walk it together."

I looked at Ben, thinking of the many chances he'd had to run from me and my messy life. Yet here he stood.

"Whatever you decide, Reginald and I will be waiting." Aiden's tone implied he'd prefer not to wait long. He entered the room and shut the door.

I reached for Ben's hand. "Hey, are you all right?"

He gave a shaky laugh and rubbed at the back of his neck. "I'm not sure. This is a little surreal for me."

"It's okay if you don't want me in there," I said. "I understand what he's saying, but I won't be angry if you need more time."

Ben inhaled deeply and looked at the door. He exhaled and squeezed my hand. "I'm ready. If you're okay with it, I'd like you beside me." He looked back at me, and my stomach did that flippy thing again.

I opened the door, and we entered the archaic room together.

Reginald greeted us, his sunny demeanor at odds with the dark and chilly stone room. "Good afternoon!"

Ben's wary look moved from the stone table to his grandfather. He tensed at my side, but for once he didn't immediately scowl at Reginald.

"I'm so pleased this day has arrived, Benjamin, and thankful I can be a part of it," Reginald said. The older wizard's eyes were bright, and he couldn't stop smiling. He looked between us. "Who would like to go first?"

I looked at Ben, struggling between letting him go first and my need to rid myself of the tether. When he didn't answer, I said, "Ben can go. He's been waiting longer."

Ben released my hand and hoisted himself up to sit on the table. When he lay back against the stone, he pulled his knees up since his legs were so long. Ben folded his hands together over his stomach and began to intermittently shake.

Aiden and Reginald approached the head of the table. "Are you ready?" Reginald asked.

Ben squeezed his eyelids shut. He swallowed and nodded.

I stood back from the table but watched closely as Aiden dipped his thumb into a shallow dish of oil he held. Ben flinched when the priest's thumb came into contact with his throat, but his face didn't communicate anything like pain. Aiden drew his thumb in a crescent over the mark Ben had hidden with tattoos.

Aiden stepped back. Reginald shook his head, smiled, and pushed some of Ben's hair away from his closed eyes. The cadence of Reginald's incantation sounded poetic as he recited the words. I anxiously looked at Ben's face. There still wasn't any sign of pain.

Reginald lowered his open palm to within an inch of the tether's mark on Ben's throat. He raised his hand slowly. The symbol, as if hooked to his palm with a string, lifted from Ben's skin.

Ben's eyes squeezed tighter and his jaw clenched.

Reginald closed his hand over the floating cross, making a fist. He turned his wrist and opened his fingers again. The symbol, now a plume of dark vapor, floated upward and dissipated.

Ben's hands clasped the edges of the table. His back arched, and he took an enormous gulp of air, as if his lungs hadn't been full in a long time.

His back dropped to the table. He rolled to his side and started coughing. Reginald placed a hand on his grandson's shoulder. My urgent questioning look at Reginald was met with a nod, and I went to Ben's side to hold one of his hands.

Ben's breath rasped, but he grinned when he opened his eyes to look at me. I blinked, startled by the electric blue color of his eyes. Even as I opened my mouth to say something, the impossibly vibrant hue faded back to a pale grey-blue color.

I helped Ben sit up, and he seized me in a tight hug. Then he started to cry. The tears were the happy kind, though, and when I looked past Ben to Reginald, I saw tears in the older wizard's eyes as well.

Still grinning, Ben drew back. "Your turn, Alex."

My heart did a somersault as I heard his true voice for the first time. I'd expected something like a gentle tenor, but it was surprisingly deep. I grinned. "Say my name again."

He rested his forehead against mine. "Alex."

I almost crawled up onto the table and made out with him right there.

Aiden spoiled my daydream by clearing his throat. "Are you ready, Miss Steward?"

Ben got down off the table, and I hopped up in his place. I settled back against the stone. Unlike my last time here, Ben's body had already warmed the stone. Ben may have been nervous, but I shivered in anticipation.

Having seen the spell prepared and cast over Ben, I thought I knew what to expect. But when Reginald pulled the mark from my skin, it felt as if a long blade were being extracted from the length of my body. I cried out in surprise at the pain.

A moment of relief soothed the hurt, like my body shed a foreign object, something that had walled me off from my true self. The part of me I'd known as my inner wolf flushed throughout my being with a delicious explosion of strength and warmth. It originated at my core and bloomed outward to the ends of my fingertips and toes, leaving my extremities tingling. A low, throaty growl rumbled from my chest and past my parted lips.

Finally, all my senses burst into color. Incredible richness and vibrance filled everything around me. The room lightened, and I could see the crevices of the stone walls. The air was so heavy with a musty dampness, I could taste the moisture in it. I rolled to my side and sat up, every nerve in my body firing.

Ben waited, grinning from one ear to the other. His arms closed around me, and I inhaled deeply. His warm, spicy scent filled my nose and poured down my throat into my lungs. I pressed a kiss or two to Ben's neck before briefly catching his earlobe with my teeth. I whispered something to him that made his body erupt with heat.

Aiden cleared his throat again to remind us of their presence, but Reginald chuckled. "They'll find their way when they're ready, Father." He ushered Aiden from the room, the door latch clicking into place behind them.

25

THE HEAT AND humidity of summer broke, and autumn drew closer. Ben and I, about to depart on a road trip of sorts, waited beside my car in Emma's driveway. We'd moved back to Ben's apartment, but when Trish finally contacted Fillip, she suggested I leave Hopewell as soon as possible. She needed time to smooth out relations with the vampire.

I'd been fired from Rear Window Records. I was disappointed, but I understood how showing up to work is a basic and reasonable job requirement. The owner of the shop adored Ben, so he was excused with the promise he'd get back to work when we returned to Hopewell.

Emma jogged from her house to us. "Okay. I think this is everything." She handed me the canvas tote bag she carried. I didn't have to open it to know its contents. The delicious scent of roasted coffee beans wafted out of it.

Ben leaned over to peek into the bag. "Is that *all* coffee?"

"What if you two stop somewhere that doesn't have decent coffee?" she said. "Do you want to be stuck with a werewolf who hasn't had her coffee?"

"Hell no." Ben grinned at me. "Especially this one. Thanks, Emma." He took the bag to the trunk to find a place for it.

Emma shook her head and smiled. "It's so bizarre to hear him talk. Does it weird you out at all?"

"No. Quite the opposite." I watched Ben and lowered my voice. "Anytime he says my name, I want to jump him on the spot."

Emma laughed. "I wonder how everyone will react at his performances. Do you think people will be asking questions?"

"Probably." I grinned. "But there's this talented surgeon in Hopewell named Charles Arztin . . ."

"Oh, dad will love that," she said.

I looked at the soft cast she wore. "How's your wrist?"

"It's fine." She waved away my concern. "It's mostly for show. Dad repaired the majority of the damage after the hospital discharged me."

"Did he say if they found the two guys who ran us off the road?" I asked.

Something darkened in Emma's eyes, reminding me of her father when I'd told him what happened. "Father has dealt with them. They won't hurt anyone else." Before I could ask another question about the men's shared fate, she smiled and took my hand. "But let's not waste any time thinking of them. How're you feeling?"

With no tether blocking my healing abilities, my body mended. "Only my shoulder and lower back are still stiff."

"How is everyone else?" Her eyebrows drew together. "I haven't seen or heard from anyone since our lunch together."

"Do you mean 'How's Sebastian'?" He'd been invited but didn't show up for the meal.

Emma's arms settled around herself and she shrugged. "Him too, I guess."

"After the questioning at the park, I haven't seen him." I glanced past Emma to where Ben closed the car trunk. "Ben met him at The Beacon for coffee."

"You were okay with that?" she asked.

"I guess Sebastian apologized for how he'd left things between the two of them. Ben told me not to worry about it." I looked back to Emma. "It scares the hell out of me, but I chose to trust him."

Emma smiled.

"When Teuling gave his confession, he mentioned his wife is sick," I said. "I wonder if that's another reason Sebastian is visiting Hopewell." I remembered Sebastian's defensive behavior when I asked about his mother. "If you see him, maybe there's something you or your dad could do to help."

"Maybe." Emma's smile twitched, and she tucked a strand of hair behind her ear. "How are the others?"

"Trish, Reginald, Joan, and the few remaining members of the Committee are busy deciding where we all go from here," I said. "I wish I could stay and help."

"There'll be plenty of *rebuilding our society* or whatever to do when you get back," Emma said. "Go practice some self-care."

"Yeah." I smiled at Ben as he rejoined us. "We thought a trip out to visit my family would be fun, and he already has a few shows booked along the way."

"I'm so envious." Emma mock pouted. "I wish I could be your roadie."

"We couldn't afford you." Ben chuckled and shook his head. "I hope I make enough along the way so we can eat."

Emma beamed at us and squeezed my hand. "Off with you, then! But of course text me whenever you can so I know exactly what is going on and all the fun I'm missing."

"Thank you for being amazing." I hugged her. "I love you, Em."

She hugged me as tight as her little body allowed. "I love you, too."

Ben and I got into the car and started toward the highway. Being a midweek afternoon, traffic on the highway was light. Warm air whistled in through cracked windows, a perfect accompaniment to The Shins crooning from the speakers.

The city skyline disappeared from the rearview mirror, and I was thankful for the small twinge of homesickness I already felt. On our return, I'd help build a new path forward for my community and other supernatural citizens in Hopewell.

But first . . . I glanced over at Ben. He watched the world pass outside the passenger window, the pleasant breeze making a dark hurricane of his hair. I smiled. "Hey, Ben?"

He turned his attention to me, mirroring my smile. "What?"

"If this trip goes well and we don't strangle each other, I think we should look for a place together when we get back. Maybe an apartment with a little more space and an actual bedroom?" My pulse skipped and my face warmed. "I gave it some thought, and I'd like you beside me, too."

"Yeah?"

"Yeah."

His eyes bright, he leaned over and kissed my cheek. "I'm up for it."

He didn't try to bail out of the moving vehicle when he heard the suggestion. Good sign. I looked forward to smooth sailing with him over the next few months. No amateur sleuthing. No pissing off bad guys. No fighting for our right to live a decent life in the city we called home. Just a lady and her guy, spending time together on the open road.

What could go wrong?

Thank You

Thank you for reading *Free the Wolf*. If you enjoyed the book, please consider leaving a reader review.

For updates on the Alex Steward series, simply scan the QR code or visit the author's website at **stefaniegilmour.com**

Acknowledgements

THANK YOU TO my husband, Josh, for allowing me the time and space to write this first arc of Alex's story. I'm grateful for your patience and support.

Like the previous books in the series, this novel went through so many revisions! Logan Austin, Rebecca Cooper, and Diane Telgen, thank you for your talent. It helped me craft a story I'm proud to pass on to readers.

Thank you to the amazing *Free the Wolf* beta readers. Each of you gave me feedback that further strengthened the story: Logan Austin, Emily Bevilacqua, Kelly Bungee Rogers, Hailey Fournier, Jen Hefko, M.A. Hinkle, Hillary Robin, and Olivia Smith.

Family and friends, so many of you supported me in ways too numerous to list here. Thank you.

Readers, thank you for your support of an indie author writing about a messy lady werewolf. Without your purchase of this book, I wouldn't be able to continue writing them.

Stefanie Gilmour

STEFANIE IS A graphic designer who enjoys creepy and fantastical stories. Her short fiction has been published in *The Quiet Ones* literary magazine.

Plants, concerts, books, and writing are a few of her favorite things. She's a Midwest native and lives there with her patient husband and their tolerant cats.

stefaniegilmour.com
Facebook.com/AuthorStefanieGilmour
Instagram: @StefGilmour

9 798990 462328